Tomorrow Comes Today

A novel by Eric Frederick

In loving memory of my mother,
Lita deVeyra Frederick

Chapter 1

Rachel's four-year-old daughter burst into the kitchen through the sliding glass doors, beaming with excitement, and slammed full force into her leg.

"What is it, honey?"

"Where's Daddy?" Cindy whimpered. "He said he'd be here."

Rachel averted her eyes, shrinking back into silence. She had been dreading this moment all afternoon.

"I'm sorry, honey," she sighed.

She felt Cindy's fingers digging into her leg, her little body shuddering—teetering on the verge of a tantrum. Rachel scooped her up, sensing her Autistic stirring, then rushed her past a group of unsuspecting guests, and into the laundry room. The hair on the back of her neck stood straight up; she knew what was coming and there was nothing she could do to stop it.

Just as the door closed, Cindy unleashed an ear piercing cry, wailing at the top of her lungs, and screaming for Daddy. Rachel pulled her close, hoping to muffle the cries in her shirt, stroking her hair, and trying desperately to console her.

"It's okay, honey. Daddy will be home soon, I promise."

The bawling grew louder, prickling her nerves, and

causing her skin to crawl. She cooed in her ear, humming a soothing tone.

"But he promised…" Cindy whimpered.

"I know, honey," she set her down, "I know."

She wrapped her arms around her, trying to absorb the pain. She stroked her hair, and told her how much Daddy loved her. After what felt like a painful eternity, the crying finally subsided.

"Are you okay?"

Cindy nodded, wiping the tears from her eyes.

Rachel kissed her forehead, then brushed her bangs aside. "How 'bout a smile for mommy?"

She pursed her lips into a half smile, her eyes drooping with disappointment. Rachel wiped her face with a damp washcloth, straightened her shirt, and combed her hair.

Just then, a bell rang in the backyard, followed by circus music and children's squeals of delight.

"Hey, you better hurry," she grinned. "You know what that means." Cindy's face lit up, this is what she had been waiting for all day. She raced through the kitchen and out the sliding glass doors. Rachel trailed behind; peeking out the bay window to make sure everything was okay.

Cindy darted straight for the gathering crowd, pushed her way to the stage, and plopped down in front of the red-wigged clown.

Rachel stared blankly at the gaggle of children jumping up and down. She bowed her head in frustration, her body slumped in surrender. As guests strolled through the kitchen, she pasted on a half smile, hoping to mask the bitterness that was festering inside.

Grasping at anything to distract herself, she carried endless trays of food to the barbecue area—burgers, steaks and marinated chicken. Within minutes, the charcoal grills sizzled with enough food to feed a small army—the smell of tangy honey-glazed chicken wafting in the breeze.

"Can I help with anything?" her sister asked.

"I think we're good," she smiled, grabbing a tissue and dabbing her forehead.

For the remainder of the afternoon, she played the role of dutiful hostess, going through the motions, and making sure the guests were having a good time. She stocked the pool bar with soda, chips and fresh fruit smoothies, keeping her teenage daughter and her friends happy. The buffet table overflowed with pastas, watermelon and a dozen types of potato salad. And the kitchen was a regular Grand Central Station—the kids running in and out, filling water balloons, and playing hide n seek.

While everyone stuffed their bellies, Rachel looked around, enjoying the success of the party. The music had everyone singing and laughing, and Cindy was chasing her friends with a super soaker, playing water tag, and having the time of her life.

Rachel ducked inside to make a phone call, slightly worried, but mostly annoyed. When the voicemail chimed in, she sighed in disgust, hung up the phone, then threw it on the counter. She felt a twinge of angst poking at her conscience, a nagging suspicion that was gnawing at her insides. She couldn't remember a time when her intuition felt this uptight.

As afternoon turned to evening, the guests slowly trickled out. Her daughter, Christy, and a group of high school friends hung around the campfire, roasting marshmallows and eating s'mores. Rachel moseyed outside for the last time, clearing the dessert table, and dumping the coolers.

With her energy waning, she blew out the mosquito candles, and turned off the lights. Her sister and brother-in-law insisted on helping with the cleanup, but she pushed everyone out the door, refusing to let anyone work.

After kissing everyone goodnight, she dragged herself into the kitchen, peering up at the clock which was pushing closer to midnight. Surrounded by half eaten trays of birthday cake, she collapsed into the nearest chair. Was it all worth it? Her head said yes, her body said never again.

She leaned forward in a half-hearted attempt to stand, when she noticed the countless empty liquor bottles and soda cans lying around. The room was a disaster area, with toys and balloon fragments scattered about the floor. Mystery liquids dripped from countertops, and the plants smelled like root beer, as did the tablecloth. The trash can looked more like the trash corner—overflowing with dirty plates, empty boxes, and gift wrap.

Her head throbbed, as it did when any part of her home was in disarray; she felt undone. She winced when she saw her favorite chrysanthemum toppled on its side; flower pedals were scattered all over the floor, right next to a puddle of melted ice cream.

After a minute of staring at the chaos, her mind drifted into a foggy blur. She hung her head, realizing that she would have to move at some point, but for the moment, she was relishing the calm.

She eventually labored to her feet, leaning against the table to keep from falling over. Her feet were on fire, cramped and stiff, and crying for a massage.

Where should she begin? With her eyes fading in and out of focus, she crumpled back into the chair. Her muscles were staging a mutiny, and she was more than willing to surrender. She reached across the table for a bottle of vodka, then poured herself a glass, the splashing sound was music to her ears. The citrus vodka rolled down so easily. She closed her eyes for a prolonged moment, allowing the alcohol to work its magic.

"I'll rest my eyes for just a second," she thought. Delaying cleanup was always an option. "Maybe if I keep my eyes closed, it'll all go away."

As she teetered on the brink of dreamland, she heard an electric buzzing noise—a static, crackling sound that was coming from somewhere in the room. She rubbed her eyes, squinting through the sleepiness, trying to pinpoint where the sound was coming from. She realized it was the countertop TV, flickering in the background, with the volume turned low.

Glancing at the screen, she saw a blazing fire, a late-night news report of an African village engulfed in flames. An elderly woman dressed in threadbare garments was howling in anguish, tears streaming down her face. She dropped to her knees, lifting the body of a dead infant out of the mud. She flinched, as gunshots ricocheted all around her, stumbling backwards, and collapsing behind a burned out truck. The coverage ended abruptly, switching from the village carnage to a reporter in the studio.

"Tribal infighting, genocide, kidnapping and crimes against humanity... the atrocities being reported from inside this border country seem to be mounting by the minute," the anchor reported.

Rachel reached for the remote, fumbling for the off switch; bad news was the last thing she wanted to hear.

She slumped in the chair, her mind floating in a daze, still holding the remote in one hand, the empty glass in the other. Her eyes grew heavy, the silence closing in around her; she thought about another drink, but her arms were glued to the table. She inhaled a calming breath, her anxieties slowly melting away.

The phone rang suddenly, jarring her from her semiconscious state. She rubbed her eyes, blinking repeatedly, then grudgingly reached over, and picked up the phone. ,

"Hello," she muttered.

"Honey, it's me."

She recognized the chipper voice. Her stupor vanished, her adrenaline flaring to life.

"Mitch—where are you?" she exploded into the phone.

"I'm sorry, honey, I was called to D.C. last minute. Senator Browning..."

"How could you miss it?"

"Didn't you get..." he stammered.

"I've been trying to reach you all day! Why didn't you call me?" she raged.

"I told my assistant to..."

"Well I never got the message. Next time you need to call me yourself. And why is your phone sending everything to voicemail?"

A surge of anger coursed through her veins. Whatever fatigue she was feeling was a distant memory. Her mind was wide awake, but her body was still sluggish—feeling the effects of a long day.

"I'm sorry," he cowered, "If I had known…"

"And Cindy's been asking for you all day. You promised her that you were gonna be here."

"I know, honey, I'm sorry. I'll make it up to you… both of you."

She dangled the phone by her ear. She was speechless, her fury overpowering her thoughts.

"How was the party? Did everyone have a good time?"

"Hey, don't try and change the subject! Your daughter's been waiting for you."

The phone line fell silent.

She staggered out of the chair, driven by a newfound adrenaline, and laboring toward the hallway. With phone in hand, she trudged through the foyer leaving the cleanup behind for another day. She was surprised that she was moving as quickly as she was.

She ignored the pain, lumbering up the stairs, then peeking into her daughter's room. Cindy shifted, half awake beneath the floral bedspread, clutching her favorite doll, and nestled between her teddy bears. When she caught a glimpse of her daughter's quiet beauty, her anger subsided, like a gentle breeze cooling the sweltering heat. She inhaled a calming breath, then nudged her on the shoulder.

"Honey, wake up." Cindy opened one eye, rolled over, then took the phone.

"Hello?" she whispered, her voice drowsy.

"Happy birthday, Pookie."

"Daddy!" she squealed. Her face lit up like a Christmas tree. The tiredness in her voice dissipated—she was ecstatic upon hearing his voice. She sat up, pulling her teddy bear close to her heart.

"How's my big girl?" he asked.

"Good."

"Did you have fun today with your friends?"

"Uh-huh," she bounced.

"I heard there was a clown, was there a clown?"

"Yeah, and Mommy pushed him into the pool," she giggled, barely getting the words out.

Rachel smirked, staring at the floor.

"What? Mommy did what?"

"Yeah, and his wig came off and everything, and he was bald!" She slurred her words—she was laughing so hard.

Cindy rambled on, recounting every detail. Barely pausing for a breath, she boasted about drenching her friends with super soakers and blowing out all the candles on her cake. Of course, the red-wigged clown was her favorite part, especially when mom shoved him into the pool—an accident according to mom.

Rachel was tickled listening to her daughter's version of the party. The knots in her stomach slowly unraveled with each passing giggle. She smiled in silence, even chuckled and rolled her eyes—reveling in the love that Cindy shared with her daddy.

Meanwhile, two hundred miles away in the Ritz-Carlton in the nation's capital, Mitch balanced the phone against his ear, slipping off his jacket and loosening his tie. He tossed his coat onto the love seat, then sank into the soft leather. After kicking off his shoes, he reached down and peeled off his socks, then wiggled his toes deep in the plush maroon carpet.

"Did Mommy tell you what I got you for your birthday?" he teased.

"No, what, Daddy?"

"You have to guess, Pookie."

"A new dollie?"

"Nope, but you're close."

"New dresses for Boo Boo and Piggly."

"Getting warmer..., I'll give you a hint. It's soft and loveable, and something you've always wanted."

"Um..."

He flinched when he heard a loud crash—the sound of glass breaking—coming from the adjoining room. He stared at the bedroom door, more curious than nervous, waiting for the door to open, but there was no sound, no movement, nothing. Finally, after a long moment, his guest appeared. She pranced through the suite, wearing a silky white bathrobe; passing directly in front of him, teasing him with a playful wink. His heart fluttered in a disjointed rhythm, his cell phone dangling by his ear. A waft of perfume lingered in the air, tickling his nose and exciting his senses. He gasped in awed silence, snapping his hand over the mouthpiece; his thoughts were adrift in another world, until the bathroom door clicked shut.

"Um, honey, can you hang on for a second," his face flushed. "I think there's something wrong with my phone," his voice cracked, his conscience teetering between two realities.

He rose from the sofa, and drifted toward the bathroom; he felt a chill run up his spine, his heart beating outside his chest.

"Daddy?" Cindy's high pitched voice pierced the silence.

"Um..., I'm sorry, honey, what, there was a clown...?" he stuttered, turning and retracing his steps to the sofa, "Wait, what happened?" he wavered, trying to recapture the moment.

"When are you coming home, Daddy?" she whimpered.

"I...uh, I'll be home tomorrow, honey."

"I miss you."

He smiled, picturing her nestled beneath her pink blanket, surrounded by her furry friends. "I miss you too, honey," his words were lodged in his throat.

"Sing me a night-night song, Daddy."

His conscience froze, speechless; he was gripped by indecision. He closed his eyes, rubbing his fingers against his temples.

"It's pretty late, honey," he stammered.

"Please, Daddy?"

His stomach tightened—he did not want to sing. He squirmed in the silence, searching desperately for a way out. He knew that if he denied her request, his conscience would haunt him the rest of the night.

"Well, okay," he gulped. "But just a short one and then its night night, okay?"

"Yay!"

He coughed in his hand, clearing his throat.

"I, uh…"

"Wait, Daddy, I'm not ready. Piggly, Boo Boo and Mr. Jammers can't hear you."

Cindy set the phone down, disappearing for a moment, then when everyone was ready, she signaled the go-ahead.

He swallowed hard. He was well aware that an additional audience member was listening in the bathroom.

He sang softly, "You are my love, my little…"

"I can't hear you, Daddy," she interrupted.

He coughed, then started over, increasing the volume.

"You are my love, my little white dove; sent from above, you are my love. You're my only delight, please hold me tight; all through the night, you are my light," He crooned with a soothing charm. He was an average singer at best, but to his baby girl he was a superstar.

"You make me smile, la, la, la, la, la…

La, la…" he stammered, forgetting the words, then becoming tongue tied. His improvisation plummeted from bad to worse.

He launched into a poorly constructed rap. "Psh, Psh. Time fo princess to go to bed, rest yo pretty head… Time fo bed…"

She chuckled as he fumbled through his rap.

"You wack, Daddy!" she blurted out.

"What?" he objected playfully.

She giggled through it all, begging for another song—but

to no avail.

"Time for bed, Pookie. It's way past your bedtime."

"I love you, Daddy," she whispered.

The bathroom door swung open. His jaw dropped when his guest re-emerged, his face lighting up like it was his birthday. The blond intern strutted through the suite, wrapped only in a towel, flipping her hair to one side. Her skin glistened with a healthy glow, her golden tan highlighted by the plush white towel.

He covered the mouthpiece with his hand, his heart racing, titillated by the inherent danger. His tongue was paralyzed—entranced by her beauty; his eyes followed her every step, as she sashayed across the suite. She flashed an innocent come-hither glance, then dropped the towel, just as she entered the bedroom.

His hormones raged like a giddy schoolboy, replaying the last twenty seconds over and over again in his mind. He stared in a daze, waiting for his quivering legs to lead the way, but his conscience was flashing warning signals, keeping him anchored to the seat of the couch. Why was he struggling with this? Surely, he was not the first man in history to indulge in all of life's bountiful riches. He wrestled through his emotions, determined to silence the voice of resistance.

He pressed the phone to his ear. "Um ..., I love you too," he choked out a generic reply.

"Don't forget to say your prayers," she whispered.

Chapter 2

Rachel's eyes glazed over as she stepped out of the car. The electricity in the crowd sent chills up her spine. Everywhere she turned, she spotted another Hollywood actress more glamorous than the last. She wanted to shout names when she recognized a celebrity, but couldn't find her voice, and the crowd noise was nearly deafening. The event was surreal— fans screaming, flashbulbs popping, and the flowing dresses worn by the women were simply breathtaking. It was more perfect than she could ever imagine.

Her knees felt wobbly, as her husband escorted her along the red carpet. She lost all sense of direction, reeling from the bright lights, the cheers from the crowd, and the butterflies fluttering in her stomach. She was well aware of who was walking in front of her and who was trailing behind her. She didn't feel young enough, pretty enough, or famous enough to be on the carpet. When she finally reached the entranceway, she lingered for a moment—reveling in the glitz and glamour— smiling at the playful interchange between the stars and the paparazzi.

"Who's your designer?" someone yelled.

Her face turned beet red—blushing like a teenager—she wasn't ready for any of this. She laughed to hide her awkwardness, then retreated into the banquet hall, anxious to catch up with her husband.

She spotted him in the welcome area, greeting guests, and fulfilling his duty as official host of the charity event. She loved being a governor's wife, especially receiving gift bags and party perks; however, serving as the unofficial hostess, was the one obligation she could live without.

She greeted the guests one by one, forcing herself to breathe, and tempering her enthusiasm. She exchanged kisses with musicians, actors and some of Hollywood's power couples. She was tongue tied around many of the celebrities, choking out superficial greetings and trying to stay calm. Why was she so flustered? She turned to jello in front of the TV cameras, while the actresses around her posed with poise and confidence—smiling for the paparazzi like they were born in front of a camera.

She snatched a glass of champagne from a passing waiter, then drank it in a single breath. She had to calm her nerves somehow; she knew it was going to be a long night.

When the line slowed to a trickle, she escaped to the grand ballroom. She waved to a few acquaintances by the bar, then scanned the ballroom for her girlfriends. She had a thousand stories to tell, and no one to share them with.

She weaved from one cluster of guests to the next, making sure that everyone had plenty of food and drinks. Party goers greeted her as she circled around the bar—friends of her husband and local media types—introducing themselves, and thanking her for hosting the event.

As the night progressed, her inhibitions seemed to melt away. She bounced around the party like the belle of the ball, sipping her third glass of Chardonnay, and chatting it up with anyone and everyone. Who knew that she could be the life of a celebrity gala? Maybe she would make the next issue of *People Magazine*. She jumped playfully into VIP photo shoots, striking poses for the paparazzi, and even pulling other celebrities into the pictures. She was caught up in the moment, relishing her semi-celebrity status and vogueing like a supermodel. All eyes were on her as she pranced around the ballroom, showing off her curves in her red designer dress.

In between photo ops, she made her way to the dance floor. For the first time in a long time, she felt like she could dance all night. She was sixteen again—swept up by the party music, the beautiful people, the flowing fashion, and the contagious laughter—she was living the dream.

The dance floor was jumping with energy—the crowd waving their hands, and singing along.

The DJ kept the party flowing, until he segued into a slow song, signaling a romantic intermission—reserved for couples only. Rachel headed to the bar for a drink with her girlfriends, when suddenly she felt a warm hand on her shoulder.

"Would you like to dance?"

She turned, and met eyes with a handsome young suitor; her breath caught in her throat, their eyes locked in a timeless gaze.

He smiled at her, as she blushed with indecision. She squirmed like a third grader, biting her lip, and staring into his eyes.

"No, I'm sorry."

The young man—easily ten years her junior and obviously a professional football player—shrugged it off and gave her arm a gentle squeeze.

"Maybe later," he smiled.

As he walked away, one of her friends stared at her with her mouth hanging open, frozen in a state of disbelief.

"Do you know who that was?"

"Who?"

"I think his name is Josh something… He was like the comeback player of the year or something!"

Rachel grinned. "So maybe he'll come back," she

smirked, turning to take a second look. It was too late; he had disappeared into the crowd.

She spent the entire song asking questions about the mystery man, gossiping like a school girl, and loving every minute.

In the midst of all the star gazing and party toasts, she realized that she had lost track of her husband. Her mind was mildly curious; she hadn't seen him for several hours as the clock approached midnight. She craned her neck, making a visual sweep of the dance floor, but all she saw was a swirl of blurred faces.

A part of her knew that there was nothing to be worried about, but something was gnawing at her conscience—conjuring up doubts—and telling her that something wasn't right. But why should this occasion be any different? She trusted her husband, didn't she? After all, he was surrounded by bodyguards, and the banquet hall was crawling with security.

She made her way to the front of the ballroom, deciding to initiate a search and put her nagging suspicions to rest. When she arrived at the welcome area, she was mobbed by well-wishers. Her search would have to wait, while she played the name game with her husband's friends.

She pushed through the dance crowd, weaving her way toward the bar at the far end of the hall.

"Rachel, honey, I love your dress," one woman gushed. "Please tell your husband I said, 'Hello.'"

"Thank you, I will," she yelled above the music.

Countless dignitaries detained her, showering her with compliments, and insisting on buying her a drink. She smiled politely, enjoying the attention—with the lone exception of a married senator who whispered a sexual innuendo in her ear.

Another politician's wife babbled incessantly about the food, praising the lobster hors d'oeuvres, and insisting that the calorie count was Jenny Craig approved.

Rachel plowed undaunted toward the far end of the dance floor, peering around in bewilderment, her thoughts quickly leaning toward curious concern. Still no sign of her husband. She sighed in surrender, deciding to abandon her search. She convinced herself that she was getting worked up over nothing.

The party music echoed in her ear, as the crowd sang and clapped along; the place was bouncing with elation—the strobe lights flashing to a hypnotic beat. With her head bopping and her hands clapping, she was seduced back into the festivities. Her eyes lit up unexpectedly when she spotted one of her favorite R&B singers smiling in her direction; her concerns about her husband quickly became a distant memory.

After downing another glass of champagne and dancing with a few celebrity crushes, she stumbled into her husband's personal confidant, the lieutenant governor.

"Jester, have you seen Mitch?"

"Wow, Rachel, you look incredible!" he schmoozed, his eyes lingering a little too long.

"I've looked everywhere."

"Sorry Rach. I've been on the dance floor all night, gettin' my groove on." He staggered, nursing a mini buzz.

"Well, if you see him, can you tell him I'm looking for him?"

"Hey, come dance with me!" He scoped her up and down.

She chuckled, amused by his brazen overtures. "I hope you have a designated driver," she winked.

"You know, come to think of it, I did see Mitch earlier," he slurred, "and he said you were dying to dance with me."

"Goodnight, Jester," she smiled, tickled by his boldness.

She grabbed a glass of red wine from a passing waitress, then scurried along, her eyes doing a second scan of the colonnade room. Where could he be? She squinted in vain, shaking her head, as the disco lights provided zero visibility. Finding another black tuxedo in the crowd was like searching for lost car keys in the dark. Her anxiety gnawed at her. Why was she so concerned? She glanced up toward the cathedral ceiling and noticed a narrow balcony jutting out from three sides of the great hall. "That's where I need to be," she thought.

She weaved through the wall-to-wall bodies until she reached the spiral staircase at the rear of the ballroom. She gathered up her full length gown in one hand, while balancing her wine glass in the other. She crept up the stairs in her high heels, wobbling slightly, but careful not to spill her drink. When she reached the top, she peered over the railing like a queen gazing down upon her kingdom. She lingered for a moment, enjoying the bird's eye view, and reveling in the success of the event. Power had its privileges, and tonight, she was feeling good.

The pleasure of the moment was short lived, however, as her suspicions continued to needle her conscience. She glanced across the crowded ballroom, but still no Mitch.

She crisscrossed along the banister, greeting everyone she bumped into; her energy waned with every stranger she spoke to, her pasted smile was working overtime tonight. When she reached the balcony's end, she shook her head, letting out a sigh of surrender. Where could he be? She decided to return to the main floor—perhaps search the banquet area or find his driver, in case he stepped out for air.

As she turned toward the staircase, she noticed three small outdoor balconies—mini alcoves that she hadn't seen before. She dismissed them initially as being insignificant, but decided to check them, since she was already there. Her heart beat faster as she approached the first balcony. She felt warm all of the sudden, maybe it was the alcohol, or maybe it was something else. She stepped through the curtain and out into the misty air. The view of the courtyard was breathtaking—a sparkling three-story waterfall, and endless rows of flowers. A young couple strolled onto the balcony behind her, then retreated when they saw that the terrace was taken.

She made her way to the second balcony, stumbling upon a few more lovebirds along the way. But there was still no sign of her husband.

She approached the third and final alcove—a secluded entranceway which was blocked off by a rope, and a maroon curtain. The hallway was cold and empty, the carpet emitting a musty odor. There was no foot traffic in the secluded terrace; it was dimly lit by a few lights along the baseboard.

She felt a chill flash up her spine, as she walked up the short staircase. She squinted into the shadows, peering down a narrow corridor. The alcove appeared to be vacant, but she wasn't sure because the door up ahead was partially closed. She inhaled a deep breath, tensing her body, and listening for any signs of life. After convincing herself that the balcony was empty, she pivoted toward the exit to resume her search on the main floor.

"Shh!"

She heard a faint noise, then a giggle. She turned back toward the dark opening, swallowing hard, a lump of anxiety caught in her throat. She tiptoed toward the balcony, her ears listening for additional sounds. As she walked closer, she noticed a dark shadow emanating from the side of the balcony's archway. It appeared to be a silhouette of a person; maybe one or two people nestled in the corner of the terrace. She crept closer to the opening, her heart thumping, stuttering, then picking up speed. The single shadow split into two, then morphed back into one. The wine glass in her hand shook involuntarily, as she inched closer into the light.

Just then, she let out a sudden gasp.

Her breathing stopped, her body shuddered; the glass slipped through her fingers, and fell, crashing to the floor. She covered her mouth with both hands when she realized that one of the shadows was her husband. He was locked in a kiss with a young blond woman, their arms wrapped around each other, his fingers entwined in her hair. A wave of humiliation flooded her mind.

She turned and fled, gasping for air, her entire body went cold, like she was being strangled to death from the inside.

"Rachel, Rachel...!" her husband cried out.

She stumbled down the staircase, nearly tripping on her dress—clutching onto the railing to keep from falling. She was trapped in a cage, clamoring to escape, and determined to flee as far away as possible. Pushing through the thicket of bodies, her mind tuned out the festivities. Everything was a blur—the party music, the elegance, the celebrity and candlelight—none of that mattered. Her conscience screamed in agony, her heart leaving a trail of blood.

She heard commotion behind her, but refused to turn around, her lungs gasping for air, desperate to flee this nightmare. She weaved her way to the middle of the ballroom, when suddenly she felt a cold hand grab her, jerking her to a halt. She spun around in a flash, with fire shooting from her eyes. When she saw that it was her husband, she lashed out with a volcanic fury, her anger burning a hole through the duplicity written across his face. He averted his glance, pleading with her in a muted voice.

"Please, don't make a scene," he begged.

"Don't touch me!" she screamed, her face crimson red, her voice seething with rage.

"Rachel, please, just..."

She ripped her arm from his grasp, cocked her hand back and slapped him across his face.

"Stay away from me!" she exploded.

She turned and plowed undaunted like a charging rhino through the crowd. Her lungs hyperventilated, her heart was an open wound. She wanted to die.

Chapter 3

Rachel erupted out the front door, a light mist spraying cool against her fury. Tears streamed down her face as she stumbled into the drizzle; losing her balance, then steadying herself against a white column. Her heart pounded faster, agonizing, like it had been punctured by a dagger. She inhaled quick, sharp breaths, desperate to keep moving and distance herself from the pain. Where should she go? What should she do? Everything was a blur, a slow painful nightmare. She peered into the darkness, gaping over endless rows of parked cars. She couldn't think straight, her demeanor transforming from dejection to determination. She shuffled across the slick pavement, nearly slipping in her high heels.

"Can I help you, Mrs. Jameson?" The valet called out, as he pulled off his headphones. She ignored him, nearly bowling him over by the hurricane force of her will.

Her eyes darted from one car to next, searching frantically for her midnight blue Infiniti. Her senses sharpened by the second, driven by a betrayal that only a spurned wife would ever know. Who was the other woman? The image of the blonde hussy flashed through her mind—a snapshot of her husband kissing the tramp was etched in her memory—gnawing on her nerves.

She spotted her car in the distance, then wiped the mist

from her eyes. She skidded across the wet blacktop, slipping twice, but eventually making it in one piece.

She jumped in, exhaling a sigh of relief, then searched for the keys. She ran her hand along the floor mat, and also checked under the seat. Her head felt dizzy—she regretted that last glass of wine. She checked her purse for an extra set of keys, then felt along the sun visor—but still no keys.

Out the corner of her eye, she spotted her husband as he burst out the front door. Her hands shook with a sense of urgency, fumbling for the light, the keys, anything.

"Where are they?" she sighed.

Mitch wobbled in the doorway, gasping for breath, then doubling over with his hands on his knees. He stumbled toward the valet attendant who was texting on his cell.

"Hey, did you see a lady come out here?" he yelled.

The attendant pointed to the VIP section. Mitch shuffled in her direction, still scanning the parking lot with a quizzical look on his face. After a few short steps, he slipped on the slick pavement, crashing hard to the ground—skinning his knuckles on the cement.

"Dammit!" he cried.

He staggered to his feet, wincing from the pain, and clutching his leg. He limped between the rows, sucking his knuckles, and wandering in a daze until he spotted her car.

"Rachel, stop!"

The moment she heard his voice, she snapped the door lock.

He hobbled over, and slapped the glass.

"Come on, Rach, open up!" He tugged on the handle.

She reached into the glove compartment, felt the metal keys, then shook them loose until she found the starter key.

"Rachel, please…, Rachel, just hear me out!"

"Leave me alone!" she screamed without looking at him.

"Please, just let me explain. It's not what you think…"

She revved the engine, switched on the headlights, then threw the car into gear. Adrenaline took over as she stomped the gas, her tires peeling out on the rain covered blacktop. Mitch leapt out of the way, smacking the trunk with his hand, then choking on the fumes as she sped away.

"Rachel…" his voice trailed off.

She raced out of the parking lot, exhaling a sigh of relief. She swerved across three lanes of traffic, nearly causing an accident but never looking back. Her resolve was locked in high gear, a surge of electricity shooting through her veins.

She sped through the first intersection, ignoring the red light, and nearly crashing into oncoming traffic. Tires screeched, as motorists barreled through the intersection, slamming on their brakes, and swerving off the road. The smell of burning rubber filled the air after half a dozen cars skidded to a halt. Drivers rolled down their windows, and poked their heads out, cursing at the top of their lungs, and flipping her the finger.

Her mind swirled like a blender—a sordid concoction of humiliation, and anger. She stepped on the gas, increasing her speed ten, fifteen, twenty miles per hour over the speed limit.

She stared blankly into the dead of night, ignoring the flashing yellow lights that signaled dangerous curves ahead. She had no idea where she was headed; her body was driving, but her mind was trapped in a fog. The reflectors, shining off the rain covered highway, streaked by like a hypnotic mirage. Her eyes glazed over as she stepped on the gas; not watching her speed, not watching the signs, not caring if she lived or died, she simply sped off into the dark.

Back at the banquet hall, Mitch limped toward the valet booth, sucking his knuckles, and fretting over what to do next. The salty blood helped to clear his head, as he stared helplessly over the endless rows of cars. He was stranded without a vehicle, cursing the name of his absent driver who was occupied inside the party.

Suddenly, the front doors flew open, and his lieutenant

governor stumbled out, with a drink in hand.

"Mitch, Mitch, where are you?" he stuttered, squinting into the fog.

"Jester, where's your car?"

Jester staggered toward him, throwing up his hands. "What's going on?" he slurred. "I just saw your wife...?"

"Your car... where's your car?" Mitch interrupted.

Jester pointed reluctantly to the black Mercedes, then pulled his hand back with tentative regret. Mitch darted toward the shiny sedan and jumped in. He felt along the floor mat, searching for the key. He popped open the glove compartment, snatched the keys and started the engine.

"Lights, where are the lights?" he grunted.

He fumbled around the dashboard, pressing every button he touched. The windshield wipers whipped full speed across the glass, catching him by surprise, and causing him to flinch. "Damn foreign car!" he growled. Finally, he switched the lights on, threw the car into gear and tore out of the parking lot.

He raced down the single lane highway, weaving in and out of traffic. His heart thumped with anxiety, as he peered off into the distance. He felt a curl of nausea in his stomach, dreading the imminent confrontation that awaited him at home.

The tiny voice in his head calculated excuses for getting out of this mess. "She'll scream at me, curse me out, vent for a while, and then I'll beg her to forgive me," he thought. "Then I'll tell her, I met this girl tonight, I had one too many beers, we kissed, and that was it."

Convinced that his plan would work, he exhaled a half-hearted sigh of relief. He gunned the engine, pressing sixty in a forty mile per hour zone. "Hey, if I have to sleep on the couch for a week, and buy a ten thousand dollar diamond ring..., so be it, whatever it takes," he shrugged.

He drove less than a mile before he was impeded by a cluster of slow drivers on the single lane road. Shaking his head in disgust, he popped his head out the window and spotted the law abiding driver who was holding up the traffic.

"Let's go! Come on!" He honked the horn. "What is this, a parking lot? Pass him!" He ducked back in, aggravated, wiping the rain from his eyes.

His eyes ballooned wide when he noticed a clear lane and a chance to pass. He swerved into the opposite lane, then stomped the accelerator to the floor. His heart beat faster, a wave of testosterone shooting through his veins—he felt like a race car driver. The moment he passed the first car, he could taste the open road. "Only three more to go, then I'm home free," he thought.

As he sped by the second car, the road curved unexpectedly to the right. Warning signals flashed inside his brain, a lump of anxiety was building in his throat. Just then, a blinding light shined directly into his eyes. He flipped the visor down to avoid the glare, when suddenly he heard a loud blast from a truck horn, sending chills up his spine. An eighteen wheeler barreled straight toward him with its headlights flooding his vision. Paralyzed by fear, he tensed his body, then slammed his foot on the brake. The lights blinded him momentarily, as his car fishtailed out of control. By some stroke of luck, he swerved back into his lane, nearly sideswiping the car in front of him, but managing to escape without a scratch. The eighteen-wheeler flew screaming by, still honking his horn, and splashing water through the open window.

His heart pounded in his throat, as he wiped the rain off his forehead. His whole body shuddered, the horn still echoing in his ears—he was astonished that he was still alive. After a few deep breaths, and a check of his stomach to make sure everything was intact, his nerves calmed down and he decided to press on.

Eventually, he found an opening and sped past the one person traffic jam. He yelled a few curse words at the old geezer, then zigzagged past, and flipped him the bird.

Meanwhile, up ahead, Rachel was speeding off to nowhere. The rain beat against her windshield, fogging up the glass, and stirring her anxiety. How long had she been driving?

She didn't want to go home; she just wanted to get away.

Her subconscious kept hitting the rewind button, replaying the painful event over and over again in her mind. Who was the young blond? Did he meet her tonight or were they having an affair? Had he slept with the tramp? Was he sleeping with both of them at the same time? Her thoughts fluctuated between anger and disbelief.

The shrill ring of her cell phone made her jump. She looked down at the passenger seat, then felt around in the dark for her purse.

"Please don't let it be him," she winced, deciding to ignore it.

She hardened her gaze on the road in front of her, trying to block out the musical ringtone. The song, which was normally one of her favorites—began to chew at her conscience.

"It doesn't matter…, it doesn't matter," she chanted, waiting anxiously for the voicemail to kick in.

She tried to block it out of her mind, but her curiosity overpowered her resistance—she had to know who was calling. She pulled the phone out of her purse, and glanced at the caller I.D. Anger exploded inside her chest at the sight of her husband's name. She didn't want to talk to him; she didn't want to talk to anybody, especially not him.

Annoyed by the ringtone, she pressed the speak button, then hung up immediately.

She lashed out at everything—the rain, the windshield wipers, the cars she had to pass, the darkness. She tried to pretend that none of this was a big deal, but she couldn't shake the feeling, that everyone knew by now. She shot a quick look in her rear view mirror, seeing only darkness—she was all alone.

After venting a few curse words, she noticed something strange in her mirror. A car in the distance seemed to be flashing its high beams. She slowed down and listened, hearing a faint noise that sounded like a horn.

Suddenly, her cell phone rang again. She glanced over her shoulder, squinting at the headlights, and shaking her head in disgust. "Could it be?" she thought. She rolled her eyes, hoping it wasn't him. She glanced at the caller ID, then threw it down—resolving to let it ring.

Her blood boiled as she tried to clear her mind. She stepped on the gas, pressing twenty over the speed limit. She approached a business section of town lined with coffee shops, fast-food restaurants and gas stations on both sides. The crowds were out in full force tonight—filled with late night shoppers, college students, and Denny's customers.

The traffic light turned yellow as she approached the busy intersection, so she stepped on the accelerator, hoping to squeeze through the light. Just as she sped up, the light flashed red.

A car crossed into her lane, then stopped, suddenly, waiting for pedestrians. She slammed on her breaks, locking her wheels and sending her car into a skid. She swerved at the last second, nearly plowing over a young mother and her daughter.

Trailing behind in hot pursuit, Mitch had his eyes fixed on the tail lights up ahead. He gunned the engine, streaking along the slick blacktop; if only he could catch her, he could make this all go away. He pressed his cell against his ear, listening anxiously, as the dial tone rang over and over.

"Pick it up, Rach. Come on, honey, just pick it up."

He squinted through the blurry windshield, still trying to convince himself that the lights up ahead belonged to her. As the dial tone repeated in his ear, he rubbed his temples, disgusted that he was even in this mess.

"Come on!" he pleaded, tapping his finger against the phone.

Click. The disconnect rattled in his ear. No voicemail, no recording, no dial tone.

"Dammit!" he growled, slapping his hand against the steering wheel. He fumbled for the redial button.

He dialed a third time, but was cut off once again.

"Ahh!" he grunted, slamming the phone to the floor.

He shook his head in a fit of rage, unsure what to do next. Where was she headed? Was she driving home? The rain pounded the windshield, impairing his visibility. He looked around at the unfamiliar surroundings, perplexed for a moment, realizing that he was nowhere near their home. He stomped on the gas, as he approached a busy business intersection.

"Where is she going?" he sighed.

His phone rang suddenly from down below his feet. The ringtone was muffled—either damaged or flipped upside down. He ran his hand along the dashboard, searching for the interior lights. He pressed multiple buttons, unlatching the trunk by mistake.

"Dammit!"

The phone stopped ringing, causing his heart to drop.

After a long minute, it rang again. His breathing quickened as he ran his hand along the floorboard. He stretched his arm toward the passenger door, patting the carpet anxiously; afraid the ringing would stop at any second.

"Don't hang up, Rach!" he blurted out, taking his eyes off the road and squinting down at the floor.

After the fourth ring, he unbuckled his seat belt, then steered with one hand while searching along the floor with the other. His heart beat faster as he stretched his arm all the way to the passenger door, zigzagging his fingertips along the carpet. "Maybe it slid under the seat," he thought. He ducked his head down, stretching his forearm beneath the passenger seat, and running his hand along the metal springs. His fingertips scratched along the carpet until eventually he felt the edge of the phone. "Finally," he thought. He popped his head up for a quick check of the road. He saw an intersection coming up quickly, but noticed that the light was holding a steady green. He ducked back under, extending his hand; he leaned as far as he could reach, then grabbed the phone.

Just then, the ringing stopped. Without warning, he heard

tires screeching. Excruciating pain ripped through his body, as he bounced like a rag doll inside the interior. Lights flashed before his eyes, and the sound of metal crunching echoed through the air. Everything went black.

Chapter 4

A dank chill lingered in the air. Rachel wrapped her arms around her body, rubbing her goose flesh, and trying to calm her nerves. She stared in prolonged silence at her husband's swollen face; his eyes were sealed shut, a breathing tube protruding from his mouth.

She slumped in a chair beside his bed, staring bleary eyed at the splints and braces that held his fractured body together. His forehead was wrapped like a mummy, the stitches along his chin too numerous to count, the result of a defective airbag.

"He's lucky to be alive," a doctor murmured, peering over at her and shaking his head.

Her mind was frozen in place, transfixed by the beeping sound that pattered from the life support machine. She struggled to process what her eyes were telling her, gaping at a face that she couldn't recognize.

"Can I get you anything, Mrs. Jameson?" the doctor asked.

She breathed a heavy sigh, shaking her head, and keeping her eyes fixed on her husband. The doctor scanned the heart monitor a final time, then exited, leaving her alone in the room.

She buried her face in her hands, too angry to cry, too scared to run away. A part of her hated him for the torture he put her through; however, another part of her was crying on the inside—this was her husband, her lover, her best friend clinging to life. "This is a nightmare," she shuddered, her mind clouded with conflicting emotions.

She traced the breathing tube with her eyes, following it from the respirator to his mouth. His chest inflated with every uptick of the machine, rising and falling, but inspiring very little hope.

She rubbed her arms again, the cold air a reminder that she was wearing only an evening gown. She crossed her arms across her chest, trying to hold herself together.

Images of the party flashed through her mind, the energy and the dance music bouncing around in her memory. She reached down and slid off her heels, wincing from the blood blister rubbing against her pinky toe. She thought about the celebrities she danced with, the neon lights, and the endless girl talk. She couldn't remember the last time she had had that much fun—perhaps not since her wedding.

"What am I doing?" she sighed, rubbing her temples to clear her mind.

She felt a twinge of guilt in her throat, recoiling as if she had done something wrong. "But, why should I feel guilty?" she mumbled, straining to suppress the anxiety welling up inside.

She grabbed Mitch's hand—his limp, unresponsive hand—then rubbed it, trying to infuse some warmth into his fingers. She reached up and caressed his face, gently stroking those cheeks that she had kissed so often. Who is this person? Is this her soul mate, the person she shared every intimate thought with?

She averted her eyes, exhausted from mulling over the entire evening.

She couldn't get the image of her husband with that woman out of her mind. How long had he been having an affair? She may never know the answer. Was it better not to know? And, how could she stay married to someone who betrayed her deepest trust, someone who lied to her and disgraced her in front of the whole world?

She swallowed hard, the lump in her throat scraping the side of her windpipe. She couldn't deny her love for him. Twenty one years of marriage had cemented their lives together; he was the father of their children, and the love of her life.

Just then the door burst open disrupting her pseudo silence.

"Daddy, Daddy!" Christy cried out.

Her daughters rushed in with tears streaming down their faces. Rachel flinched the moment she heard their voices, then reached out and grabbed them, one in each arm, keeping them away from their father's bed.

"Daddy! No, please, no." Christy bawled.

Her daughter covered her mouth, staring at the countless tubes jutting from her father's mummified body. She turned away in horror, cringing at the sight of his swollen face. Rachel pulled her close, wrapping her arms around her, trying her best to absorb the pain. Christy sobbed hysterically, burying her face in her arms, and holding tight around her waist.

"Shh, it's okay, honey, it's gonna be okay," Rachel whispered. The assurance in her voice was poorly disguised. She closed her eyes, knowing that her words were hollow.

The door cracked open, and her sister, Jennifer, slipped inside the room. Aunt Jennifer gasped when she saw Mitch's battered body, then walked over and embraced the family.

Rachel peered up at her sister with tears in her eyes. Her sister shook her head and looked away; they both knew there was nothing to be said.

She dabbed her daughters' eyes with a tissue, content to let them grieve as much as they needed. She knew she had to be strong for her children, not only physically, but emotionally as well. She picked Cindy up in her arms, stroking her hair, and cooing in her ear.

As the early morning hours wore on, Cindy fell asleep on her lap; she decided to send Christy home with her sister, there was no sense in having everyone stay. The waiting was the hardest part, waiting for answers that perhaps they didn't want to hear.

The room was calm with the lights turned off—a blanket of serenity, a respite from reality. The heart monitor echoed in the background, its haunting rhythm ticking like a time bomb, counting down the final seconds.

She stared out the window into the bleak unknown. The sky was pitch black, with no moon, and no stars to wish upon. If she had one wish, it would be to turn back time. But time was at a standstill, stuck in a nightmare.

She squirmed in her chair, careful not to wake her daughter. She couldn't decide if she even wanted to sleep.

Her eyelids grew heavy, but her mind refused to let her rest. Where would it all end? She was desperate for this night to end, but fearful of what tomorrow would bring.

Chapter 5

Rachel woke in a cold sweat. Her thoughts were hazy, still clouded in a web of confusion. She looked around through drowsy eyes, struggling to process the strange shadows and flickering lights. She reached down and picked up the blanket that had fallen off the recliner, then adjusted the pillow behind her head, hoping to drift back to sleep.

Cindy fidgeted on her lap, curled in a ball and squirming to find a comfortable position. Rachel wrapped the wool blanket around her daughter, shading her eyes, and protecting her from the cold reality.

The room felt clammy, shrouded in darkness except for a small TV flickering inconspicuously in the corner. The beams of light served as a subtle nightlight; the low volume adding a whisper of life to a room heavy with anxiety. Rachel closed her eyes, drifting in and out of consciousness, longing desperately for some peace of mind. Just as she was about to nod off, a breaking news banner flashed across the screen.

"We interrupt this program to bring you breaking news," the anchor cut in.

Rachel flinched out of her stupor, turning her head and gazing bleary-eyed at the screen.

"We have received tragic reports that a private jet has crashed about sixty-five miles southeast of New York City."

Rachel's brain was slow to respond—annoyed by the interruption, and piecing together every third word.

She laid her head against the pillow, regretting that she had turned the TV on in the first place. Her eyelids drooped, on the verge of closing, but she was semi-curious about what was going on. She peeked with one eye partially open, trying to make sense of the grainy video. She watched as rescue workers scurried through the woods; the picture was dark and jittery, the frame was shaking as if the cameraman was running with a sense of urgency. Being careful not to wake her daughter, she reached for the remote—increased the volume, then inclined her ear toward the TV.

Photos of several national celebrities popped onto the screen. She furrowed her brow, still confused as to what the reporter was saying. What's the big emergency, and what did the celebrities have to do with the mad dash through the woods? She increased the volume again, sorting through the images in her mind.

"Officials are saying that national talk show host Balinda Summers, civil rights activist Dr. Tony Chambers, and author and televangelist David Connolly are among the missing passengers on board," the anchor reported.

Rachel's jaw dropped.

Video highlights of the celebrities flashed onto the screen. Balinda Summers was one of her personal heroes.

"Oh, my gosh!" she gasped.

Helicopters shined spotlights through the trees, lighting the way for rescue workers who were chopping through the brush. Emergency crews scampered toward the fiery wreckage, dragging rescue equipment—oxygen tanks and stretchers— through the tall weeds.

Rachel shook her head, wincing in horror. She muttered a reactionary prayer, hoping that somehow, someone would survive the crash.

"What is going on?" she whispered.

She glanced down at her daughter, breathing a sigh of

relief that she was still asleep.

The footage turned grisly, zooming in on the plane's fuselage which was burning out of control. Rescue workers battled the flames with fire extinguishers, scrambling around the crash site, and searching for survivors. Rachel cowered in disbelief; she couldn't stand to watch anymore, but she couldn't look away.

She grabbed the remote, her fingers quivering, as she flipped through the channels, curious to see if the other stations were covering the story. She was amazed that nearly every network was broadcasting the crash. "Just turn it off," she thought, "or at least switch it to an infomercial, or something else."

Her hand was frozen on the remote, she had to watch, this was too huge to miss. She flicked it back to the network.

The fire raged on as rescue workers coordinated their spotlights between the trees. Jagged shards of steel jutted from the fuselage, metal burning white hot against the backdrop of the forest. The fire burned out of control, the jet fuel leaving a fiery wake in its path.

Fire fighters screamed at reporters and camera crews, ordering them to move back and stop impeding the rescue effort. The news coverage seemed as chaotic as the incident itself.

"We are looking at live footage of the crash site," a correspondent reported, "as rescue workers are searching frantically for any signs of life. We're told that firefighters, and search and rescue teams, are scouring every inch of the woods... in and around the twisted wreckage... combing the area for any survivors."

Rachel winced at the sight of what looked like a body bag, listening intently for any details. She turned away for a moment, averting her eyes at the sight of a possible victim, and catching a glimpse of her husband across the room. What was happening to her? Death was closing in from every side.

She felt a chill run down her spine, her body flinching,

knocking her blanket to the floor. Cindy awoke from the cold, rubbing her eyes, and looking around in confusion.

"Mommy, where are we?" she slurred, staring at the blinking lights from the life support machines.

"Shh, go back to sleep, honey. It's okay, everything's okay." She pulled the blanket back over her, covering her eyes, and shielding her from the TV. Cindy shifted slightly, then curled back into the fetal position.

The news coverage switched from the crash site to the news desk. Producers scrambled in front of the camera, shuffling fresh updates to the anchors.

"We just received the latest from the crash site...," the anchor hesitated. "Local authorities are now reporting that there are no survivors. Every person aboard the private jet has been accounted for including the pilots and crew members. We repeat there are no survivors. Among the passengers... talk show host Balinda Summers, civil rights activist Dr. Tony Chambers and televangelist David Connolly... all among the dead."

Rachel's jaw dropped. Her heart caught in her throat from disbelief. "What is going on?" she sighed.

She turned away, searching the room for any semblance of relief—desperate to clear her mind with even the smallest distraction.

She clicked off the TV; she couldn't bear it anymore. Her lungs began to hyperventilate—her body shuddering from a sudden panic attack. She wrapped her arms around herself, trying to hold her world together.

Her mind spun like a whirlwind—flashing from anxiety to disbelief. Where was life's off switch? She was tired of crying, tired of hating, too frightened to even think about tomorrow.

She buried her face in her hands, hiding behind a veil of self-denial. There was no one to reach out to. For the first time in her life, she felt all alone.

Chapter 6

Darkness flashed into instantaneous white light. Balinda's eyes fluttered in wonderment, as she soared high above the ocean, through the warm summer sunshine. She felt a soft brightness all around her, enveloping her in celestial warmth—soothing to the skin. Her heart raced as the all-encompassing radiance permeated her soul like an early morning sunrise. She flew higher and higher, floating in a carefree weightlessness—a feeling of serenity and rapturous joy. She inhaled deeply, her lungs filling with the fragrance of pure happiness. Her body tingled, her senses surging into hyper real, a mix of laughter and deep satisfaction. Images flashed before her eyes, bright colors of a flowery meadow; her nostrils filled with the smell of sweet perfume—pleasure beyond compare. "Is this a dream?" she wondered. Caught up in the moment, she could not remember yesterday. She felt waves of exhilaration washing over her—the sensation so overpowering, there was no past, no future, only the present.

Dr. Chambers blinked repeatedly, opening his eyes as if waking from a deep sleep. His senses sparkled with heightened elation, his adrenaline pulsing through his veins. He held his head high, soaring like an eagle high above the green pastures.

A gentle breeze brushed against his cheeks; the sights, the sounds, his entire being was enthralled by a sense of total freedom. He raised his arms in victory, the sound of millions upon millions, cheering in his ears. Jubilation swept through his soul; his emotions bursting with unending joy, as he soared ever higher through the boundless heavens.

David Connolly ascended high above the snowcapped mountains. His smile was radiant, his eyes were mesmerized by the breathtaking scenery. His thoughts were flooded with childhood memories of warm embraces and Christmas mornings. He heard the sounds of children laughing, church bells ringing, and stadiums filled with millions of cheering fans. Rising ever higher into the heavenly realms, he was overwhelmed by a wave of all-consuming happiness.

All three celebrities shined brighter than the stars, their journeys transcending the glories of the heavens. They gazed in wonder at the beauty that surrounded them, rising ever higher through the royal blue skies. They were engulfed by a calm serenity, experiencing a soothing comfort unlike anything they had ever felt before.

They soared toward what appeared to be a bright light, a brilliance as beautiful as the sun. The luminous glow before them was both strange and wonderful—a beacon of splendor, so familiar, so divine. As they drew closer to the light, the clouds began curving into a tunnel formation. Their spirits ascended with anticipation, captivated by this warm radiance that shone before them. What were they seeing? What was this brilliance they were journeying toward—so irresistible, so completely enthralling?

Balinda drew closer to this mysterious light, a smile beaming across her face, her spirit giddy with expectant joy. As an international celebrity, she had been loved and adored by millions of fans from all over the world, but for all the adulation she had received in her lifetime, nothing compared to the jubilation she was feeling right now. As she approached this glorious radiance, the inexplicable brightness began to take shape. She opened her eyes wide, sharpening her focus, her heart fluttering as she absorbed this vision of loveliness. The gleaming brilliance began to centralize, revealing the unexpected form of— a man. Her cheeks flushed as she glided forward, anxious, like a beautiful bride approaching her awaiting groom.

Finally, she arrived at her appointed destination, coming to a gentle stop and standing alone before this man. She felt a sense of awe as she absorbed this vision of loveliness. The first thing she noticed was the jagged scar marks embedded in his hand. She winced momentarily, as the blemishes seemed out of place in light of perfection. His appearance took her breath away, dressed in a gleaming white robe that shined brighter than the sun. She gazed into his eyes for a brief moment, her heart shuddering, overcome with feelings of majesty and awe. She was breathless, as if staring at the most beautiful diamond she could ever imagine. She knew who this was, there was no doubt in her mind. She had heard stories about him since she was a little girl, and even attended a few Sunday school classes. Although she did not attend church regularly as an adult, his name was brought up during virtually every holiday. This was Jesus—celebrated at Christmas and Easter, along with Santa Claus and the Easter bunny.

She peered down at her clothes, noticing her familiar designer dress. Somehow the fabric felt softer against her skin, more luxurious than any silk she had ever worn before. The colors were vibrant and majestic, reflecting the brilliance coming from Jesus.

As she stood speechless in place, she heard a voice whispering inside her head. The voice was not coming from the person standing before her, but from a semi-familiar voice from her distant past. Trying to think it through quickly, she faintly recalled the speaker. It was a nameless pastor, who spoke at a funeral which she attended as a child.

"The very second you die, each of us will stand before a man with scars in His hands. The Bible says, 'Man is destined to die once, and after that to face judgment,'" the pastor quoted.

Dr. Tony Chambers and David Connolly also arrived at their destination, marveling at the beauty that surrounded them. They too heard the same words from the pastor, whispering to their soul.

All three stood tall with eager expectations, excited to be welcomed into the comforts of heaven. All three felt like they belonged in this haven of glory, displaying excellent records of generosity, doing good, and thinking of others. All three had been recognized for their outstanding charity work, living lives of good karma, and spirituality.

They peered around, shaking their heads, unsure of the existence they were witnessing—or the ground they were standing on. Celestial music filled their ears, the most pleasurable sounds they'd ever heard. Their souls leapt with joy, captivated by the magnificence of the sights and sounds surrounding them. With their mouths agape, they stood silent, soaking in the overwhelming grandeur. But the surroundings took on a lesser significance—as their eyes were enthralled by the person standing before them.

Alone before Jesus, each newcomer leaned forward with bated breath. All were speechless, their hearts tugging with eager expectation. For one of the new guests, the wait was over—their euphoric experience had reached its culmination. Jesus looked deep into the eyes of one of the attendees, as they felt his gaze peer directly into their soul.

The voice of the pastor suddenly resonated in their thoughts. "The Bible says that it is God's desire that everyone... everywhere... would come to know the greatness of His love, and spend eternity with Him in heaven. But sadly for some... this will not be the case."

In a blinding instant, one of the attendees trembled violently like a mighty earthquake, their whole body imploding, being ripped apart from the inside.

Their face disfigured, their voice screaming in excruciating pain. Their clothes transformed into disease ridden excrement—sewage dripping from their dilapidated corpse. Then twisting like a tornado, they were suddenly whisked away as though being sucked through a vacuum, cast into eternal torment.

"Ahh! No!" they shrieked.

Their soul plunged into a bottomless pit of fiery torture. Their body infested by a skin-crawling rash, of festering blisters, and prickly hives. Screams of insanity echoed throughout the empty chasm. Their blood-curdling cries were silenced when a thundering boom crashed in the darkness—like a metal door the size of a mountain slamming shut and sealing the abyss for all eternity.

Chapter 7

"What a nightmare," the editor-in-chief grumbled, as he pushed his way through the crowded sidewalk. His skin crawled when strangers pressed against him—having other people touch him annoyed him to no end. This was not the way he wanted to start his day. The faces were a blur of yuppies and sightseers, all crammed together, waiting for the light to turn green.

One Month Earlier

"What is going on?" he growled.

He scooted along the curb, nearly being run over by college students waving picket signs. The protesters all wore bright orange t-shirts bearing the slogan, 'Hey Governor…Bite me!' scribbled in magic marker.

"Ah, yes. The great minds of tomorrow," he scoffed.

The protesters closed in around him, jostling and spinning him in every direction. He felt a dry tickle in his throat, undoubtedly the result of someone's cologne shower. He held his breath, squeezing through the myriad of perfumes and body sprays. His lungs were about to burst so he resorted to breathing through his nose.

He turned the corner catching a waft of fresh air, then weaved through the normal foot traffic—women speed walking in their sneakers, and young men sporting early morning gel-looks. The smell of mocha lattes tantalized his taste buds, tempting him to make a pit stop, but he was already running late.

He quickened the pace, feeling a slight breeze blowing through his white hair; he enjoyed the brisk jaunt as he called it, chalking it up as his cardio for the day. After scurrying half a block, he slammed into another wall of bodies. He rolled his eyes in disbelief, flabbergasted at the never-ending congestion. The sidewalk swarmed with pedestrians who were texting and donning earphones, all shuffling to their cubicles in the sky.

He waved to the bagel vendor who was cooped up in his silver cart.

"Muffin today, sir?" the vendor called out.

"Not today, I'm watching my weight."

His stomach growled as he waited for the walk signal. He raised his eyes skyward, smiling in awe at the towering obelisk—the twenty-first century corporate cathedral, rising to the heavens before him. The imposing girth of this modern-chic castle epitomized strength and sophistication, the heartbeat of Yuppieville, and the centerpiece of Metropolis.

Waltzing through the front door, he was greeted by the doorman. He exhaled a sigh of relief, like a king entering the plush comforts of his own castle. The concierge welcomed him with a warm smile, handed him a newspaper, and escorted him to the elevator. The lobby teemed with tourists, all milling about and marveling at the priceless paintings and contemporary works of art being displayed between the arches. This midtown skyscraper was home to several Fortune 500 companies, a prominent five-star restaurant, and the esteemed Legacy Gold Magazine Inc.

After breezing through security on the top floor, the editor-in-chief sashayed into the corporate boardroom, fashionably late as always, turning heads and relishing the attention.

He waved to a few colleagues—his way of signaling to the top brass that it was time to get the party started. Dozens of chief executives and their ostentatious colleagues buzzed with anticipation. Staff members nibbled on buttery croissants, while others picked at fruit platters—anxiously awaiting the big announcement.

The editor sauntered toward the head of the table, offering a kiss to his assistant, then settled comfortably onto his magisterial throne.

"Good morning, everyone." His booming voice commanded attention.

"Good morning."

The room fell silent; the bourgeois shuffling to their assigned seats.

"As you all know, today is the big day," he grinned.

The room rustled with a burst of expectation.

He stood and walked toward the giant plasma TV—the media center that resembled a small movie theater. He took his time, primping and posturing, flaunting his tailor-made pinstripe suit, gold cuff links, and silk bow tie.

"Well, boys and girls, let the wagering begin," he smiled.

"After much heated debate and backroom dealings, I am pleased to announce our finalists for this year's Legacy Gold Magazine's Person of the Year award."

The room erupted into applause. He soaked in the adulation, winking at his subordinates, and basking in the spotlight. Eager to keep the momentum going, he raised his hand high in the air, then pointed to the plasma screen that suddenly flashed to life.

The staffers hooted and hollered, never ones to hide their enthusiasm.

The silhouettes of four mystery faces burst onto the screen. Staff members raised their eyebrows, smiling and pointing at the mysterious figureheads, shouting names and voicing their guesses.

The editor signaled for the lights to be dimmed, as the surround-sound speakers rolled out a heavy drum roll.

"Are…you…ready?" he boomed with his rich baritone

voice.

"Yes," a spattering replied.

"I can't hear you!" he raised his voice. "I said, are... you... ready?"

"Yes!" they roared.

The overhead lights faded to black as the plasma screen flashed like lightening with blazing special effects.

"Of course we begin with the queen of daytime television... Ms. Balinda Summers."

The room burst into applause, as staffers lauded their hearty approval.

"Balinda, Balinda!" several supporters chanted.

A large portrait of Balinda filled the screen. A video montage featured quirky outtakes from her award winning daytime show. She laughed and danced with Hollywood celebrities, ran around the studio chasing exotic birds, and engaged in a silly-string battle with her studio audience. The staffers laughed at her carefree love of life.

"Balinda is one of a kind. She has ruled the airwaves for nearly twenty years, and is loved and adored by yours truly," the editor crowed.

"She has donated millions of dollars of her own money and raised countless millions toward opening hospitals and emergency medical clinics in many of the poorest countries in the world... including Haiti, Bangladesh and Sudan."

The room stirred with unbridled enthusiasm. Executives smiled at one another, casting glances of appreciation and support—affirming Balinda's nomination.

"I hate her for her 'Succes dans la Vie,'" he flashed a wry smile, "But she does have a heart of gold and a knack for fashion."

Staffers resumed chanting her name, clapping in unison, and whipping the crowd into a frenzy.

"All right, here we go kiddies."

The drum roll thundered in the background, as the editor-in-chief waved his hand high in the air, then swung his arm with a grand flourish as the next silhouette lit up the screen.

"Next, we have bachelor number two," he quipped. "In order to please our loyal paying subscribers in Middle America, we offer our religious zealot of the month."

A tepid applause rose up from the group, accompanied by grumblings that could be heard from the back of the room. The always diplomatic editor-in-chief proceeded cautiously. He teetered the proverbial middle road when it came to religion—laboring to remain objective—but his true unfavorable sentiment was vaguely concealed.

"He is the controversial and bestselling author, Mr. David Connolly," he announced. "Regardless of one's religious affiliation, of which I have none, we cannot deny that Connolly has been filling arenas from Hicksville, Mississippi, all the way to Podunk, Idaho, conducting his alleged healing services."

A chill permeated the air as a few staffers rolled their eyes and cringed in disgust. The majority, however, seemed to accept the token nomination realizing that he played a representative role in the eyes of small town subscribers—after all, money was money.

A video montage of the televangelist burst onto the screen featuring highlights of the faith healer's TV specials. He hugged senior citizens, laughed with students and children, and knelt beside wheelchair patients kissing cheeks and shaking hands.

Some staff members around the conference table looked on with professional tolerance, while others picked at their food and grumbled under their breath. One heckler in the back coughed in his hand, then uttered a playful obscenity, garnering a few chuckles from those within earshot.

"Also, his recent book has been on the New York Times best seller list for fifteen weeks," the editor said. "Has anyone read his book?" He scanned the room for a split second. "No, I didn't think so."

Hearty laughter swept across the room.

"Moving right along."

The disapproving majority applauded mockingly, anxious to ride roughshod over this controversial nominee.

"All right, settle down, you heathens," he chuckled.

He waved his hand high in the air, then gestured toward the next silhouette which burst onto the screen.

"And behind door number three we have our beloved Governor Mitch Jameson."

A mix of applause and groans dotted the conference room. The peanut gallery was quick to cast aspersions and voice their disapproval of the state leader.

The editor felt a tickle from his funny bone, flashing a sardonic smile, and relishing the opportunity to berate a public official.

"Slick Mitch, the independent, is hated by political pundits from both sides of the aisle. This slippery son of a public servant is still taunted by roundtable opponents—many of whom claim he won his election by a bogus recount."

Confetti blizzards filled the screen as the governor hugged his wife and family, and blew kisses to zealous supporters. Continuing highlights showed the governor shaking hands and posing for pictures with constituents along the campaign trail.

The air in the conference room took on a lukewarm indifference as disgruntled staffers watched the governor's victory footage with a smirk and a yawn. Others crossed their arms and snickered, exhibiting their partisan bent against most politicians—but especially for the sitting governor.

The ensuing video segued to a children's hospital filled with clips of autistic children.

"The Teflon governor has his many warts," the editor continued, "But there are two sides to this chameleon. Jameson is highly respected for his fight against Autism on behalf of his four-year-old daughter. He has raised tens of millions of dollars and has spearheaded countless fund raising events."

Continuing highlights showed boys and girls in rehab

facilities playing games and exercising with physical therapists. Even the hardest cynics in the room bit their tongues, empathizing with the plight of these children.

"Here, here," a timid voice in the back chimed in. The female voice was anonymous; perhaps the mother of an autistic child, or simply someone with a conscience.

"Has anyone ever been to one of his fundraisers?" the editor asked. "Now, I will deny that I ever said this, but we all know that Slick Mitch is a frat boy at heart…, and well, enough said." A few staffers smirked.

"And finally…," the editor exhaled a sigh of relief, "My personal, impartial and unbiased favorite…" he paused, raising his hands and waiting for the drums to crescendo, "…I give you… Dr. Tony Chambers."

The room erupted in applause as supporters unleashed their pent up enthusiasm.

The plasma screen lit up with throngs of cheering crowds. Great multitudes surrounded Dr. Chambers as he led protests in front of the U.S. Capitol Building, blocked traffic in front of a State Supreme courthouse, and passed out winter coats and food boxes in some of the nation's poorest neighborhoods.

The next video showed Dr. Chambers being handcuffed by riot police, which elicited boos and catcalls from staffers in the boardroom. Onscreen, the doctor was carted off in a police paddy wagon as thousands of protesters chanted his name.

"The good doctor and I happen to share the same alma mater," the editor boasted. "Go fighting Jabberwockies!"

Parade video followed with the doctor waving American flags with some of Hollywood's A-list celebrities. He stood arm-in-arm with protesters in front of the Statue of Liberty, at the Lincoln Memorial, and in other notable cities.

"He's the People's Champion!" the editor roared. "Loved by Americans everywhere, Tony the Tiger fights corrupt politicians, fights greedy special interest groups, and fights on behalf the homeless and the poor."

The editor raised his hands signaling the end of the nominations, as fireworks exploded on the big screen.

"So let the games begin!"

The staffers buzzed with excitement.

"Oh, and let me remind you before you peons commence with your wagering and office pools. Make sure you get your official guesses into Maria before the deadline. The rules are the same as always. Whoever picks the winner and comes closest to the total number of votes will win the grand prize." He peered about. "Now we've thought long and hard about this year's top prize, and I think you're going to like it. This year we are giving away...are you ready?" he smiled. "A cash prize of fifty thousand dollars and ...," he paused, "An all expenses paid trip for two to paradise... to the beach resort of your choice.

The staffers jumped out of their seats, high-fiving each other and hugging and cheering.

"And remember...," he shouted above the hoopla, "In the end ..., there are winners and there are losers... so who's it gonna be?"

Chapter 8

The crowd erupted in anger as the motorcade rounded the corner. Mitch flinched when he heard the screams, then peered over at his driver, flashing a cynical grin.

"Curtis, you told me my approval rating was up," he joked.

His driver stuttered, "What can I say, it's a fickle crowd."

"Well, you better hope there are no coffee showers today."

Curtis smirked under his breath.

The convoy of black SUVs slowed to a crawl as they approached the impending mayhem.

Mitch squinted at the blur of faces—the hundreds of protesters who were shouting obscenities and wielding picket signs. He exhaled a long sigh, trying to prepare mentally for the verbal assault. He sank back into the soft leather, the air conditioner wafting against his face. Protesters dangled from the trees—screaming curse words and flipping him the bird. He shook his head in disbelief, then let out a nervous chuckle.

"Ah, yes. Even my friends the tree huggers showed up," he scoffed. "You feeling the love, Curtis?"

His chauffeur flashed an employee grin.

"Come on Curtis, feel the love, I want you to feel the love." Mitch reached over and squeezed his shoulder.

He popped the glove compartment open, scrounging around with a determined look on his face. He pulled out a small cosmetic bag, unzipped it, then grimaced in disgust.

"Damn, we're out of earplugs," he sighed. "Make sure you write them on your grocery list."

Chanters yelled through megaphones, the noise rumbling between the buildings. Police officers shoved the crowd back with their nightsticks, trying to clear a path for the governor.

Mitch's convoy approached with caution, pulling into the designated parking area between the orange cones. The shouting escalated to a fever pitch, growing riotous and more venomous by the second.

Mitch grabbed the door handle, hesitated, then cracked the door open. He was blasted immediately by a barrage of insults. He smiled outwardly, but winced inwardly. Shading his eyes from the sun, he inhaled a deep breath of the morning air before tensing his body for the pushing and shoving. As his security team gathered around him, he scanned the crowd, doing a quick assessment of the situation. Waiting for him at the curb was a lone friendly face, his Lt. Governor, Jester Bragdon.

"Welcome to the party!" Jester shouted above the obscenities, his tone thick with sarcasm.

"Five hundred of my closest friends." Mitch smirked.

He conjured up his pasted smile, then raised his hand, offering a pageant wave to the spiteful masses. The pandemonium stirred like a beehive; police officers clearing a path and pushing protesters into the street. As the governor's cluster plodded toward the front door, the thicket of bodies parted like the Red Sea. The dissidents were driven backwards, screaming profanities, and being squashed against the building. Journalists jockeyed for position in front of the governor— flash photographers and cameramen tussling about in a scrum.

Mitch and his posse—half a dozen heavies in dark sunglasses—were being squeezed from every side. The group trudged through the media frenzy, bombarded by noisy reporters who shouted questions above the ear-piercing screams.

As they inched their way toward the building's main entrance, he didn't mind the verbal attacks, it was the flying food and impromptu beer showers that kept his eyes shifting from side to side.

He ignored the reporters, as they shouted questions with machine gun rapidity.

"Governor, two of your staff members have just been accused of money laundering... any comment?" a reporter yelled.

"Your honor, what are your ties to the banks?" another shouted.

Pretending not to hear above the mayhem, he grimaced, then pointed to his ear while shaking his head. He actually enjoyed the mini confrontations—feigning ignorance and practicing the art of avoidance.

Jester chimed in, yelling, "No comment, the governor has no comment."

As they proceeded up the walkway, his group inched closer to the ringleader, Dr. Chambers, who was locked arm-in-arm with some of the governor's political opponents. Mitch covered his ears, trying to block out the escalating noise—his ears throbbing from the painful blasts of nearby fog horns. He stretched his neck trying to gauge the distance remaining to the front door; he was somewhat relieved that he was beyond the halfway point.

"You're a coward, Governor," the doctor shouted through a bullhorn.

Mitch flinched from the abrupt sound.

"How does it feel to be Wall Street's puppet?" the doctor yelled.

He recognized the doctor's voice, but shaded his face to

avoid eye contact. Struggling to project a look of courage, he smiled and pointed toward a reporter, as if to acknowledge a longtime friend.

"Any comment, Governor?" the reporter asked, "What's your response to...?"

"No comment," Jester interrupted.

Dr. Chambers waved his arms, stirring the crowd, "How does it feel to hide in your fancy office while someone else pulls your strings?"

Mitch shuddered at the contention that he was anybody's puppet. Something snapped inside of him, his pride bubbling to the surface. The accusation demanded a swift rebuttal. He shot a defiant look in the direction of the doctor; his face was stone cold, his eyes spewing fire.

"Be a man for once, governor, it's time to resign!" the doctor shouted.

He stared at the doctor with a steely resolve, his blood boiling, his sweat glands perspiring beneath his Italian suit. As thoughts of vengeance simmered in his mind, he placed his hand on Jester's shoulder—cueing his assistant to stand down. He would indeed address the mob.

The plodding cluster of black-suits sputtered to a halt, the rabble rousers cheering and celebrating a premature victory. He raised both arms high in the air, gesturing for the crowd to quiet down. Reporters anxiously clicked on their audio recorders in anticipation of the governor's comments.

A hush fell over the crowd with the exception of a few hecklers who delighted in cursing during the impromptu silence.

"Shh, quiet, let him speak! He's gonna give a statement," a reporter yelled.

Flashbulbs flickered all around him. He held both arms above his head, like a maestro in full control, then cleared his throat to speak.

He jutted his chin out, scanning the peasants, and flaunting an air of confidence in the face of resistance.

Just then, he noticed a TV camera from one of the major networks, and his demeanor changed at the flick of a switch. He softened his reaction, nodding to the crowd, and displaying a mild look of empathy; but beneath the facade, he relished the attention, enjoying the power he wielded over the multitudes. 'What a bunch of saps,' he thought, 'Who's the real puppet?' He pivoted three hundred and sixty degrees, until he was convinced that everyone's attention was on him. He lowered his arms, stared at the doctor, then unleashed a mocking grin.

"I have no comment," he smirked.

The crowd exploded in anger, the agitators roaring and shrieking obscenities. He nodded to his henchmen, then resumed his journey toward the front door. Hecklers and reporters alike shook their heads in disgust, with the media screaming questions even louder than before.

"How do you sleep at night, Governor?" Dr. Chambers shouted with repugnance, "Millions of Americans are thrown out of their homes while you and your bank buddies keep getting fatter, how do you sleep at night?"

Mitch and his group finally arrived at the entrance, stepping through the glass doors and into his haven of refuge. He exhaled the moment he set foot inside the sound proof lobby, relieved that he was dry and in one piece. Brushing off his jacket sleeves, he chuckled beneath his breath. He thought about skipping his morning workout, and instead, ordering a second breakfast.

"How do you sleep at night?" he snickered to Jester.

"Never alone," Jester cackled.

Mitch peered back at the crowd, a rush of satisfaction flowing through his veins. He felt like a mountain climber grabbing hold of the top ledge, then pulling himself over the pinnacle and resting on the summit.

He glared at the protest leader, determined to mete out some retribution; a swift response was in order, and he had an appetite for vengeance. He grabbed Jester's arm and whispered, "See that the good doctor spends the night in the pokie," he smirked. "Oh, and make sure the food is extra spicy, no bathroom privileges, and cut the hot water."

Jester nodded in agreement, then turned to carry out the order.

"Wait, where are you going?" Mitch raised his eyebrows. "That's only step one. I'm just getting started."

Chapter 9

"Bad doggie, I said, bad!" Cindy scolded the barely two-month-old Golden Labrador pup.

The sun had set on Mitch's swanky suburban home, and inside the family room, four-year-old Cindy was showing Goldie who was boss. As she tugged on the choke chain, she flashed a quirky grin.

"Sit! I said sit!"

The pup tilted her head in bewilderment—as it turned out, English was not her second language. Cindy picked up a tennis ball, then flung it across the room, and into the kitchen.

"Fetch! Fetch, Goldie!"

The puppy's ears perked up when she heard a noise in the backyard, so she leapt onto the couch, and peered out the window. Cindy grunted in frustration. She grabbed the leash—dangling from the couch—and dragged the pup into the kitchen. Being pulled around the house was not Goldie's idea of playtime.

The pup dry heaved after being yanked across the linoleum. Cindy spotted the tennis ball in the hallway, then jerked the leash again.

"What's wrong with you!" she yelled. The pooch cowered, as Cindy cocked her hand back, ready to unleash some childhood motivation.

"Cindy, honey, what are you doing?" Rachel shouted, as she peeked over her shoulder, while stirring the rice.

Rachel knelt beside the traumatized pup, swept her up, and cradled her like an infant.

"See, honey, you have to be gentle with Goldie."

She unfastened the torture collar, then fluffed the matted fur around her ears.

"Look, honey," she settled into a kitchen chair, laying the puppy on her lap, "She just wants to be petted, like this, see?"

A grateful Goldie sprung up and unleashed a waterfall of nonstop licking all over her face. Cindy stretched out her hand and stroked her fur gently.

"See, that's better."

Goldie wagged her tail, cowering away from her daughter, and snuggling up to her—her haven of safety.

The puppy flinched when she heard a noise, then began barking in the direction of the front door. With her tail flailing like a helicopter, she leapt from Rachel's arms, skidded across the linoleum, then disappeared into the hallway.

"Anybody home?" a voice echoed from the foyer.

"In here, honey," Rachel smiled with expectancy, returning to the oven to check the sweet potatoes.

Her husband peeked his face in the doorway—playing hide-and-seek. He spotted his daughter and his face lit up like the sunrise.

"Got any sugar for papa bear?" he raised his eyebrows.

"Daddy!" she squealed in her high pitched voice.

Mitch squatted, throwing his fatherly arms open wide. Cindy darted across the kitchen and leapt into his waiting embrace. He tilted his head with a smile, inviting a peck on the cheek.

"Mmmaa." She planted a big kiss.

Rachel beamed with joy; she was tickled watching her little girl get excited when daddy came home. She folded her arms, and enjoyed the moment. Cindy bounced in his embrace, giddy with euphoria, like she was on a carnival ride.

"Mm-ma!" He unleashed a big kiss on Cindy's silky-smooth cheek.

"Oh no!" he crinkled his nose. "You smell like doggie breath!" He covered his mouth.

"No, I don't," she giggled. "You do."

He tickled her little armpits, triggering uncontrollable laughter. While Cindy squirmed in his arms, he waddled over to Rachel, and gave her an 'I'm home peck on the lips.' She smiled warmly, absorbing his affection.

"How was your day?" she stroked his arm, gazing into his eyes.

"It'll be better, once Pookie gets a breath mint!" he tickled her tummy. "Whoa mama!" Cindy giggled incessantly, then began brushing her fingers along his five o'clock shadow.

"All right, honey, it's time to get washed up for dinner." He gave Cindy a final kiss, then set her down.

"Wow, what a day." He loosened his tie, stretching his arms overhead.

"Still fighting off groupies?" she joked.

"Psh…, I wish."

"Oh, really?" she glared.

He winked, as he strolled to the fridge. He stooped down to pet the puppy, who was camping out by the refrigerator. After grabbing a beer and pulling his head out of the chill, he peeked out the corner of his eye, and noticed her grinning—holding up a full page 'Person of the Year' article.

"Hey, …," she beamed with pride.

Pretending not to hear her, Mitch turned away. "Hey, any mail, honey?" He feigned ignorance, stumbling over to the table. He picked up the mail and started flittering through it, acting nonchalant.

He angled toward her, lifting his eye briefly as he sifted through the letters. "What's that, what you got there?" he asked coyly.

"Don't give me that!" she smirked.

"That's right," he chuckled with over the top elation.

"Big daddy's bringin' home the bacon!"

She gushed with pride, reveling in his silly banter. She enjoyed his little mind games.

"When did you hear about it?" she asked.

"They called me this morning at the office. Yeah, but don't hold your breath." He scoffed.

"Why not?" she feigned a look of surprise. "Too many skeletons in your closet?"

"Yeah, I wouldn't know. My wife fills the closets."

She turned away quickly, hiding her smile. Unable to contain her glee, she strolled over and gave him a warm kiss on the lips.

"Well, you know, it's not easy being a trophy wife."

"Mm…" he smiled. "Smells incredible," offering his intimate approval.

"Why thank you," she blushed.

"Is that rotisserie chicken I smell?"

She scoffed, landing a loving slap on his bicep. She grinned, taking great pleasure in his teasing ways.

As she turned to check the oven, he spun her in a dancer's twirl, then pulled her close. He looked deep into her eyes, causing her to blush as she melted in his embrace. Time slowed to a standstill as he leaned in and kissed her with a soft passionate kiss, nearly taking her breath away.

"Wow, what was that for?" she smiled, opening her eyes.

"Just because," he whispered, pressing his lips to hers once again.

Her whole body tingled, enveloped in his loving affection. Swaying in rhythm, he slid his hands around her waist, her body temperature was rising.

"How 'bout we postpone dinner till later?" he intimated.

"Are you serious?" she blushed.

"Of course, I've been thinking about you all day."

His words stirred her heart. "But it's almost ready." She licked her lips, breathless.

"That's okay, that's what microwaves are for."

"Aren't you hungry, after a long day?"

He smiled, "Yes."

She chuckled, amused by his bad behavior.

"Why am I sensing resistance?" he quipped.

"I'm not resisting, honey, I just know that you're probably hungry, and I cooked one of your favorite meals..., and besides, we have all night."

"But man does not live by bread alone," his eyes begged.

"Wouldn't you rather wait for dessert?"

"How about a little appetizer and dessert?" he reasoned.

"What about Cindy, she hasn't eaten?"

He paused, thinking on the fly. "Let's just send her to her room with a bag of Oreos, she won't mind."

She laughed. "We have all night, honey. I promise, you can climb on me later, just as I'm about to fall asleep, just like you always do."

After giving him a peck on the cheek, she returned to the salad preparation. She smiled inside. She loved to control his desire, keep him hungry; it empowered her, and gave her a sense of sway. He may be the governor—ruler over millions—but she ran the show, she was in control.

"Oh, and just so you know," he whispered, slipping up behind her, "I plan on eating as fast as I can, and then I'm sending Cindy straight to bed."

She chuckled, stroking his cheek. "Honey..., there's something burning." She hurried to the oven.

He picked up the full page add that had his picture along with the other three nominees.

"Not a bad picture of me. I gotta be honest with you, your husband is one good looking guy."

"I didn't realize it came with a million dollar prize?" she raised an eyebrow.

"That's right. Have you spent it already?" he teased.

"No! Well, maybe half," she smiled.

"Wow, only half?"

"Uh-huh, your half."

He chuckled. "Does that mean I have your vote?"

"Nope. Unless we go to Maui."

He nodded, offering a congratulatory grin.

She grabbed the salad bowl and headed into the dining room. She cleared the table, then straightened the red tablecloth.

"Where's Christy?" he asked.

"School. She said something about a chemistry project."

A whiff of skepticism lingered in the air. Their sixteen-year-old daughter had stretched the truth in the past, especially when it came to boys—bad boys.

When the dismissal bell rang at school, Christy burst out of the building like a trapped animal being sprung from her cage. She raced down the crowded stairway, her heart leaping inside her chest. She stumbled as she weaved through the stragglers—nearly tripping—then catching herself on the railing. She paused for a second to gather her bearings, then headed straight for a pimped out silver sedan parked in front of the school. She could barely contain her school-girl elation, when she saw her crush-of-the-moment through the partially tinted windows. She flung the passenger door open, jumped in, and then embarked on a different kind of chemistry than her parents had envisioned.

Meanwhile back at the ranch, Mitch removed the assumed plate from the dinner table. It would be dinner for three this evening, plus the two-month-old beggar camped underneath the table.

"Yeah, Christy said she might be late and wanted to finish some experiment with Natalie," added Rachel.

"On a Friday night?" he scoffed.

"What? You don't trust your daughter?"

"I don't trust sixteen-year-old boys who walk around

with their pants sagging off their backsides and their underwear hanging out," he snickered. "And I don't care for her new rapper boyfriend, what's his name... Rickety Rick?"

"His name is Tereek."

"Whatever," he scoffed. "Kid needs to pull up his pants. I'm gonna sic one of my bodyguards on him."

He settled in at the head of the table, his stomach growling as he caught a whiff of the rotisserie chicken. She set the chicken in the middle, between the marshmallow covered sweet potatoes, the Cajun rice and the broccoli polonaise. The mouthwatering aromas wafted throughout the room. Goldie bounced around in a beggar's frenzy, following the dishes from the kitchen to the dining room.

"Smells incredible, honey." He proceeded to carve the chicken.

"What are you drinking?" She called from the kitchen.

"I'll have whatever you're having."

She picked up a couple of wine glasses, then grabbed the remote to turn off the countertop TV. She enjoyed watching the daytime shows; they kept her company while she cooked dinner. As she fumbled for the 'off' button, she noticed an intriguing figure on the screen. She recognized his picture as one of the nominees running against her husband for the 'Person of the Year award.' He was the guy she had heard about in the news recently—a faith healer something or other, David Connolly, featured on Nightline and 60 Minutes. She turned up the volume.

"There's no such thing as a small miracle," Connolly said. "All you have to do is believe. A miracle may be waiting for you today."

Mitch walked in, and grabbed the pitcher of ice water.

"Do you believe that quack got nominated?" he scoffed.

"I saw an interview with him; I think it was on Sunday night. Intriguing guy," she said, squinting, and watching with attentive curiosity.

"Have you sent in your donation?" he joked.

"I did. I put your name on it. Love Mitch, with lots of hugs and kisses."

"Well, don't book those Hawaii tickets just yet," he replied. "Vegas odds are picking Balinda, two to one."

She flashed a provocative grin. Knowing her husband, she knew he was toying with her. As long as she had known him, he was never one to back down from any challenge, especially one with so much notoriety and national acclaim.

"And what, you're gonna just roll over?" she scoffed.

"What can I do?" he shrugged.

"Please, have you ever lost at anything?" she quipped, giving him a look like 'the game was up.'

"Anything?" he squinted, pondering deeply. "Nope. No," he shook his head. "Wait, there was this one time, I wanted to date this incredibly gorgeous girl, stunning, the most beautiful girl I had ever seen. But I couldn't... cause she was going out with the captain of the football team."

She froze, genuinely dumbfounded.

"No, wait that was you," he teased.

She grabbed a dish towel and flung it at him, hitting him in the chest.

"You always have to get the last word, don't you?" he smiled.

"Always," she grinned.

Chapter 10

Mitch's stomach growled, his appetite was insatiable. After an early morning swim and a deep tissue massage at the health spa, he was craving something sweet. He strolled into his office after skipping a morning meeting, chomping on a strawberry—one of his healthier guilty pleasures. His secretary and Jester were sorting through the morning mail, systemizing a stack of contracts, and setting his agenda for the day.

"Good morning, Bernice," he flaunted his smile. "Did you fight the crowds this morning?"

"No," she chuckled. "But they like me."

"I'm gonna tell everyone you're with me... I don't want you to miss out on the fun," he smiled, peering through the window at the protesters below.

Bernice grinned, amused by his carefree attitude. She finished organizing the documents, aligning every folder with the edge of the desk.

"No egg throwers this morning?" she quipped.

"No, I was a little disappointed. I think they're starting to warm up to me," he winked.

She grinned, setting down the last document marked 'urgent.' Before she left, she reminded him of his afternoon appointments, then handed him a napkin to wipe his strawberry fingers.

"Thanks, Bernice."

As soon as she left, Jester blurted the latest news. "You were right, Mitch. Good ole Dr. Cellblock made it official. He threw his hat in the ring a few minutes ago, and he's coming out swinging."

Mitch stared at the TV, unfazed by the news. He removed his suit jacket, then flung it on the couch. Jester looked on intently, silently gauging his reaction.

Mitch shuffled through the contracts fanned out on his desk. He pondered the latest challenge, sifting through any foreseeable obstacles. The competitor inside of him welcomed the competition, almost scoffing at the pressure—he had never lost a race.

He licked the residue off his fingers, crumpling the napkin, and flinging it into the garbage. He snuck a quick glimpse at the TV, forming a strategy in his head. Dr. Chambers was holding a press conference, and fielding questions about his candidacy. Mitch felt his heart rate jump, his muscles tighten, his adrenaline surge.

"Damn," he grumbled with disgust.

"What, what is it?" Jester flinched with concern.

"Strawberry seed is a bitch," he muttered. "Got any floss?"

Jester mockingly felt his suit pockets. "Yeah, I'll get right on that."

He pressed the intercom, buzzing his secretary.

"Bernice, you got any dental floss?"

Jester furrowed his brow, still curious about the Dr. Chambers' announcement.

"What do you think, Mitch?"

He ignored him, gathering the contracts into a single pile. He plopped into his chair, trying unsuccessfully to relax. He let out a sigh, then leaned back as far as his chair would allow. Just as he was about to speak, he reached in his mouth, and picked at a seed that was stuck between his molars.

"That's two in a row," he grinned, his eyes relishing the moment.

Jester begrudgingly pulled out a wad of cash. He snapped off the money clip and peeled off a twenty.

"Apparently stupidity runs in his family," Jester grumbled bitterly. "And I'm tired of buying your lunches."

Jester extended the money across the desk; Mitch gloated, as he claimed his prophetic winnings.

Bernice popped in, handing him a roll of dental floss.

"Yeah, I don't think you're ready for your big boy pants yet," he chided Jester. "Thanks Bernice."

He flicked the lid off the floss, extracted a ten inch string from the roll, then clicked the cap back into place. He tossed it back to Bernice. She fumbled it, barely catching it—athletics was never her strong suit.

"Governor, I'm going to step out for lunch, if that's okay."

"Enjoy, Bernice."

Jester paced in front of the TV, his eyes fixed on the press conference.

Mitch worked the floss back and forth between his molars, still calculating in his mind the political hurdles ahead.

"Should we send a fruit basket?" Jester quipped, champing at the bit. "Maybe a nice bouquet…welcome to the neighborhood?"

"You're getting soft Jester, I like that."

"Hey, a little house warming gift," Jester grinned. "…maybe a little something for the wifey. Schmoozing goes a long way, what can I say?"

"Yes!" Mitch finally jimmied the seed loose.

He looked intensely at the speck, shook his head, and thought, "How could something so small be so freaking annoying?" He exhaled a sigh of relief, enjoying his mini conquest even more than taking Jester's money. He flicked the seed into oblivion, then smirked at his restless assistant.

"You okay, Jester?"

"I'm just anxious to win my money back," Jester grumbled.

"Oh really, what's the new bet?"

Jester hit the mute button, then conjured up a big smile. "I bet we can force him out of the race in a month."

"One month?" he sounded surprised, "Wow, are you serious?"

"What, we took Peterson out in a month." Jester bragged.

"Yeah, but Peterson was a schizoid alcoholic. I don't know…, four weeks is pretty ambitious."

"You don't think we can do it in four weeks?" Jester raised an eye brow.

Mitch stared for a long moment, contemplating the bet. He stroked his chin. "No, I say two."

Jester's eyes lit up, his smile beaming with a look of shock. "Two weeks!" he laughed, "Are you kidding me! Wow, has someone been doing his homework?"

Mitch meandered in front of his desk, rolling up his shirtsleeves, and leaning back. He nodded with certitude, flashing the same swagger he always projected.

"This weekend, in D.C., there's a march." He grabbed another strawberry, and bit into it. "Let's send our friend a little complimentary room service."

Jester, who had one eye on the TV, suddenly relaxed, giving him his full attention. His face began to exude mischievous pleasure in anticipation of a plan.

"What are we gonna send him, Chinese? Sushi?" Jester's eyes widened.

"I hear he prefers Spanish cuisine," Mitch's smirk grew more pronounced. He stroked his chin with puckish delight.

"Maybe a little bonita Mamasita."

Chapter 11

D r. Chambers grimaced, his feet were on fire—with every muscle in his toes screaming for relief. Inside the penthouse, he collapsed onto the couch, then peeled off his socks, and sunk his toes deep into the plush maroon carpet. He closed his eyes, feeling the tension drain down through the soles of his feet. All he needed was a stiff drink and he was set for the night.

He leaned against the armrest, his muscles begging him to call it a night. His eyelids grew heavy as his mind debated whether to eat or sleep.

He slipped off his suit jacket, which required a monumental effort, then slowly stretched his arms overhead, wincing from the pain. His back muscles clenched like a steel trap, in fact, every muscle in his body tightened up—cramping into double knots. He closed his eyes, then sank deep into the couch, vowing to never move again unless a giant earthquake shook the world.

As he started to doze, he caught a whiff of pasta wafting from the nearby dinner cart—exciting his taste buds—and distracting him from his misery. He loosened his necktie, then inhaled deeply, his mouth watering from the smell of the vinaigrette dressing.

A room attendant, dressed in a penguin uniform, laid out the food—the grilled shrimp appetizer, the covered entree, and the chocolate cheesecake dripping with strawberry puree. The waiter plunked a few ice cubes into a glass tumbler, then filled it to the rim with the hotel's finest Scotch.

Dr. Chambers chugged it without blinking, drinking in the cold comfort, and rinsing his stress away in one shot.

"Leave the bottle," he motioned to the waiter.

He slumped against the armrest feeling satisfied, then picked up his cell, and hit the speed dial.

He closed his eyes, massaging his temples.

"Hey, it's me. I'm exhausted," he groaned, "and my feet are killing me. What's our start time?" he hunkered over, resting his elbows on his knees.

"Six a.m.," his assistant said.

"Stop scheduling these long days," he grumbled. "I'm dying here."

A knock at the door startled him, causing him to loose his train of thought.

"Now what?" he moaned.

He reached into his pocket and pulled out a wad of bills. He peeled off a ten, then gestured to the waiter.

"Can you see who that is, and send them away?" He handed him the bill, followed by a friendly wink.

The attendant filled his glass, then headed for the door.

The doctor covered his eyes, pressing the phone against his ear.

"I'm sorry, go ahead."

"Six a.m."

"You're killing me," he shook his head.

"Actually, we should leave at five thirty."

"Whatever, I'm too tired to argue." He rubbed his eyes, exasperated.

"You know the Vice President doesn't like to be kept waiting."

"Yeah, well life is rough," he scoffed. "Anything else?"

"That's about it."

"Oh, and one other thing," he sighed. "Next time I want

a room with a Jacuzzi."

"You getting old on me, Doc?"

"I'm serious," he smirked.

"Get some sleep."

"Alright, bye." He hung up, tossing the phone aside.

His stomach gurgled, unsettled by the Scotch; he was craving something savory, something chewy with a spicy kick. He could smell the french fries with Tex-Mex spices, causing his mouth to water, stirring his appetite into a frenzy. He lifted the metal cover, inhaling a whiff of the lasagna, and smelling the rich tomato sauce, sprinkled with zesty parmesan. He grabbed a hand full of cheese fries, stuffed them in his mouth—savoring the tangy cheddar on his tongue.

The waiter gathered the empty dishes, balancing plates on each arm. When he opened the door, his jaw dropped in disbelief; the dishes wobbled in his arms, with one plate bouncing off the floor.

"Gracious muchacho. Como estas?"

The doctor heard a soft, feminine voice coming from someone at the door. He stopped chewing and looked up, his ears tingling with curiosity. His eyes widened as his desire for food quickly became an afterthought.

The waiter set the dishes down, then pulled a masseuse cart into the center of the room. The spa carrier was fully equipped with a massage table, exotic oils, lotions, candles, towels and bathrobes.

The senorita stroked the waiter's arm, causing him to smile from ear to ear. He flushed as he gathered the dishes, trying not to stare at the twenty-something goddess. Before he left, he turned for one last look, and she blew him a kiss, sending him out with a smile.

Dr. Chambers sat speechless, his heart racing as he watched her move with the grace of an angel. She checked the door to make sure it was closed, then sashayed over to her massage table.

"Buenos noches, Senor," her accent flowed like honey.

"Usted debe ser cansado despues de un dia largo."

He raised his eyebrows, spellbound by her beauty and the lyrical sounds dripping from her lips. Her eyes were dark and captivating, her smile was radiant—outlined by a warm red lipstick. She had the face of an angel—a flawless complexion, golden brown, and beaming with the innocence of youth. Her hair was black as midnight, silky smooth, and swept up in a ponytail. Her tan shoulders were bare, a red satin chemise clinging to her body, accentuating every curve of her feminine beauty. Her mini skirt complimented her long slender legs, and her black designer heels displayed a delicate rosette bloom, highlighting her golden tan.

"Pueda relleno su bebida?" She gazed deep into his eyes, refilling his drink, then handing him the glass. His hand shook as he sipped a nervous swig, trying to fill the silence with something other than words. With his hormones heating up beneath his suit, he blushed like a schoolboy, barely mustering the courage to speak.

"Um, how are you?" he stuttered—more interested in who she was, and less of how she was feeling.

"Soy maravilloso, gracia." Her words melted him.

He couldn't speak a lick of Spanish, but he sensed that they were feeling each other between the words.

"Are you sure you're in the right place?" he fumbled.

"Quiero masaje y he sido enviado para que se sienta major cualquier forma puede."

She spoke with her hands, and her gestures were just as fluid as her words.

His eyes glazed over, locked in a hypnotic stare. Half of his brain was trapped in a seductive fog, and the other half was languishing in a sleepless stupor. In the midst of the silence, an ounce of doubt crept into his mind. He inhaled a deep breath, trying to organize his thoughts, his conscience firing off a caution signal, sending a shiver up his spine.

"Um, I didn't…, ah, I'm actually good. I'm bueno," he stammered.

"Si, bueno," she laughed in agreement, causing him to blush involuntarily. He was mesmerized by her eyes, his body stirring with a passion that he had not felt in a long time. She kneeled beside the cart, rubbing her hands with a scented lotion, then pulling out a plush bathrobe and setting it on his lap.

"Puedo hacer que usted se sienta mejor asi que relajese," She spoke with her eyes and he understood every word.

Floating in a hypnotic haze, his heart sped up—his breathing grew heavy, as his fatigue melted away. Delicate fragrances floated all around, the sweet smell of perfume casting a spell on his senses. With his mind wandering, he wasn't sure if the scents were emanating from the oil collection or from this goddess kneeling beside him.

"I'm not sure who... I mean, I didn't...um," he stuttered. "No, no. No, thank you. No gracious, no," he insisted with hesitation.

His brain wrestled with an overwhelming desire to indulge. Every fiber in his being wanted to taste, touch, and be touched.

It was just an innocent massage, right? What could it hurt?

He tugged on his collar, his imagination indulging in the tantalizing possibilities. His wedding band weighed heavy on his finger, triggering resistance in his mind, drawing a lump in his throat.

With sweat beading on his forehead, he heaved a heavy sigh of regret. He knew what he had to do, and the longer he waited, the harder it would be. Since he didn't speak her language, he knew that dismissing her would require him to show her the door. Such a herculean effort would be a painful trip in more ways than one.

He closed his eyes, inhaled a deep breath, then summoned the courage to suppress his inner stirrings. He labored to his feet, hesitated, then ambled to the door, opening it with a shaky hand.

Her eyes drooped with sadness. She sat stunned for a long moment, then reluctantly rose to her feet. She took her time folding the bathrobe, packing away the oils, and finally, pouring him another drink. She swung the cart around, then walked sheepishly toward the door. He smiled graciously, with a hint of regret, then retraced his steps back to his dinner tray. As he sat down, he noticed out the corner of his eye, that her handbag had fallen off the side of the cart.

"Um, Senorita, is this your...?"

He bent down slowly, his back muscles clenching as he picked up the purse. She turned and approached him with a look of apology on her face.

"Lo siento mucho, gracias por su amabilidad."

She smiled with her eyes, gazing deep into his schoolboy stare. He handed her the purse, his palms sweating, his emotions reeling with excitement. She laid her fingers on top of his hand—her feminine touch sent waves of elation through every ounce of his body. The energy transfer overpowered him, causing the hair on the back of his neck to stand up. The room blurred into slow motion—perhaps it was the Scotch, or perhaps it was something else.

"Gracious, senor. Muchas gracious," she whispered. "Usted es amable como mi papa."

Releasing his hand and also his gaze, she leaned in and kissed him on the cheek. He caught a whiff of her perfume—so feminine, so seductive; he was intoxicated by her beauty, soaking in her sensual allure. She spun toward the door, then leisurely made her way to the exit. He swallowed hard, his eyes indulging the entire scope of her posterior beauty. He stood frozen, spellbound, as she pulled the door closed behind her. The click from the door was deafening, the echo lingering in his ear.

"Are you insane?" he heard a voice bellow inside his head.

He peered around the empty room, the floral fragrance still tickling his nose. His heart thumped unsteadily, shaking like an internal earthquake, his stomach growling for something to eat. He scratched his head, pondering the loneliness that surrounded him. He realized that his deepest craving was not for food—he was looking to order off the menu. Her soft voice lingered in his ear. He was desperate to see her smile again, to drink in her beauty, and feel her hands against his skin. Like a dog in heat, he dashed to the door and flung it open, without hesitation.

"Senorita!" he cried out.

The masseuse stopped when she heard his voice, startled for a moment, then smiling at his apparent change of heart.

He waved his arms, beckoning her to return. He tried to mask his excitement, but his smile betrayed him—he knew he wasn't fooling anyone. He held the door as she wheeled her cart back into the middle of the suite. His heart was racing a mile a minute, nearly bursting when she stroked his arm. She whispered in his ear, something he didn't understand; she could've asked him for the world, and he would've handed it to her on a platter.

She offered him the bathrobe, which he snatched with both hands. She smiled at his giddiness, squeezing his bicep as he blushed with embarrassment. She unfurled the robe for him, kissed his cheek, then nudged him toward the bedroom. He scampered through the door, like a toddler on Christmas morn.

When he emerged from the bedroom, his face beamed with expectancy. Scented candles flickered all around, the lights turned low, creating a warm ambiance. He inhaled a soothing breath—his senses enveloped by a bouquet of exotic fragrances. He stifled any voices of resistance, then scurried to the table, and lay across the masseuse's web.

His eyes grew heavy as he rested on the table. He barely noticed the flashing lights that flickered between the curtains.

He felt her hands slide softly across his shoulder. He closed his eyes, surrendering all suspicions to the night. Her fingers were warm against his skin; his senses were overwhelmed by pleasure, drifting slowly into ecstasy.

He sunk deep into the bowels of oblivion, and there was no turning back.

Chapter 12

Everything went pitch black with people screaming at the top of their lungs. The rumblings grew louder by the second, vibrations rippling all around as if it was a cattle stampede. She felt the excitement building as she peeked between the crack in the door. She let out a nervous laugh—butterflies fluttering inside her stomach. She had done this a thousand times before, but somehow, it always felt like the first time.

A voice cried out, "Places everyone!" The tension thickened, when suddenly the lights flashed on and the stage manager shouted, "Cue announcer, and go."

"Ladies and gentlemen, you know her, you love her. Here she is... Balinda Summers!"

The audience erupted with screams of hysteria. The rear doors burst open and she emerged from the shadows. Her heart leapt within her, surrounded by cheers from every side.

Party music filled the air as she started down the aisle. She hugged the women along the way, shaking hands and touching as many as she could reach.

Spotlights zigzagged around the room, turning the studio into a dance party.

When she arrived up front, she hopped onstage, striking a pose in her crimson dress. She waved both hands above her head, mouthing the words 'thank you,' and blowing kisses all around. As the music climaxed to a crescendo, she was eager to get the party started.

"Thank you. You'all are too much!" she laughed. "Please have a seat. Thank you."

The audience was reluctant to end the celebration, clapping and laughing till the music finally stopped.

"I'm more excited about seeing you!" she joked.

The audience whooped it up one last time, before they took their cue, and settled into their seats.

"Thank you. You're too kind," she smiled. "How ya'll doing?" she greeted them with a southern drawl.

"Great," they yelled.

"You 'all are amazing." she chuckled.

"We love you Balinda!" The back row yelled.

"I love you too," she laughed, waving to the back. "Well, I've got some good news to share, but…, I'm afraid I also have some bad news," she cringed. "I feel kinda guilty having to share bad news with you after such a wonderful welcome." She rubbed her arms, fending off a sudden chill.

"As you know, we are celebrating 'Anniversary Week,' all this week. We've been on the air…, how many years?"

"Twenty." The audience applauded.

She shook her head. "I still can't believe it…, especially since I turn twenty five next month," she joked.

"Well, as you know, we've been giving away a trip a day to one lucky audience member in celebration of our anniversary. If you remember, on Monday, we gave away a trip for two to Paris…"

The plasma screen flashed to life behind her, showing an audience member jumping up and down, hugging her family, then running onto the stage.

"And on Tuesday, we gave away a trip to the beautiful port city of Monte Carlo, along the exotic shores of the Mediterranean."

The audience shuffled with excitement.

"Well, the bad news is…that we have no more trips to give away."

The audience groaned.

"I need to apologize to you 'all, because this morning I attended a very painful meeting with our promotions and tourism division, and they informed me that our budget for European vacations has exceeded our limit," she paused, "I am so sorry…, I know many of you were looking forward to possibly winning a wonderful prize."

The audience stared in stunned silence.

"So why am I sharing this with you? Because you know that our motto around here is, that 'we try to keep it real,' and unfortunately the recession has taken a heavy toll on all of us. So I wanted to apologize for that. Also, we never let you leave the Balinda Show empty handed, so we do have some t-shirts and…" She looked at her stage manager, "What else do we have?"

"T-shirts, DVDs, and key chains," the assistant said.

"That's right, DVDs, and key chains. So you can pick those up on the way out," her enthusiasm trailed off, waiting for the silence to set in.

"Oh, and by the way," she spoke apologetically, "at the end of today's show, one of you will be adding a new key to your key chain when you drive away in this… new car!"

The big screen burst to life. A sleek, beautiful sedan whooshed along the country road, rustling up the autumn leaves, and gleaming in the sunshine.

The audience jumped out of their seats, hugging and cheering in disbelief.

"That's right…, today, one of you will be cruising home in style!" she shouted, "So cross your fingers, because it could be you!"

The crowd bounced up and down on the risers, sending vibrations throughout the studio.

She spoke directly into the camera, shouting over the jubilation. "We have an incredible show for you today. We are going to take a short break, and let our audience catch their breath, but when we come back…, we have a Balinda exclusive that you're not gonna want to miss…, today's show is red hot! That's all I'm going to say. We'll be right back."

"And we are off the air," the director yelled.

"Three minutes," the stage manager called.

Balinda hurried offstage for a quick touchup of hair and makeup. She grabbed a sip of water, then briefly scanned her notes.

"Thirty seconds, Balinda," she heard the director call.

She scooted back to center stage and inhaled a deep breath.

The stage manager cued her, "Counting down in five, four, three …"

"Welcome back, everybody. There are two or three major stories in today's headlines, and as you know, we here at The Balinda Show pride ourselves in going to the heart of the matter, so we asked ourselves, 'What is the number one story… the must-talk-about story of the day?' And we decided to bring it front and center. So, are you ready?"

"Yes," they replied.

"Are you sure?"

"Yes!"

"It's gonna be juicy," she teased. "Then let's get right to it. Unless you've been living under a rock, you know that another sex scandal has rocked the political world."

The audience gasped from recognition.

"Will these men ever learn?" she scoffed. "Let's take a look."

The screen lit up behind her.

"The number one trending topic the past few days has been Dr. Tony Chambers."

The audience chattered, as they watched the video.

"For those of you who don't know…, Dr. Chambers has been a leading civil rights activist for decades. He has been happily married for nearly thirty years, and recently announced his candidacy for governor. Well, guess what?" she smirked. "Surprise, surprise… three days ago, these shocking pictures hit the tabloids."

Photos of the doctor and the masseuse flashed onto the screen. Close-ups of his face were interspersed with full length shots of him sprawled out on the massage table. Additional photos and tabloid covers revealed a topless masseuse, with body parts covered by blur marks and black squares.

The audience was glued to the video—some were incensed; however, no one turned away.

"When these photos hit the internet a few days ago, Dr. Chambers conveniently disappeared from the public eye, and has not been seen since…" she paused, "that is… until today."

The audience let out a collective gasp.

"That's right, he is here…, and speaking out today for the first time, to address these salacious allegations."

The crowd recoiled—a mix of excitement and moral repugnance.

Beneath the cover of darkness, a skittish Dr. Chambers walked quietly to the corner of the stage. He settled inconspicuously on the interview couch, bowing his head, with his eyes glued to the floor.

Balinda paused for a moment, peeking over, then turning away. Her conscience was torn, struggling to set aside her fifteen year friendship with the doctor and his wife. As a journalist, she knew she needed to grill him, lest she face a backlash from the mainstream critics.

When the video ended, the studio lights flooded the stage, revealing a hunched over Dr. Chambers, with a downcast look on his face.

Audience members gasped when they saw him—the atmosphere taking on a sudden chill.

"It must be noted for full disclosure that I have known Dr. Chambers, his wife and family for many years," she confessed.

She glanced at the doctor, offering a courteous nod, but

being careful not to show any signs of favoritism. The audience murmured, shifting uncomfortably in their seats. The doctor, who had a well-known track record of humanitarian acts and charitable contributions, sat frozen in the silence, while the audience sat on their hands. The snub spoke volumes about how far he had fallen.

Balinda shook his hand, sensing the awkwardness in the room, then settled into her seat. She inhaled a deep breath, trying to clear her mind of any sense of allegiance, then reminded herself that she had a job to do.

"First we want to welcome you Dr. Chambers."

"Thank you," his voice cracked.

"Let's forgo the pleasantries, and cut to the chase, if you don't mind."

He nodded sheepishly.

"Like most Americans, I was shocked and appalled when these pictures surfaced... and I have to be honest with you, a part of me is still disgusted." She looked him directly in the eye. "And you want to say what?"

He took a deep breath, hesitating before he spoke.

"First I want to say, thank you for having me on your show, and allowing me to speak the truth about these ugly rumors. Secondly, I want to say clearly and unequivocally that I did nothing inappropriate."

The audience snickered.

He raised his voice above the chatter, continuing to press his case.

"I love my wife with all my heart," his eyes glazed over. "And we've been together for almost thirty years and I have never cheated on her. And I did nothing sexual or inappropriate with this or any other woman."

Balinda watched intently, sensing the audience's cynicism. She was surprised that his first words were not an apology. She was willing to grant him the benefit of the doubt, but his margin for error was slim to none.

"Why should America believe you?" she probed. "I

mean, we just saw the pictures."

He shook his head, heaving a heavy sigh of frustration. "Balinda, you've known me for years. And you know that I tell it like it is... I have nothing to hide. When I make a mistake, I am the first to admit it."

"Did you make a mistake?" she pressed.

He averted his glance and swallowed hard. "I do admit that I was in the wrong place at the wrong time."

"Well, I'm relieved to hear you say that," she rolled her eyes. "But in the end, what...? All we have is your word against hers?"

"Well, actually, all you have is my word."

"She hasn't spoken?"

He shook his head. "She has mysteriously and conveniently disappeared."

"Well, I'm sure some tabloid is out there tracking her down as we speak," she quipped.

He smirked, hanging his head.

"Okay fine," she continued. "Let's say she never shows up. You still haven't proven anything. Why should we believe you?"

"Balinda, you know I'm a fighter," he sighed. "I come from the streets, and I don't mind getting dirty." He straightened up. "Now there are some people who fight the right way, but there are others who hide in the shadows and fight like cowards."

"What are you suggesting?"

"Hey, I'm just saying..., if it walks like a duck, acts like a duck, quacks like a duck and craps like a duck..., it ain't no chicken.

The audience snickered, whispering among themselves.

"You think someone set you up?" she pressed.

"I'm saying that the hotel has no record of this woman as a masseuse, or as an employee. And secondly, my people are telling me that the security tapes may have been tampered with. These pictures that were leaked to the public, were pictures photographed through a window… I mean, come on."

The whispers in the audience grew louder.

"Well, I'm not going to lie to you," she chuckled. "If I was your wife, you'd be sleeping in the dog house just for getting caught up in this mess."

"Fair enough," he nodded with a slight grin.

She stared for a long second.

"I will tell you this," she hesitated, "these pictures are pretty damning," she looked on, reading his reaction. "So let's wait for the facts," she paused, "because in life… nobody gets a free pass."

Chapter 13

Mitch's blood pressure rose, his head throbbing as he squirmed through the angry crowd. The late day tussle left him winded, along with a mild case of indigestion. He shuffled off the elevator toward his office, eager to sprawl out on the couch and call it a day. After his secretary mouthed some meaningless messages, he dropped his brief case by the door, then headed straight for the mini bar.

"We need to tighten security," he yelled to Jester, who was camped in front of the TVs.

"Why, what happened?"

"Apparently hurling insults isn't enough anymore."

"Tomatoes?" Jester chuckled.

"A couple of eggs."

"Did you get hit?"

"Curtis caught it in the ear."

Jester smirked, "Now see, Mitch, why do you get all the fun?"

"Just lucky, I guess." He rolled his eyes. "Maybe I need a disguise. You got any wigs lying around?"

Jester smiled, "Yeah, I'll check my closet."

Mitch grabbed a drink and sauntered to the couch. He peeled off his suit jacket, kicked off his shoes, then sank deep into the soft leather—his body unwinding, sensing the end of the work day. He let out a loud growl, still smarting over the flying egg assault. He grabbed the newspaper and perused through the sports section, searching for anything that was not work related.

Jester was glued to the TVs, catching the end of Dr. Chambers' interview on Balinda's show.

Mitch peeked from behind the paper, snickering at the sight of his political rival.

"Ah, Senor Tony. How's he doing, has he buckled yet?"

"He's squirming," Jester said.

"Lucky dog. He should be thanking me. From the pictures I've seen, it looks like margaritaville lasted all night."

"Yeah well, he's begging like a dog."

"Sometimes it's just too easy, Jester," he grinned.

"Don't be so sure, you haven't won yet."

"Double or nothing?" he quipped, ducking behind the sport's page.

"Maybe," Jester wavered, "I think Balinda might actually be bailing him out."

"Naw, that bird is basted." he scoffed, "Oh, and by the way, that reminds me…, that's what we need."

"What, a masseuse?" Jester joked.

"Well, that too," he grinned. "No, if I could get her audience on my side…" His mind strategized like a chess master, the wheels turning as he contemplated his presidential run.

Jester hit the mute button, squinting with a quizzical look on his face. "A national audience, already?"

"Apple trees don't grow overnight…, and neither do presidents. After November, it's full speed ahead."

Jester offered a half nod.

"The women's vote is huge," he said. "It's never too early to work those demographics, get a little exposure."

Jester turned back to the news, flipping to an international channel. He watched as an elderly woman was pushed around by villagers. She was knocked to the ground as townspeople wrestled over food supplies. She groveled in the dirt, while a few small children tried to help her to her feet. They were swallowed up in the pushing and shoving—the food lines exploding into a full blown riot.

"What are you watching?" Mitch asked.

"Your ticket to the White House."

"What are you talking about?"

"If you want Balinda's audience," Jester suggested, "it's all about compassion with these ladies, a little soft sell. Just make a little charity visit to one of these poor countries. Play the game. Take some TV cameras, and snap a few pictures with Tarzan and the gang."

Jester tossed him the remote, basking in the certitude of his pseudo-charity plan. Mitch chuckled at his gloating, shook his head, and returned to his paper.

"I'm serious," Jester insisted, "Build up your international cred, Mr. Ambassador, and you'll look like a freakin' hero."

Mitch yawned at the idea. "Yeah well, let's put Tarzan on hold. Besides, it's dirty over there," he grimaced.

He threw his feet on the coffee table and took a long chug of his beer. A nap sounded pretty good right about now, especially since his reelection was a virtual lock.

"You want glamour?" Jester chimed in. "How about a good scandal?

"Scandal?" Mitch snickered.

"Absolutely, you toss in some false accusations…, and boom, instant sympathy vote.

He pondered the idea for a second, then averted his eyes.

"People love to support victims." Jester insisted.

"Scandals are messy."

"Are you kidding, it's brilliant," Jester protested. "I'll set up a dinner with a former beauty queen, toss in some photos, circulate some rumors, and then concoct a trail that leads back to the doctor."

"Is this your first day?" he chuckled.

He stretched out on the couch and closed his eyes, hoping to catch a breather before he faced the crowds.

"What are you talking about?" Jester quipped. "Scandal means face time."

"Yeah, I'm thinking, no…" He shook his head, wanting to put the discussion to rest.

"Come on, Mitch, just give it…"

"Hold that thought," Mitch looked at his watch. "Just take a breath…"

He walked over to his desk, plopped in his chair, and buzzed his secretary.

"Bernice, do you have a second?"

He looked Jester in the eye, like a seasoned veteran schooling his young apprentice, "Let me bring you up to speed, Jester. You see, if you want to win your way into a woman's heart…"

Bernice popped in, interrupting his mini lesson.

"Bernice, I want you to call Balinda Summers' people, and tell them we're interested in doing a show on children… and autism."

He smiled at his protégé. "You see, Jester, the way to a woman's heart…is through the children. Just show 'em you care," he winked.

Chapter 14

"You've got to be kidding me," Rachel rolled her eyes, deeply annoyed. After waiting more than twenty minutes in the cold cut line, a tidal wave of customers swept in from out of nowhere.

"Are they giving money away?" she sighed. Feeling penned in, she decided to avoid the front of the store, which was crammed with wall-to-wall bodies. A group of high school kids clogged the magazine aisle, moms were pushing strollers, and senior citizens were swapping coupons in slow motion. She peered at her wristwatch, sighing in disbelief—it was five-thirty. Great, now she had to face rush hour traffic too. She shook her head in dismay, still fuming about Cindy's therapy session running late. She pushed her cart through the produce aisle, weaving past a dozen shoppers who felt the need to touch every head of lettuce.

"Excuse me, please?" she asked with forced politeness, bumping baskets and plowing through the herd.

Cindy fidgeted inside the shopping cart, anxious to climb out and run around. She attempted to stand, pulling her legs up through the wire openings.

"Honey, stay seated. Mommy's almost done."

"No!" Cindy's face shriveled in defiance.

"I said, sit, we're almost done." Her temples throbbed.

"I want down!" Cindy's high pitched voice screeched, as she struggled to stand.

"Fine!" She relented. Her energy was drained; she was too tired to fight. "But stay close to mommy. Don't wander off, do you hear me?" She lifted Cindy out, and set her down.

She crossed a dozen items off her list, anxious to leave as soon as possible. She circled the necessary items, along with her must-have guilty pleasures.

"This is ridiculous," she muttered, turning into a crowded aisle. "Just get in and get out," she grimaced.

Sprinting through the frozen food section, she made a beeline for the ice cream freezer.

Cindy straggled a few steps behind, poking packages and sliding her hand along the shelves. She was cranky after therapy; definitely in need of a nap. She picked up a family size jar of red maraschino cherries and then hoisted it above her head. She inspected the bottom, licking her lips and nearly licking the jar.

"Cindy, please don't touch those," she cringed. "Come on, we have those at home."

She snatched the jar, and placed it on the nearest shelf. Cindy's face twisted in anger, folding her arms in defiance.

"Come on, honey, we're almost done."

She hustled through the frozen food section dragging her daughter close behind. A misty chill lingered in the aisle as she scanned the glass freezers—frozen pizzas, green beans, juices, frozen dinners... ah ha, the dessert section. There was one item left on her list, and then it was straight for the checkout. As she opened the freezer door, the cold air wafted against her face—a refreshing coolness. She shuffled the containers around, pushing the boring flavors to the side. Her eyes lit up when she spotted the last available canister of Chunky Monkey. She stared at the cylinder, a bit perplexed. "Only one left... what's wrong with it?" she wondered. She flipped the tub over, examining it for any tampering or seepage. After a quick check, she was relieved—convinced it was safe. She tossed it in the cart, then exhaled a sigh of accomplishment.

When she closed the freezer door, she looked around, then suddenly let out an audible gasp. Her daughter was gone.

"Cindy?" she called out, more concerned than panicked.

No answer. She pushed the cart with urgency toward the back of the store. Cindy appeared from around the corner, waving a box of Lucky Charms in one hand and a bag of family sized M&Ms in the other.

"Cindy, what did I tell you?" the skin shivered on the back of her neck. "You need to stay with mommy."

She snatched the cereal and candy out of her hands and threw them on a display case.

"What did the doctor say...? You're supposed to listen!" she grit her teeth.

Cindy's face burned with rage. She exploded into a tantrum—category high. She crossed her arms and stomped her feet, her body shuddering like a pent up volcano. Her high pitched scream uncoiled softly at first, then reverberated off the ceiling and throughout the entire frozen food section.

"Stop it, honey. I am not in the mood for this!" She clenched her jaw, staring her down.

Cindy's wailing bounced between the freezer aisles, ricocheting louder and faster by the second. Rachel tossed the groceries that were in the child's seat into the main basket, then snatched Cindy up, and plopped her into the cart. With her adrenaline pumping, she steered the cart down the aisle, heading straight for the checkout counters.

When she reached the front, her face twisted in anguish, as each checkout was at least four customers deep. She rolled past the express lanes, pausing to consider the possibility, then forged ahead with her fifteen-plus items.

Cindy's screaming intensified, causing her to shudder inside. She pulled into aisle five, avoiding all eye contact, and knowing full well what everyone was thinking. Cindy's tirade increased in volume and irritability, as people turned away, murmuring under their breath.

"Shh. Honey, please stop crying," she pleaded.

"I wanna go home! I don't wanna stay here. I wanna…"

"We will, honey, in a few minutes. Please, Mommy just needs to…"

"No, I wanna go now!" she whined.

"How about some animal crackers?" She tore open the box.

Cindy grabbed the animal crackers, raised them above her head, then flung them into aisle nine hitting several shoppers in the head with flying monkeys and elephants.

Rachel flushed with humiliation.

"Cindy!" she cringed, covering her eyes. "I am so sorry." She apologized, wanting to crawl in a hole and die.

Desperate for peace, she lifted her daughter out of the cart and set her down. Cindy was now out of sight, but unfortunately not out of mind, or earshot. The wailing continued—heightening to an ear piercing level.

Rachel gnashed her teeth, shaking her head in surrender. She felt the eyes of people around her, judging her with condescending glares.

Customers whispered to one another, peeking occasionally, and trying to sneak a glance without being noticed. She struggled to remain calm, inhaling several deep breaths, and praying that the line would move quickly. Her temples tightened, feeling a wave of self-consciousness—she was keenly aware of her semi-celebrity status as the governor's wife.

"Maybe I should just leave, abandon the cart and head out to the parking lot," she speculated. She looked around, contemplating a run to the door, as the line inched closer to the register. She vetoed the plan, since she was hemmed in on every side. Besides, she was almost to the front, and leaving an abandoned cart with melting ice cream was not ideal. She decided to tough it out.

"Honey, please," she begged, "When we get home, I'll ask Daddy to buy you a new dolly. Would you like that?" Cindy covered her ears and continued to scream.

They finally reached the conveyer belt, after what seemed like an eternity, and she began to unload the groceries. One by one the cashier scanned the items, the sweet sound of each beep meant she was one step closer to home.

As she placed the last item on the counter, she peered down at her daughter, when her face turned ghost white. Without warning, her worst nightmare unfolded before her eyes. Next to the checkout stand was a six-foot-high glass tower of apple juice that was stacked neatly beside the counter.

"Cindy, No!" she screamed in horror.

Cindy wrapped her fingers around one of the bottom jars, then tugged, until she pulled the bottle free. In eerie slow motion, the entire pyramid came crashing down like a house of cards. The six-foot structure collapsed, with bottles crashing on top of bottles. The crowd around her retreated like ripples in a lake, jumping out of the way as juice washed in every direction. The sound of glass breaking only added to the chaos— combined with the screaming symphonics that were coming from Cindy.

Rachel snatched her daughter up from the broken glass, pulling her from harm's way, and clutching her against her body. She hopped away from the register, doing the tip toe dance to avoid the apple juice river. Unable to outrun the deluge, her socks were soaked to the bone, only adding to her misery.

The store fell into a ghastly silence, as shoppers stared with wide eyes, gawking in horror. Rachel's face blazed beet red, her body stiffening, her emotions seized by utter humiliation. Her heart stopped beating. She wanted to die, as every eye in the store was staring at her.

Chapter 15

Rachel burst through the front door, still shaking with humiliation, her feet making a squishy sound as she stepped into the foyer. She peeled off her shoes and socks, then stormed into the kitchen.

Cindy tramped close behind, still screaming her head off, and spreading an ample supply of dry tears to anyone and everyone.

"I can't take it, Mitch!" she shouted, her voice cracking on the verge of a nervous breakdown. "I'm through, this is the last..."

Mitch spotted her from the family room, his cell glued to his ear. He looked on with puzzled concern, not sure what to make of her distress.

"What is it, honey?" he covered the phone.

"I'm done! I can't take it anymore."

"What happened?"

"Everyone was staring," she stuttered, choking back tears.

He turned away for a second, covering his eyes, and pondering his options.

"I'm sorry, I'm gonna have to call you back," he winced.

He hung up the phone, then headed toward the hallway,

slamming face first into the brunt of Cindy's high pitched rant.

"Christy!" he called up the stairs, "Come get your sister!"

Rachel opened the kitchen cabinet, deciding to soothe her anxiety with a cup of premium java. In haste, she ripped open a new bag, which exploded onto the counter. She growled in frustration.

"That's it, I'm taking her to see David Connolly," she blurted out, struggling to regain her sanity.

"Okay, that's fine," Mitch agreed, helping her clean the spill. "No big deal. I'll give Dr. Connolly a call. Is he like a specialist?"

She swallowed, averting her eyes. "Yes."

"Okay, just tell me where he is. Is he with Presbyterian Medical, or is he downtown?"

"Sort of." She tore open another bag.

"What do you mean? Where is he?"

She hesitated. "He's the guy on TV."

Cindy appeared in the doorway, screaming a few new syllables. She raised her hand over her head, then chucked a set of keys across the floor—adding an aerial attack to her verbal assault.

"Christy, come down here, please!" Mitch called out. "Wait, what?" he turned to her.

"David Connolly," she replied, briskly stirring her coffee.

"TV…, what are you talking about?"

"He helps people."

"You mean the religious quack?"

"Hey, you don't know that," she objected.

"Are you serious?" Mitch scoffed at the absurdity. He shook his head in disbelief, pulled out his cell and headed back into the family room.

Rachel closed her eyes, trying to block out the screams, but the persistent wailing triggered flashbacks—the embarrassment embedded in her memory. She cringed, as she recalled the whispers and stares, the glass crashing, the oceanic spill, and people cursing as they ran out the store. Just thinking about it made her skin crawl. She refused to relive that nightmare ever again.

"I can't take it anymore, Mitch," Her voice cracked on the verge of tears. "You weren't there, you didn't have to…"

"Rachel, honey," he interrupted. "But he's not even a doctor. He's a quack."

"He's not a quack," she dug in. "People all over the country are going to see him."

"Honey, no… no… we can't."

"Why not?"

"This guy is a snake oil salesman. If you're photographed near this guy, it's gonna be all over the front page."

She crossed her arms, determined not to back down. Her mind raced for a response, searching for something, anything.

They stared at one another, wrestling in a silent impasse. Her eyes filled with anguish, but her mind was made up.

"I've had it, Mitch! You weren't there. There were a thousand people staring at me…"

"Look, honey," he replied. "I'll hire another nanny. We'll get a nurse to be here full time, so you'll never have to take her shopping again."

"We tried that," she winced. "I'm tired of pushing her off on other people. I want her to get better. Honey, don't you want her to get better?"

"Of course I do," he insisted, implying it should be obvious. "Look, if you want I'll arrange a private meeting with this guy sometime next year, but we cannot be seen with him. He's too extreme. And, honey, we are so close."

She shook her head, distraught that he was ignoring her pain. She retreated inside; she didn't have the emotional strength to wage another battle.

She walked away in frustration, staring blankly out the window. Her skin shivered as the room temperature dropped a few degrees. Her eyes glazed over, feeling alone—abandoned.

He approached her slowly and gently rubbed her shoulders. She breathed a little easier, watching the sun as it dipped behind the trees. The smell of coffee and the caress of her husband's touch began to slowly loosen the tension. She closed her eyes. A calm serenity washed over her senses as her breathing returned to normal.

"Look, let's go out to dinner," he whispered. "Just the two of us. We'll have some drinks, a nice relaxing evening... maybe dance a little."

His caring voice soothed her, causing her body to relax, like a blanket of safety enveloping her and keeping her warm.

He twirled her around and embraced her in his arms. She laid her head against his shoulder, feeling his heart beating next to hers.

"Honey, you gotta trust me on this," he assured her, kissing her gently on the forehead. She inhaled a deep breath, then closed her eyes. She loved the close compassion, absorbing his trust—for the moment.

Chapter 16

Christy dawdled down the stairs—her fingers flittering across her cell. She was annoyed that she had to clean up after her sister; she was missing her favorite show. Her mind was preoccupied, giddy, in anticipation of going to the movies with her new boyfriend. Her sister pouted on the bottom step, pulling off her wet socks—still dripping with apple juice. The foyer finally breathed in silence; however, the hallway looked like a disaster area—littered with shoes, jackets, boots and umbrellas.

"Cindy, what did you do?" she grumbled, flipping a plant right side up.

"Christy, honey," her dad called from the kitchen. "Can you come in here?"

She rolled her eyes, scooping up Cindy's shoes, waiting anxiously for an important text. She tarried in the doorway, her eyes glued to her cell.

"What?" she sighed.

"We need you to babysit tonight. Your mother and I are going out for dinner."

Her jaw dropped to the floor, gasping as if she had been punched in the stomach. Her world had just imploded. She dropped everything, then lashed out in disbelief.

"I can't! I'm going to the movies with my boyfriend!"

"Well plans change."

"What?! That's not fair!" she rebutted, crossing her arms in defiance.

"What's not fair? Family?"

She growled in disgust. She had been looking forward to this night all week. Her heart rate sped up, the sobs building in her throat; if she didn't see her boyfriend tonight, she would die.

"Why can't you bring in a babysitter?" she argued.

"It's too late. Come on, honey, this is an emergency." He raised his eyebrows, not expecting a debate. "Plus, Cindy listens to you, she looks up to you."

Her mind was paralyzed by anger. Once her father played the dominant family card, she knew she was cooked—game, set, match. She grumbled in silence, wanting to argue, but nothing was coming out. She switched strategies quickly employing the guilt maneuver.

"You never let me go out," she whined.

"Hey, family comes first," he insisted. "End of discussion."

"You only let me go out on weekends as it is, and now I can't even do that," she fumed, storming out of the kitchen.

"Um, excuse me. We're not done here." His voice stopped her in her tracks.

She slinked back to the doorway, staring at the floor.

"What?" She refused to look at him.

"When you have teenagers of your own, you'll understand."

She rolled her eyes, tired of that lame excuse. She wanted to vent, but she bit her tongue instead.

On the verge of tears, she held out one last hope—it was now or never. Going to the movies with her boyfriend was a lost cause, but she had to recoup something, anything.

"Mom, please?" she whimpered.

Her mother looked on with empathy.

"Sweetie, what if your boyfriend comes here," she

suggested. "You can watch a movie here."

Christy sighed loudly. It was not what she was hoping for, but at least there was a breach in the wall.

"You know it's not the same," she pouted.

"It's either that or nothing," her father chimed in.

"Fine," she relented.

She picked up her sister's belongings and dragged her feet toward her decreed banishment. But just when she thought it couldn't get any worse, further stipulations were piled onto the carnage.

"And listen to me," her dad called out. "He is not to go upstairs. He is to stay on this floor. Is that clear?"

"What, you don't trust me?" she snapped.

"I don't trust Rickety Rick, or whatever the hell his name is."

"His name is Tereek."

"Whatever. Is that understood?" His glare pierced right through her.

She was tempted not to answer. She had to flex her independence somehow—assert her teenage autonomy. She pivoted away, throwing up the silent treatment.

"Is that understood?" he walked slowly toward her.

"Yes!" she grunted. "You treat me like I'm a baby," she muttered. She stormed up the stairs, stomping her feet the whole way. Her show of disgust was nominal at best—her socks generating very little noise on the plush carpet stairs. She slammed her bedroom door.

"You never let me do anything!" she screamed, knowing full well that her father couldn't hear her.

She cranked the stereo full blast, the noise easing the frustration that churned in her mind. She texted her friends, her fingers fumbling over the wrong letters; she couldn't think straight now that her whole world had just collapsed.

With her heart crashing in her chest, she groaned, desperate to exert her independence—somehow, somewhere. The question was not if, but when?

Chapter 17

Christy flung open the bedroom door, her heart beating out of her chest. She scurried down the stairs, nearly tripping before she caught herself on the banister. Her smile lit up the darkened staircase as she fumbled for the light switch.

"I got it!" she yelled.

She scampered in front of the mirror for a final hair check. She felt good in her tight blue jeans and clingy tee from Abercrombie.

The puppy raced into the foyer, barking incessantly as the unofficial welcoming committee.

"Goldie, get back. Hey, Goldie!" she shooed her away.

Her heart fluttered, partly because of the stairway dash, but mostly due to her giddy expectation. She opened the door and beamed with excitement at the sight of her saggy pants knight-in-shining-armor.

"Hey," she smiled, biting her bottom lip.

She threw her arms around his neck, giving him a shoulder leading hug. He flashed a half smile, masking his eagerness, until their eyes met, then his enthusiasm was exposed.

"Hey," he grunted.

She loved his street swag, and the smell of his cologne. Along with his saggy blue jeans, he wore a faded blue tee with Aeropostale written across the front. His dark brown hair was cropped short and tight.

She glanced sideways and saw her mom descending the stairs like a beauty queen, touching every step with elegance and style. Her sleek evening gown accented her curves in all the right places, her bare shoulders revealing a hint of sexiness.

"Hi Tereek, it's finally nice to meet you." She extended her hand.

"Hey, Mrs. J.," his eyes lit up.

"Have you eaten dinner?"

"I ate before I came."

"Well if you get hungry…, Christy can heat up some lasagna, or you two can order a pizza."

"Thanks, mom."

"Now, honey…," her mom said. "All the emergency numbers are by the phone…, and we should be home before eleven.

"I know, mom," she grumbled, still feeling the stigma of untrusting parents.

Her dad strutted down the stairs in his crisp Italian suit. He walked with a Wall Street swagger—more commanding than her street savvy boyfriend. Mitch paid no attention to Tereek, strictly adhering to his own appearance; he straightened his tie and checked his cufflinks—exuding a VIP aura that demanded respect.

When he touched down at the bottom, he towered some five inches above her boyfriend. He stared into Tereek's eyes, locking his gaze until her boyfriend averted his glance. Tereek fidgeted with his clothes, shifting nervously back and forth.

"I understand you weren't in school on Monday, son," Her father greeted him with a contentious tone. "What…, long weekend?"

"No, sir," the Tereek smiled with a nervous laugh.

Mitch stared expressionless into the boy's eyes.

Christy grew antsy at her dad's interrogation. Tereek's eyes glazed over, like a deer in the headlights.

"Mom?" she pleaded, intervening to break the tension.

Her father crossed his arms, then fired another warning shot.

"And you got a parking ticket last Wednesday…," he pressed. "No quarters?"

"Um, no sir," he stammered, staring at the carpet.

"Mom, please?" Christy begged.

Her mother stood silent for a moment, choosing not to interfere.

"Oh, and by the way, I've contacted the United Way," her father said, "about donating a thousand belts to your school, since you boys are having trouble…"

"Honey, let's go," Rachel chuckled, tugging Mitch's arm, "We're gonna be late for our reservation."

Mitch's eyes were locked in a rock hard stare, until he broke his gaze with a grin of satisfaction. He shook Tereek's hand with a grip of steel, squeezing tight for a prolonged moment until he saw the boy flinch.

Her father kissed her cheek, then looked her in the eyes, "You call us if you need anything."

He embraced her with an extended hug, making her feel safe and loved. Her mother followed up with a hug and a kiss, then whispered in her ear, "We love you."

Christy closed the door behind them, releasing a heavy sigh of relief.

"I am so sorry." She squeezed his arm. "My dad is weird like that. Are you okay?"

"Naw, I'm good," he shrugged, trying to act nonchalant. "I thought he was gonna have me arrested for that parking thing," he smirked.

"Come on, are you hungry?" She led him to the kitchen.

"I'm always hungry." He grabbed her around the waist, tickling her, then wrapping her in a bear hug.

"Stop it." She giggled, pushing him away. "Seriously,

what do you want to drink," she opened the fridge, "We've got everything, soda, juice, iced tea, energy drinks?"

"Oo, energy drinks!" he grinned. "Naw, I'll just take a beer."

She smiled. "Be serious."

"Come on, let's splash a little rum in our cokes."

"Obviously, you don't know my dad." She popped some ice in a glass. "If one of those liquor bottles is moved even a whisker, my dad will kill me."

He pulled a beer from the bottom shelf.

"Tereek, stop! I'm serious," she giggled, snatching it from him. "Now just go... go and pick a movie." She pushed him toward the family room.

Tereek did a superman dive onto the couch, then threw his legs haphazardly onto the coffee table. Cindy was sprawled out in front of the TV, teasing the puppy with a tennis ball and a bone.

Christy walked in, balancing an armful of soda, cookies and several bags of chips. She plunked down next to Tereek who was stretched out like it was his bed. He tilted his head toward her, ogling her curves with a hungry eye. He kicked off his shoes, flicking them into the center of the room; his swagger seemed to be back, like he was the king of the castle. He grabbed a cold can, then lifted the back of her shirt and pressed it against her skin.

"Tereek!" she gasped, "Stop it." She pushed him away.

He laughed as she recoiled.

"Come on, pick a movie." She shuffled through a stack of DVDs.

"Whatever," he grunted, leaning back.

"What are you in the mood for? We've got everything," she smiled, glowing with pent up excitement.

He shrugged, tearing open a bag of cookies. She could feel his eyes staring at her—scoping her from head to toe.

"Let's go for a swim," he suggested.

"We can't." She popped open a can of cherry soda.

"Come on, a late night swim."

"We can't, I gotta keep an eye on my little sister and she's not allowed in the pool."

"So let her run around in the grass and we'll chill in the Jacuzzi." His eye twinkled.

She blushed, enamored by his boldness.

"I'm sorry, we can't," she sighed. "She might wander off."

He pouted, feeling the sting of rejection. He stretched his arms across the top of the couch, still staring her up and down as she pulled a DVD from its cover. He tore open all the bags of chips at once, then started flinging popcorn at her, popping her in the head.

"Tereek, stop it," she giggled.

She blocked the incoming fire with her hand, then snatched a throw pillow and bopped him in the face. He abandoned the snack attack, and instead, pounced on her for a little close contact. The wrestling escalated into a tickle-fest that traveled from the couch, down to the carpet, then tumbled across the room. Goldie was a huge proponent of the popcorn battle, hoovering up the buttery snacks and an occasional flying cookie.

They rolled across the floor, pulling and tugging, then tickling—much to his delight. They laughed hysterically, jumping around, dodging Cindy and stirring Goldie into a barking frenzy. Pillows were tossed back and forth, as the room became a full-fledged battle zone. She scrambled back to the couch before Tereek dove on her—engaging in some tight, in-close maneuvers.

During the mayhem, he spun off the couch in a reckless spin, when suddenly his flailing leg whacked Cindy on the arm. She toppled over, landing on her butt, then burst into tears.

Christy let out a gasp, then sprinted to her side. She wrapped her arms around her, stroking her arm in an effort to calm her down.

"Shh, it's okay, Cindy," she apologized profusely.

The crying turned into ear-piercing shrieks, which led to a chorus of high pitched wailing.

After several minutes of screaming and blubbering, Cindy eventually calmed down, thanks to a candy bribe.

Christy taped a band aid onto an imaginary cut, and order was restored in the combat zone. Tereek resumed his original position, fanned out on the couch with a sour look on his face.

"She'll be all right. She's tough," he smirked.

Christy opened a can of soda for Cindy, then proceeded to clean up the battle zone. She gathered the stray pillows that were strewn about and scooped up the popcorn that Goldie had not eaten. Her boyfriend was content to watch her do all the cleaning—busy channel surfing, texting on his cell, and stuffing his face with chocolate chip cookies.

"Let's check out your room," he suggested.

"We're not allowed." She rolled her eyes.

"You're not allowed in your own room?"

"No, you're not allowed," she giggled, trying to cushion the rejection.

"Come on. I'm gonna see it eventually."

"We can't. Look, just pick a movie." She was anxious to change the subject.

He squirmed on the couch not sure what to do next. He chugged one of the sodas, then bounced up, plodding toward the kitchen.

"Where are you going?"

"Man business," he grunted.

He waddled toward the kitchen in his saggy jeans, then disappeared into the hallway. Christy munched on potato chips, feeling skeptical, and listening for the bathroom door.

Is he really going to the bathroom? As the crunching sound echoed in her head, she decided that she didn't trust him. She hopped up, and ran into the hallway, only to catch him with his hand on the railing, about to climb the stairs.

"Tereek, no!"

"What?" he smirked.

"What are you doing?"

He shrugged. "I got lost."

"Yeah, whatever." She crossed her arms, glaring at him. She grabbed his arm, pulling him away from the stairs. She knew that if he took one step on the second floor, her dad would find out about it, somehow. Tereek resisted, he was loving the challenge.

"Come on. Just a peek," he pleaded, grabbing hold of the railing.

"You don't understand, my dad is going to freak." She tugged his arm.

"I don't see him. Mr. J.?" he shouted up the stairs.

She pulled his arm, but her efforts were futile—her socks were sliding on the marble floor.

He snickered, enjoying the tug-of-war; his swagger was a little more confident then the sniveling sap who crumbled in front of her father.

"I told you, we can't," she whined. She tried to remain upbeat, but was growing weary of his persistence.

"Two minutes, then I promise we'll leave."

She looked into his eyes, feeling charmed by his tenacity; she wanted to say 'yes,' but her father's words weighed heavy on her conscience.

"Come on," he pleaded.

She shook her head in frustration, sighed, and then finally caved.

"Just a peek, and that's all," she relented.

He raced up the stairs, skipping every other step, shooting to the top like a rocket. She chased close behind, nervous that he might stumble into her parent's room or break a vase or something expensive. Her heart beat faster, her blood pressure rising, but not from sprinting up the stairs.

After crisscrossing back and forth, Tereek stumbled into her room. He flicked on the light, then surveyed the teenage décor. Convinced it was the right room, he hoisted his hands in the air, basking in his victory, having entered the forbidden zone.

"Wow, it's purple." His eyes lit up.

"What, I like purple." She slapped his arm. "You don't like it?"

"No posters of me?" he scoffed.

"Yeah, well karaoke at the school talent show doesn't make you a celebrity," she mocked.

"Oh, she's got jokes?" he smiled at her boldness.

"Come on, we have to leave."

"What's with all the build-a-bears? What are you like ten?" he teased.

"What? I like them. Don't be making fun of me."

He strutted about, checking out her personal photos, rummaging through her CD collection.

After poking around, he launched into a spread eagle and landed on her bed, bouncing, then flipping onto his back. Her eyes lit up, she was mortified and amused at the same time.

"Tereek, no, we have to go!" She grabbed his leg, tugging half-heartedly.

"Come on, let's chill," he insisted, sinking his head into her pillow.

"No, Tereek," she sighed. "You said a quick peek and that's it. You don't understand, my dad is gonna kill me."

"You do everything your daddy says?" he teased, scooting to the end of the bed, then grabbing her hand.

She sighed. "No."

"Come here. Stop being weird." He smiled with his boyish charm.

She wrestled in her mind, rubbing her temples and thinking, "He's gonna find out, I know it."

He held her hand, clasping his fingers between hers. She loved the closeness, his touch felt electric. Why was being in her room such a big deal? She exhaled a sigh of confusion. "What if her dad did find out?" she thought, "So I get yelled at, big deal." She could endure that, especially for Tereek. After all, her parents were being unfair, making her stay home in the first place.

She tried to silence her father's voice in her head—to no avail.

"Come on, you promised," she leaned away.

"What are you so afraid of, why you acting weird?" He squeezed her hand.

She twirled her hair between her fingers, the pressure of the moment was invigorating; she grew tired of resisting. She thought, "We've already broken the rules, so we might as well make the most of it." She stared into his eyes, inhaling deeply, her emotions stirring with excitement. It felt exhilarating to rebel against her father.

"Two more minutes, then that's it." Her voice reclaimed a newfound strength.

She plunked down beside him on the bed. She felt chills running up and down her spine; she was addicted to him like candy.

"Relax. Why you so uptight? It ain't no thang," he whispered in her ear.

His voice melted her. When he touched her arm, her whole body shivered. He leaned his head against her forehead, then kissed her softly on the cheek. He raised his hand to her chin, then turned her face slowly toward him, leaning in to kiss her.

Just then, a loud bang erupted from downstairs. She flinched from the noise, her body stiffening. The thud sounded like the TV fell over, or worse, like a car smashed into the side of the house. Suddenly, she heard a high-pitched scream.

"Oh, no!" her breathing stopped.

She bolted into the hallway, heading straight for the stairs.

"Cindy!"

Chapter 18

Rachel's head throbbed, her nerves still frazzled from the afternoon fiasco. With the embarrassment still lingering in her mind, and the screams ringing in her ear—she was desperate for a change of scenery, something to wash away the pain.

She held her husband's hand as they strolled through the dimly lit restaurant, escorted to their private table by the maître'd. She eased gracefully into her chair, assisted by a tuxedoed waiter.

"Thank you," she smiled, her tattered emotions beginning to soak in the pampered life.

Flickering candlelight bathed the couple in a warm glow, her eyes relaxing amidst the peaceful surroundings. The palatial interior was furnished with mural sculptures, elegant chandeliers, and a panoramic view that overlooked the moonlit harbor. She was mesmerized by the soft music and the antique candelabras—her senses saturated by the romantic ambiance. She peered out over the ocean, the sparkling seascape to the left and the city skyline to the right. The view was breathtaking.

The waitress uncorked a bottle of red wine, filling their glasses halfway. Rachel closed her eyes for a moment, absorbing the tranquility that surrounded her. She felt like a queen, her skin tingling beneath her silk evening gown. She breathed easy, catching a whiff of the French cuisine, then opened her eyes and met her husband's loving gaze.

He raised his glass to offer a toast, his smile glimmering in the warm candlelight.

"I couldn't get a reservation at Chucky Cheese. Will this suffice?" he grinned.

"We'll make the best of it," she smiled.

Their glasses clinked. Their eyes were locked in a passionate union—a joining of hearts, beating in perfect harmony. She savored the smooth wine on her lips, wet and dry, sweet and rich, causing her to swoon—a moment of lighthearted giddiness. She gazed affectionately at her husband, her lover; so handsome, so powerful, so perfect. His eyes spoke volumes, expressing an intimate language, a personal poetry that only they could understand. He gazed deep into her eyes, stirring feelings of passion—an excitement that she had not felt in a long time.

"Isn't this better?" he smiled softly. "No drama, just candlelight, soft music…"

His cell rang suddenly, jolting her out of her peaceful bliss.

"I'm sorry, honey," he shook his head, reaching for his phone, then checking the caller I.D. "It's one of my security guys."

Her face dropped at the flip of a switch. How could he be so insensitive? Her eyes blazed with disgust. An inner rage swelled in the pit of her stomach, and the throbbing tension returned to her head. She covered her eyes—her journey into timelessness was shattered, the room returning to a simple restaurant once again.

"Hey, Teddy," he turned aside. "Yeah, just hang out. Use the eagle eye." He listened. "That's right, you have my permission. And if you see a light on, you let me know." He paused. "Thanks."

He tucked the phone back in his jacket.

"I'm so sorry, honey," he sipped his wine, "Where were

we?"

Her fury burned like a volcano about to erupt; she averted her eyes—her gaze fixed on her wine glass. She was speechless, not sure what to make of the conversation she just heard. What was all of the covert lingo? And why was his phone on in the first place?

She peered across the harbor, wishing for just one thing to go right in her life. She felt the dark clouds creeping back into her thoughts.

The waitress served the first course, setting the soup in front of her—the aroma smelled divine. Her husband lifted the bread basket, peeling the cover, and offering her a piece.

"What was that?" she rolled her eyes, rejecting the bread.

"What was what?"

"That eagle eye something or other...? What are you doing?"

He chuckled at the Sherlock Holmes assumption, shaking his head.

"What every responsible father should do." He laid his napkin across his waist.

"Spy on their children?"

"Come on, you know this rapper wannabe is just a phase... some bad boy nonsense," he insisted. "He's gonna be gone in like two weeks. I just wanna make sure she doesn't get hurt before she dumps Rickety and kicks him to the curb."

He smiled. "Bon appetite."

She blushed with unexpected amusement, covering her mouth with her hand, and then her napkin. The air deflated out of her anger, her dismay disappearing almost instantly. She grabbed her wine glass and took a sip—partly to wet her lips, and partly to hide her smile. She fought internally to regain her outrage, but her funny bone was being tickled, much to her chagrin. She chuckled inside at his confident assertion. She found his relational insights both amusing and liberating. She peeked up, catching his gaze.

"What's so funny?" he flashed a grin.

She shook her head, still giddy inside; straining unsuccessfully to conceal her smile. She sipped her soup, savoring the flavor on her tongue, content to keep her secret to herself.

"All girls go through a bad boy phase, even you," he smirked.

"Nope, never had one." She shook her head in denial, tickled by the truth.

"Oh really," he raised his eyebrows. "You were never attracted to the bad boy type?"

"Nope." She blinked.

He turned to the waitress. "Um, excuse me, could we get a few more drinks for the young lady."

She blushed at her husband's wit and charm, trying not to laugh at his playful banter. She swore that somehow he could read her thoughts—even her secret musings—and she loved that about him. The cell phone annoyance began to fade, and she gradually returned to the land of enchantment.

"I remember when you used to take me out to dinner." She indicted him playfully.

"What are you talking about, we go out all the time?"

"Oh please. When was the last time we had a romantic dinner just the two of us?"

Without having to think, he blurted, "Last weekend, we went to the Palisades, last weekend."

"Um, that was a fundraiser, honey, and that doesn't count."

He conceded, nodding in half-hearted agreement. He sipped his wine, then glanced up with a look of bewilderment. She chuckled at his lack of response.

"Well, last week was a great dinner," he muttered, pointing out the silver lining. "I mean, there were celebrities there."

"I wouldn't exactly call the naked cowboy a celebrity," she scoffed.

"What are you talking about, that's America's finest right

there."

She grinned, turning away in silence.

He leaned back, trying to read her expression. "Really, has it been that long?"

She averted her eyes with a look of disappointment.

"Come on, we still go out." he insisted.

She sipped her soup, offering a silent rebuttal.

"Wow, honey, have I really been that distant?" he asked.

She deliberated in her mind, whether to enjoy the peaceful ambiance, or tell him how she really felt. She peered up, searching his eyes, and feeling along the edge of his heart.

"The first year we dated," she began, "you took me out all the time, and you would leave little notes and surprises everywhere, and I looked forward to every weekend because you made them so special."

"And now?"

She shrugged, "I miss the magic we shared."

He sat frozen, her words weighing heavy in his mind. He averted his eyes, with a dejected look on his face.

"You're right," he whispered apologetically. "I've been so caught up at work lately, that I've been neglecting you." He slunk back in his chair, shaking his head in silence.

"Honey, I know your job is demanding…" she empathized.

"No, you're right," he interrupted, "There's no excuse, I haven't been paying attention to you or the girls the way I should."

She looked in his eyes, caught up in his heartfelt admission, unsure of what to say or do.

He sighed, "I do love you, and I hope you'll find it in your heart to forgive me."

He motioned to the waiter to approach the table. The waiter handed him a large black velvet jewelry box with the word 'Tiffany' engraved in silver letters.

She gasped when she saw the size of the case, covering her mouth with her hand—her fingers shaking, her eyes misting over.

"Here." He handed it to her, his eyes locked in hers. "I am sorry, and I love you."

Her heart raced inside her chest as she accepted it.

"Oh, Mitch." She had to force herself to breathe. "I can't," her words quivered in her throat.

"Okay, I'll take it back." He reached for it.

"No, don't you dare!" She grasped it with both hands. She exhaled, waiting for her nerves to calm down; her hands were shaking, overcome by the moment.

"Go ahead, open it," he whispered.

She lifted the lid slowly, as the candlelight revealed the most beautiful thing she had ever seen. Her eyes widened in shock. She was speechless, her body trembling with disbelief.

Chapter 19

Christy streaked down the stairs, her heart beating outside her chest. She nearly tripped as she ran through the hallway, the high pitched shrieks growing louder by the second. Her mind was caught in hysterics, a lump of anxiety lodged in her throat. What was that loud crash? Her mind raced through the possibilities.

When she reached the family room, she froze in her tracks, gaping in horror at the ominous red pool in the middle of the carpet. The den was a disaster—littered with chips and cookies, overturned plants, and papers scattered all over the floor.

She spotted Cindy hunched over in the darkness, wailing by the fireplace, a red trickle oozing down her hairline.

"Cindy!" she screamed, rushing to her side.

"Shh, it's okay, Cindy, I'm here." She cooed in her ear, trying desperately to calm her fears. Cindy's shirt was dripping wet, with a jagged tear on one of her sleeves.

Christy felt along her forehead, examining for cuts or contusions. She exhaled a heavy sigh of relief when she realized that the liquid was cherry soda, the result of a can explosion.

She examined the rest of her—feeling along her neck, her arms, and her back. There appeared to be no injuries, except for a minor scrape on her arm—a tiny cut that was more bruise than blood. It took her a moment to catch her breath, realizing that her sister was in one piece.

The solid oak bookcase that held her dad's trophies was lying face down. Popcorn was scattered everywhere, along with soda cans, chips and DVDs. Goldie ran back and forth, crunching potato chips and licking the empty cans.

After several minutes of blubbering, Cindy's crying tapered into sniffles. She plopped onto the carpet, then began scooping up popcorn, pushing them into piles as if she were playing on the beach.

"Cindy, come on, we have to get you out of those wet clothes."

She dragged her sister to the kitchen sink, grabbed a washcloth and wiped her face. The sticky mess was everywhere; a trail of soda was dripping from her clothes. She gave Cindy a quick sponge bath, then sent her to her room to change.

Christy returned to the disaster zone, staring wide-eyed at the mini lagoon that had congealed in the center of the room. How could this happen? She was gone for a second, and now her world was turned upside down.

Stumbling in was her boyfriend, who smirked at the chaos, then proceeded to pick a popcorn kernel out of his teeth.

"No offense, but your family is kinda messy," he snickered.

She rolled her eyes, praying that none of her dad's trophies were broken. If one of the statues was cracked or broken, she would be grounded for a year, and never hear the end of it.

Tereek helped her lift the bookcase, picked up a few trophies, then found his way back to the couch. She straightened the bookshelf the best she could, exhaling a sigh of relief, realizing that all the statues were intact.

"My mom is gonna freak when she sees that stain," she whined.

"Just say the dog did it... it ain't no big deal," he

quipped, kicking his feet onto the coffee table.

"Yeah, well you don't know my parents."

He reclined against the back of the couch, then picked up the remote, and started surfing through the channels.

"Wow, I really do have to take a leak now," he chuckled, as he waddled into the hallway.

She knelt down on her hands and knees, sponging up the puddle with dishtowels and napkins. The towels absorbed much of the liquid, but the crimson stain was enormous—the size of a beach umbrella. After scrubbing until her fingers ached, the spill appeared to be getting darker.

She felt a curl of nausea in the pit of her stomach, picturing her parent's reaction when they walked into the room. What was she going to say?

Tereek moseyed back in, carrying a can of cherry soda and another bag of chips.

"Hey, it looks a little better," he shrugged, plopping back on the sofa.

She sprayed the stain with half a dozen cleaners, hoping that the chemical combination would remove the stain. She inhaled a whiff of the toxic cloud—the fumes scraping against her throat, sending her into a coughing fit. Her eyes burned from the ammonia, like cigarette smoke being blown into her eyes. She pried the windows open, sucking in deep breaths of fresh air, and gasping for relief. Maybe mixing the cleansers was not a great idea.

"Are you trying to kill me?" he choked.

"Shut up, it's not that bad," she giggled between coughs.

He covered his face with a pillow, then continued surfing through the channels.

"I don't know what I'm gonna do," she whined.

"Just dye the whole thing red."

"You're so stupid," she smirked.

"You know what..., just tell them I did it," he offered. "They already don't like me."

"What are you talking about," she scoffed, "They like

---

you."

"Yeah, right."

"They do like you," her voice wavered, trying to sound convincing.

"Your dad almost crushed my hand."

"Yeah well, I know my mom likes you," she insisted. "And my dad…, um, he doesn't trust you, but that doesn't mean he doesn't like you."

"Same thing."

"No, it's not."

"Whatever," he sighed, dropping the remote, then texting on his cell.

She shook her head in frustration, recognizing his discontent. The carpet was ruined, the evening was ruined, this was the worst Friday night in the history of the world, and it was all her sister's fault.

"Cindy!" she yelled, "Get down here."

Her sister bounced in with another soda in her hand, then plopped onto the floor and started playing with Goldie.

After two broken nails, and a torn blood blister, Christy surrendered in defeat. Her wrinkled fingers smelled like bleach, and her back was sore from bending over.

She tossed the supplies under the sink, changed her shirt, then came back and plunked down next to her boyfriend. She stared bleary eyed at the ceiling, exhausted, the smell of ammonia seeping through her skin. He put his arm around her, which made her feel good; the night was a disaster, but a good cuddle was just what she needed. Why couldn't this be a normal night? Why couldn't she just chill at the mall like everyone else?

She rested her head against his chest, it was the first time she felt relaxed all night. Her eyes grew heavy, she was more tired than she realized. Maybe the evening was not a total loss after all. She closed her eyes, listening to his heartbeat. She chuckled when his stomach growled, a much needed laugh on an otherwise dismal night.

"Do you wanna order a pizza?" She patted his tummy.

He smiled, looking her in the eye, then scoping her body. "Let's go back to your room." He started rubbing her back.

"What? We can't do that, what's wrong with you?"

"What's wrong with me? What's wrong with you? This is wack." He leaned forward, as if to leave.

"I told you. My parents said...."

"Yeah, whatever," he scoffed, "This is lame, I'm outta here."

She grabbed his arm and pulled him close, not wanting the night to end.

"Look, let's order a pizza. And we'll go to the movies next weekend, I promise," she squeezed his arm.

"Next weekend there's a party..., and I ain't gonna be stuck babysitting."

"What are you talking about? I'll go...," her voice wavered. She knew full well what party he was talking about.

"You sure you won't have to stay here, you know, on the first floor?"

"No!" she smiled angrily.

She wrapped her arms around his waist, snuggling close and holding tight. She couldn't believe this was happening. The room smelled like Clorox, her throat burned from the chemicals, and they were staring at an infomercial about how to tone your double chin. Could it get any worse?

His arm suddenly felt cold around her shoulder. Her thoughts began to waver, churning up feelings of doubt and insecurity. Was he slipping away? She had to go to that party— missing it was not an option. If he went without her, she would die.

"Where's the party again?" she asked.

"Forget it," he shook his head. "You know where it is."

She winced, stung by his rebuke. Her life was a disaster, and getting worse by the second. She hated being treated like a child. There was no way her father was not gonna let her go.

Chapter 20

Rachel's skin tingled, the ice around her neck sending shivers down her spine. The diamonds sparkled in the candlelight, creating a majestic aura all around. The gold chains lay soft upon her skin, adorned with four strings of diamonds, and a Burmese heart-shaped ruby surrounded by an additional twenty diamonds. She trembled with excitement, forgetting where she was, when her husband wrapped his arms around her, then kissed her with a long passionate kiss. She melted in his embrace—feeling dizzy, but in a good way.

"What's this for?" she whispered.

"Because you are you," he smiled.

"I don't know what to say."

"Just tell me you like it."

"I love it."

She lost herself in his eyes—absorbed by his charm, his playfulness, his smile. She felt butterflies fluttering in her stomach, the same exhilaration she felt the first time they fell in love.

A violinist strolled between the tables, serenading the couples, and filling the air with timeless love songs. The posh restaurant was nearly empty, with a few love birds huddled in private nooks. The candelabras flickered like stars up above, the moonlight cascading through the window, casting shadows along the mahogany dance floor.

Rachel's heart was at peace, breathing in the soft serenity of a perfect evening. This was the life she had always dreamed of, filled with romance, elegant evenings, and unexpected pleasures.

Just then his cell rang again. Her face fell when she heard the intrusion, the sound triggering a sharp pain inside her chest.

"Honey, please." She shook her head in disgust.

"I'm sorry, honey, I promise, this is the last one."

She covered her eyes, deeply annoyed by his blatant insensitivity. Anger welled up inside, as he turned his back to answer the call. She felt like she was being abandoned, cast aside as if she meant nothing. What could be so important that he couldn't turn it off?

"Thanks, Teddy," he wrapped up. "Appreciate it, nice work."

With a chuckle he hung up the phone. He caught a glimpse of her simmering rage, as he tucked his cell inside his jacket. To avoid eye contact, he sipped his wine, then gestured to the waiter to refill his glass. Her volcanic restraint bubbled; she was on the verge of ripping the necklace off and walking out.

"I'm sorry, honey, I promise that's the last."

She glared at him, burning a hole through his glance, her anger seething like a pointed laser. How could he be so insensitive? The necklace felt more like an albatross than a gift; it was the only thing keeping her from bursting out the door.

She turned away in disgust, her muscles tensing; the fuse was all but lit. The wait staff kept their distance, sensing a glacial atmosphere. She refused to look at him.

"Wow, that was some dessert," he tried to soften the mood, scooping up the last of his cake. He sighed, inclining his ear toward her, listening for a hint of benevolence.

She withdrew deep inside, cringing in silence behind a wall of frustration. Maybe she was overreacting, but, maybe she wasn't. As far as she was concerned, the evening was over. She was tired of the drama, tired of being battered by disappointment.

"Honey, look…" he stuttered.

She turned away, staring into the pitiless sky—she was done. She scooted her chair back, preparing to leave, when he blurted out a desperate plea.

"Honey, please… just hear me out."

She exhaled, exasperated, the necklace weighing heavy around her neck.

"Here." He pulled his phone out, sliding it to the middle of the table.

"I don't want that," she lashed out, rolling her eyes.

"Put it in your purse," he insisted. "I promise, this evening is about you."

"It's too late, Mitch, I'm done." She leaned forward as if to leave.

"Rachel please, what more can I do?" his voice cracked. "What will it take?"

His question froze her in place, her emotions wavering from mental exhaustion. Wasn't it obvious? Did he not know her at all? What was more important, buying expensive presents, or being in tune with a person's heart?

"On second thought," he said, "just throw the damn thing away, just throw it away."

She scoffed at the lunacy, closing her eyes, and drifting into numbness.

"Honey, I'm begging you. Everything I do is for us, for our family. I love you and Christy and Cindy so much, that if anything ever happened to any of you—I would die."

She peeked into his eyes, her lips sealed from anger.

"Please Rachel."

Her mind suppressed the sound of his voice, barely hearing every other word.

"What more can I do?" he pleaded.

She was tempted to answer, but held her tongue. She searched his eyes, trying to gain a sense of his heart.

"Go ahead," he insisted, "just throw it away, if that's what it takes." He slumped backwards with a look of defeat.

She stared wearily at the phone, stretching the silence, and waiting for her anger to subside. His words lingered in her ear, seemingly rife with sincerity. A part of her wanted to leave, but her heart was convincing her to stay.

She turned and spotted a nearby waiter, then motioned for him to approach the table. She glared at the phone, signaling to the server to remove it. The waiter raised his eyebrows in bewilderment.

"The lady would like for you to take the phone and discard it." Mitch said. She felt her husband's eyes locked in her gaze, but she looked away, peering out over the harbor.

The waiter picked up the phone, turned apprehensively and walked away.

They sat at a silent impasse, their hearts searching for something to fill the void. Her patience was spent—she didn't care anymore. Life wasn't supposed to be this hard.

"Honey, I'm sorry," he whispered, "You're right, I should have turned it off. But believe me when I tell you, that I'm only interested in our family's safety. If that idiot boyfriend of hers ever hurt her..., I could never forgive myself. You and the girls mean everything to me. You are my life."

She lifted her eyes to meet his gaze, examining his thoughts—peering deep into his soul. Maybe she overreacted—maybe it was the stress of the day. She inhaled deeply, trying to clear her mind. It's not like he took a business call, after all, his heart seemed to be in the right place. She loved her husband, and she knew he loved her too. She swallowed hard, convinced of his sincerity.

"Sir." Her soft but commanding voice resonated across the vacant dining room.

The waiter returned, then stood at attention.

"I'll take that." her eyes never left her husband's gaze.

The waiter set the phone next to her wine glass, then left.

They looked at one another, both sharing the other's

frustration. The silence brought a greater peace then any words they could say. When did life get so complicated, so tedious? This was no longer about a phone, but about two hearts searching for one another in the dark. She yearned for something more, something deeper—a kind of oneness that would lift their hearts to a transcendent love. She sensed an honesty in his eyes, a kind of compassion she had not felt in a long time.

"I do love you, I hope you know that," he whispered.

"I know you do," she nodded.

She picked up the phone, then slid it into her purse.

"I'll hang on to it, in case of an emergency," she tempered a smile.

He nodded his approval.

"Will you dance with me?" he asked.

She blinked twice. "Only because I've had a few drinks."

He offered his hand and escorted her toward the dance floor. Something wonderful was happening inside of her, like she could breathe again. Her body relaxed as they made their way to the center. The entire floor was their canvas, the soft music enveloping them with open arms.

He held her close, their bodies moving as one, gliding effortlessly in perfect harmony. She felt alive in his arms, her heart soaring beyond the dance floor—out over the ocean, and beyond the bounds of ecstasy. The rollercoaster evening had been a journey of unpredictability, but a part of her wouldn't have wanted it any other way.

"This is just the beginning," he whispered.

"What? Date night, every night?" she brushed her cheek against his.

"Dining at fabulous restaurants all over the world; kings, queens, heads of state. Servants will bow at the first lady's beckon call."

"You're pretty sure of yourself," she said with a loving smile.

"Never a doubt," he grinned.

"How can you be so sure?"

"You know what they say... 'Behind every successful man...'" he kissed her cheek.

"Yes?"

"You know the rest."

"But I want to hear you say it," she insisted.

"Behind every successful man...something, something," he grinned.

"Is that what I am...something, something?"

He looked deep in her eyes, "You're my heart and soul."

She melted into his arms, and whispered, "And don't you forget that."

Chapter 21

As midnight closed in, the couple crept through the front door. Rachel peeked into the hallway mirror, still marveling at the sparkling diamonds. Her husband tiptoed behind her, kissing the nape of her neck, giving her shivers once again. She noticed the home was completely dark with the exception of a single light streaming from the family room. She walked toward the beam, her feet levitating as though she were floating on clouds. Peeking through the doorway, she looked up and saw the solitary light source—the TV flickering in the corner.

She peered about, surveying the quiet darkness, then spotted a blanket covered heap bulging up from the couch. She smiled, assuming it was Christy and her boyfriend asleep on the sofa—snuggled in a ball.

"Anybody awake?"

Christy poked her head from under the blanket, squinting into the light. Her boyfriend groaned, his hair matted to one side with a pillow line streaked across his face.

"What time is it?" Christy mumbled.

"Almost midnight," she grinned. "Did you put Cindy to bed?"

"No, she's right…" Christy froze, pointing at the crumpled afghan in the middle of the floor. Her eyes grew wide, her mouth gaping in fright. Christy shed the blanket, whipping her head around in a state of confusion, then leapt off the couch and rushed into the kitchen.

"Oh my gosh! Cindy!" she panicked. "She was right here," her voice trailing behind her.

Rachel's stomach tightened from the sporadic activity, her mind puzzled as to what just happened. Suddenly, she couldn't breathe, choking back the rising anxiety. She kicked off her shoes, then hurried after her daughter.

"Christy...!" she screamed. "Mitch, do you see Cindy?"

Christy zipped past her father in the foyer, brushing by without saying a word. She flew up the stairs, heading straight for Cindy's bedroom. Rachel followed a few steps behind, her mind racing with endless possibilities—none of them good. Christy whipped open Cindy's bedroom door, flicked the light on, then searched from side to side, her jaw dropping from what she saw.

Rachel stumbled in, her eyes wild with desperation.

The floral bedspread lay untouched, perfectly smooth; the stuffed animals and teddy bears aligned neatly against the pillow. The vacant bed sent shockwaves through her body— her legs dissolving into jello.

"Cindy!" she screamed, "Where are you?"

Christy staggered into the hallway, darting from room to room, flicking on every light she came to.

Rachel hurried down the stairs, then backtracked into the kitchen, the living room and the den, flinging open every closet and cabinet door.

"Cindy!" she cried.

Christy reappeared in the kitchen, laboring to breathe, her face flush with a look of shock.

"What happened?" Rachel shook her by the shoulders. "Where was the last place you saw her?"

"She fell asleep on the floor," Christy stuttered, "and I covered her with a blanket while we watched the movie. I swear, she was right there."

Rachel stared at the blanket, not knowing which way to turn; she rubbed her eyes in despair, desperate to avoid the fears that were creeping into her thoughts.

"Cindy!" her voice cracked.

Her breathing became constricted, her throat tightening from the unthinkable. She stumbled into the laundry room and flung open the hamper, the washer and dryer.

"Cindy!" she cried out. "Cindy, honey…!"

Nothing, no response; only dead silence.

Her husband trailed behind rechecking every room. His cell was glued to his ear, calling his security guards who were stationed within a two block radius. Where could she be?

Rachel doubled back into the family room, guest room, and living room, turning on every house lamp she came to, shouting her daughter's name at the top of her lungs. She staggered into the kitchen, bending over to catch her breath. She leaned against a counter; wobbling from dizziness, the blood rushing to her head.

"Cindy! Cindy, honey…!" the pain in her voice scratched raw against her throat.

She noticed that the venetian blinds were opened slightly; the back door appeared to be unlocked. She yanked on the string, the blinds swinging wildly from side to side. She flicked the patio light on, illuminating the back deck and the picnic area beside the house. She threw open the sliding glass door, her heart pounding against her rib cage.

"Cindy! Cindy!" she called out in desperation. The cool air tickled her throat, provoking a sudden coughing attack, her lungs hyperventilating. She massaged her neck to alleviate the scratching; she needed a drink, but backtracking into the house was unthinkable. Her eyes watered from the coughing as she searched the darkness for any signs of life. There was no movement, no response, only crickets chirping in the dark. Her mind was gripped by fear, her fingers shaking as she wiped away the tears.

Out of the corner of her eye, she saw something move—

a foreboding shadow near the swimming pool's edge.

She heard a faint bark coming from somewhere in the dark—a muffled yelp from Goldie—as if she had something in her mouth.

"Goldie! Goldie, come here girl!" Her voice cracked, her emotions grasping for a glimmer of hope.

Goldie emerged from the shadows, the porch light twinkling in her eyes. She dropped a swimming flipper from her mouth, then started barking and zipping around the yard.

Next to the swimming pool's edge Rachel spotted a shadow in the distance, a silhouette of something or someone, lying on the ground. She squinted into the darkness; it looked like someone was huddled near the diving board—scooping water with their hand.

"Cindy, honey!" she called out with panicked alarm. "Stay right there. Don't move!"

She bolted across the grass in her bare feet; forgetting that she was wearing an evening gown. She hiked up her dress with both hands—allowing her legs to move freely. Her heart pounded faster and faster, her face flush with expectation. She swooped down and snatched up her little girl like a mother hawk rescuing a fallen chick. She pulled her close, wrapping her arms around her—squeezing the life out of the bewildered child. She smothered her with kisses, her emotions pouring out unabashedly—tears of joy, panic and relief. Cindy, who was covered in sand, extended her hand, reaching out for her beach toy in the grass.

"It's okay, honey." Rachel bawled uncontrollably.

"Mommy's here, don't worry, I will never leave you again, ever."

Chapter 22

Christy brooded alone in the kitchen, sulking after her father kicked her boyfriend out—she didn't even get a chance to say goodbye.

"What a disaster," she rolled her eyes in disbelief. She leaned back against the sink, the fan hissing above the stove, creating an ominous buzz in the dimly lit kitchen. She waited restlessly for her father to return, after he stepped away to answer a call. The specter of guilt weighed heavy on her conscience—her mind anxious to suppress an evening she would rather forget. She crossed her arms in front of her, shivering slightly—but not from the cold.

Lingering in silence, she felt a touch of stickiness between her fingers—a painful reminder of the soda catastrophe she endured a few hours earlier. She rubbed the fatigue from her eyes, wishing she could wash away the entire night.

Her father strolled in, tucking his phone away, his demeanor hardening the moment he peered in her direction. He stood silently at a distance, staring at her, with his arms crossed in front of his chest.

Her eyes were downcast, she was afraid to lift her chin; she couldn't bear to look up and see the disappointment on his face. She wrapped her arms even tighter around her body to fend off the chill.

Still dressed in his suit pants and dress shirt, he pulled off his necktie, then folded it neatly, placing it on the table. He glanced over, but didn't say a word. His expression was stone cold, indiscernible. He unbuttoned his cufflinks and rolled up his sleeves; his mind was churning, but no words were forthcoming.

She became antsy, self-conscious, waiting for him to say something—anything that might give her a clue as to what he was thinking. The silence was deafening, endless. Shuddering from guilt, she couldn't take it anymore. Her feelings blurted out like a runaway flood.

"I'm so sorry, Daddy," she cried. "We were asleep for only like fifteen minutes, and Cindy was right in front of us, curled under her blanket." She wiped her nose, waiting anxiously for him to respond.

He leaned against the wooden table, watching pensively with a furrowed brow. He raised his eyes to meet her gaze, then let out a loud sigh, thinking twice about what he was going to say.

She inhaled a deep breath, trying to calm herself; the anxiety was eating at her nerves—she wanted to crawl in a hole and hide.

"This was the worst night of my life," her voice broke. "I left the room for two seconds and she spilled cherry soda everywhere, and when I came back, there was popcorn and chips scattered all over the carpet. I spent the entire night cleaning up after her. I just wanted to have a nice evening with my boyfriend, but instead it was the worst night of my life."

He listened thoughtfully, looking on with a somber stoicism. The oven fan shut off automatically, leaving the room dead silent—the air thick with distress.

She clammed into a ball, her lungs suffocating from a guilty conscience.

"Daddy," she lamented, "I am so sorry, I swear she was fast asleep on the floor for like an hour, and we were watching the movie and I just fell asleep for a few minutes."

She bowed her head in dismay, rubbing her eyes, then retreating deep inside.

He exhaled a loud sigh, then cleared his throat to speak. "Your sister could have drowned, do you realize that?"

Her heart sank beneath the sound of his voice. The disappointment was more crushing than the words.

"She could have died," he said. "Is that something you could live with?"

Struggling hard to restrain her tears, she raised her gaze to meet his eyes. When she saw the despondency on his face, she could no longer bear the guilt—her pain came pouring out.

"I know. Daddy, I'm so sorry, I promise..."

"You have to be more responsible, honey," his voice was hard but caring.

Her knees shook; the anguish in his voice pierced her heart, her body crying out for a forgiving embrace. Black spots blurred her vision, her eyes straining to focus through the shame.

"Come here," he extended his hand. She rushed to his embrace, threw her arms around him, and buried her tears in his chest. She clung to him tightly, her soul begging for a second chance; her cries grew louder, pouring out pain and regret. She held on as if she were a four-year-old child, sensing his love—his strength and forgiveness. He was her protector, her life, her everything. They embraced in the darkness—her tears becoming a glue that bonded them together.

She didn't want to let go, holding tight until her crying subsided. She could fall asleep in his arms, knowing that he loved her no matter what.

He lifted her chin, then gently wiped her tears.

"Are you okay?" his voice was calming. She nodded, her eyes still misty.

"Now, honey, I love you and Cindy, and you've got to be more responsible around her. She needs you, do you understand that?"

"Yes." She bowed her head.

"All right, well, it's important that you learn this lesson, so next week, after school I want you to come straight home. Do you understand?"

"Yes," she sighed.

"Okay, time for bed," he kissed her forehead. "I love you."

"I love you, too." She half smiled, heading to her room.

A calming peace returned to her conscience as she left the kitchen. She walked past the bathroom, when her breath caught suddenly, freezing her in her tracks. Her body shuddered, letting out a frantic gasp. The party with her boyfriend was Friday night. If she missed it, she would die.

"Wait…" she reappeared in the kitchen doorway. But it was too late, her father was gone.

Rachel dragged her body up the stairs, relieved that the day was finally over. Her throat was raw from screaming, her mind exhausted, paralyzed by a nagging sense of guilt.

She helped Cindy get ready for bed—washing her face, then sliding into her footie pajamas. She yawned repeatedly, fighting to stay awake for her daughter's sake; her body languishing, her mind adrift in a fog. As she zipped up Cindy's jammies, she noticed a scrape on her arm.

"Honey, what happened, there's a bruise here and it's bleeding?" she winced.

Cindy shrugged.

Rachel moseyed into the bathroom, then returned with first aid supplies—a wet washcloth, some cotton balls and a bottle of rubbing alcohol. She dabbed the wet washcloth lightly against the abrasion, trying not to inflict any pain.

"Does that hurt?" she raised her eyebrows. Cindy shook her head.

She soaked the cotton ball with alcohol, then gently blotted the antiseptic against Cindy's arm.

"Ow!" Cindy flinched, jerking her arm away.

"I'm sorry, honey, I know," she winced. "All done."

She pursed her lips and blew on the damp area until the moisture disappeared. Cindy giggled, the gentle breath felt ticklish against her skin. Rachel kissed her fingers, then placed them lightly on the scrape. "All better." She covered it with a cartoon bandage, evoking a giggly smile.

"Okay, time for night night," she said in a quiet, soothing voice.

She pulled the floral bedspread aside, smoothing out the crisp cool sheets. Cindy hopped in bed, sliding her feet under the fold, then sinking her head deep into the pillow.

Rachel smiled, cherishing her role as Dr. Mom—fixing boo boos and making everything better. She pulled the covers up and over, then tucked her daughter in, a ritual she performed every night. Cindy grabbed her dollie, then tucked her under the sheet. She gathered her teddy bears and stuffed animals together and made sure everyone was sharing the pillow.

Satisfied that the whole gang was bundled under the blanket, Rachel kissed her forehead, then brushed her bangs to the side.

"Where's Daddy?" Cindy asked.

"He's talking to your sister."

"Is he gonna sing me a night night song?"

Rachel averted her eyes. "Um, not tonight, honey."

"Why?"

"You've had a busy day, time for night night."

Cindy's eyes drooped.

Rachel sighed. Her heart ached every time her daughter looked sad. She walked to the door and clicked off the lamp; a small ray of light peeped through the crack in the door.

"Mommy, don't leave."

"I'm right here…shh…time for night night," she whispered. She sat on the edge of the bed, running her fingers through her daughter's hair.

She watched and waited as Cindy drifted off to sleep; she couldn't help but wonder what the future held for her little girl. As she rose to leave, Cindy felt the shift on the bed and opened her eyes.

"Mommy?" She extended both arms, requesting a final hug. Her wish was granted.

Chapter 23

"I have a confession," the reporter smirked, "If someone told me a month ago that I'd be interviewing you, I would've laughed in their face.'"

"I'm flattered," David smiled through the insult.

"Hey, I'm just being honest," she snickered. "I mean, if you were given the choice between interviewing Morocco's royal family along the Mediterranean or interviewing a televangelist..." she shook her head, "...it's a no brainer."

David nodded along, holding his tongue, and playing the gracious host. He wasn't used to backhanded compliments, or the brash candor of big city journalists.

"So what changed your mind?" he asked.

She averted her eyes. "My six year old niece."

"She's a fan of mine?" he joked.

The reporter hesitated, swallowing hard. "My niece, Theresa, was born blind—congenital blindness. My sister took her to one of your healing services last month and now she can see. How is that possible?"

He deliberated for a moment, sensing the cynicism in her tone.

"You don't believe in miracles?" he asked.

"I have to now, don't I?" she scoffed.

"You don't sound convinced."

"I've been a journalist for twenty-seven years. I get paid to expose government liars and corporate swindlers, and to eat people like you for lunch, then spit you out on the evening news.

"And now?" he grinned.

She stared for a long moment. "I'll tone it down a notch".

He was tickled by her brazen attitude. He found her skepticism both amusing and presumptuous.

After their initial meet and greet, David made his way to the back patio which was being transformed into a makeshift interview site. The TV crew buzzed about setting up cameras and lights, turning his backyard into network central. He settled into a director's chair, loosening his collar, and gathering his thoughts as the top of the hour approached.

The makeup girl powdered his face with a brush the size of a small feather duster.

"Not too much," he joked. The girl flashed a friendly wink.

As the sun arched behind the trees, he took his place in front of the camera.

"Quiet on the set..." the producer yelled. "And here we go...counting down in five, four, three..."

The intro-package hit the airwaves featuring a video montage of David's nationwide crusades. The video showed family members from all walks of life, hugging and laughing, as they filed into crowded arenas. The ensuing shots showed patients in wheelchairs, children on crutches, and an elderly woman toting an oxygen tank toward the front of the stage. The reporter narrated beneath the video montage.

"Whether you agree with his beliefs or not," she began, "People are traveling hundreds of miles to see this unusual evangelist. Some call him a snake oil salesman, while others call him a saint. He is filling large sports arenas all across the country in every state... and most nights it's standing room only. His name... is David Connolly."

She turned and greeted him with a cordial smile.

"You've been nominated for Legacy Gold Magazine's Person of the Year…," she grinned.

"So I've heard," he smiled.

"Why do people love you so much?"

"Wow," he chuckled. "I, uh…, I don't know, how do you answer a question like that? Why do people love you?"

"They don't."

"Oh, come on…"

"This isn't about me, it's about you," she smirked. "City after city, people travel hundreds of miles to see you. What's that about?"

"Yeah, well, I…, I thought about setting up a twitter account, but I was afraid that no one would follow," he grinned.

She nodded along, engaging in the playful banter.

"Have you always wanted to be a televangelist?"

"In high school I wanted to be a football player."

"Really?" her eyes widened, not expecting such candor.

"Oh yeah, when I was in school the football players and basketball players…, they got the cheerleaders."

"What happened?"

"I played video games all day," he shrugged. "And I also played the trumpet in marching band. Not exactly a babe magnet."

"Did you date much?"

"Next question, please," he blushed.

Following the casual ten minute exchange, the network broke away for a commercial. He was surprised at how well the interview was going. Based on what he had heard, he was expecting to be dragged through the mud.

During the break, he moseyed in the house with the reporter to a second interview location that was set up inside the living room. He sipped his water bottle, then took his place on the couch, feeling a bit more confident, but still leery about what she might ask.

"Okay, here we go folks, we're back," the producer signaled.

A video package hit the air, showcasing highlights of his personal life. The footage featured him carousing with his wife at a family picnic. The two shoved cupcakes into each other's mouths—making a mess and loving every minute of it. The family video showed their children splashing in the swimming pool, climbing on top of him and soaking him with supersized water guns. The reporter chimed in with her voiceover.

"David Connolly was an above average student... and self-described video game enthusiast who grew up in a small Midwestern town. He may not have scored dozens of dates in high school, but he did marry his college sweetheart. Today, he is a devout husband, and father of three, and is highly respected for his wholesome family values."

His wife, Patricia, sat next to him on the couch, her face beaming as the camera zoomed in for a close up. She was a southern belle with a bubbly personality; a natural beauty, both charming and sophisticated. David squeezed her hand, his energy perking up, feeling much more at ease with his wife by his side.

"Patricia, you two have been married for what..., eighteen years?" the reporter nodded with a congratulatory tone.

"Wow, it's been that long?" she blushed, offering a hint of a southern drawl.

"And three beautiful children..." the reporter smiled.

"You can see they take after their mother," he gushed.

"What's it like being married to this guy?"

"It's a nightmare," she scoffed. "No, it's wonderful," she flashed a playful grin. "We have a good life; it's not much different from everyone else's. Sometimes it's tough with David traveling, but we manage."

"How do you feel about his traveling?"

"Honestly, I hate it. I wish he was home more, but you take the good with the bad."

"Yeah, traveling makes it hard," he nodded.

The reporter seemed to relish the personal details, engaging with a softer tone when she conversed with his wife.

"What was he like when you first met him?"

"He read a lot," she smiled, sneaking a peek at him, not wanting to embarrass him.

"Was he kind of a nerd?"

"Let's just say he read a lot. He didn't pay much attention to me..., at first."

He chimed in, "She had a lot of guys chasing her. I had to wait in line."

"That's not true," she slapped his arm.

"Well, you got her."

"I did." He nodded, a little embarrassed.

"And now he's a celebrity..."

"I guess." Patricia smiled, rolling her eyes.

"Has your life changed much?"

"It has," she nodded. "A lot of people say 'Hi' to us on the street and in restaurants."

"Is that a good thing?"

"For the most part," she looked at him. "It's different. Different for us, different for the kids...but we're happy."

"That's great," the reporter nodded. "David, let me switch gears, because I want to ask you about your crusades, and get to the heart of the matter."

"Okay." He leaned forward, releasing his wife's hand.

The reporter shuffled her papers, her face hardening—taking on a serious tone. David braced himself, recognizing that the meet-and-greet was over.

"There are some folks who hear the word 'televangelist,' and immediately think...con man...greed...con artists who ask for money, then live in mansions and fly private jets. Are you a con man?"

"I'm not," he said calmly.

"Do you ask people for money?"

"We do have operational costs, yes. But the money we

raise barely covers the cost of the arenas and the TV air time. In fact, I fly coach wherever I go."

The reporter eyed him with skepticism.

"I will say this," he added, "The two books that I've written have generated some income, but when you look around, I think you'd agree that our home is fairly modest by most standards."

The reporter pressed on. "Has your organization released its tax records?"

"We have."

"All right, fine...," she took a deep breath, "I actually want to get to the single question our viewers are curious about most, if you don't mind." She squared her shoulders.

"Okay."

"These physical healings, these alleged miracles if you will..." Her voice carried a subtle sneer. "Some claim that you've healed them," she looked deep in his eyes, "Is this true?"

"I haven't healed anybody," he replied without blinking.

She flipped through her notes, scanning the top page, her eyes landing on a specific list.

"Including my niece, Theresa, there's another woman, an actual medical doctor in Topeka who claimed that you cured her of cancer. In Missouri, a small boy healed of autism. The list goes on and on... do you heal these people?"

"I don't heal anyone." His face was calm, his voice serene.

"Then how do you explain it? Is it a miracle?"

He inhaled, taking his time. "I would call it a miracle, yes."

"Can you tell us what happens..., I mean, what do you do? Do you splash them with magic water, do you smack their forehead, what do you do?"

He smiled, shaking his head. "When people come to the crusades, many suffering from chronic pain or potentially fatal diseases, I am there to believe with them and for them."

"But what does that mean?" the reporter pressed.

"I do believe in miracles, absolutely," he insisted. "I am a spiritual person. I think most people would say they are spiritual in some sense. When you travel all across this country to some of the poorest, rat infested neighborhoods in America... you meet elderly people, grandmas and grandpas who suffer from cancer and arthritis, and it breaks your heart. You see children who suffer and can't run around like normal kids because of asthma, autism or blindness... What do these innocent children and these parents want most in life? These precious elderly folks? Your niece and your sister, what do they want more than anything?"

The reporter shook her head, her eyes misting up at the mention of her niece.

"They want hope. All they want is hope. That's it. Why do you think people who can't afford food, can't afford to pay their monthly bills... go out and spend five dollars, ten dollars on lottery tickets?"

"And you give them hope?"

"I hope to give them hope," he replied. "The golden rule."

"All right fine, enough with the preaching," she waved her hands. "But how do you explain the actual physical healings, let's cut to the chase, how do you do it?"

"Do you believe in karma?" he asked. "If you put goodness out there, goodness will come back to you. If you treat people well, you'll be repaid with kindness somewhere down the road.

"Yeah, yeah, I get all that, be good, blah, blah, blah..." she interrupted. "But how...medically, scientifically?"

"Please, let me finish," he insisted. "These people who come to the services..., like your niece... if they're living right, then they deserve good things, wouldn't you agree? Do you think your niece is a good person? Does she deserve to suffer the way she did? I mean, think about it for a second. Can you imagine what it would be like to be born blind?"

The reporter shifted in her seat.

"Are there good people out there who deserve good things? I think so. Well, I believe for them, and with them. Listen..., our minds have healing capabilities that we haven't even begun to tap into... And sometimes if you believe hard enough, and if you believe in karma... then anything can happen—the power of positive thinking, the power of the human mind, and the human spirit. Sometimes dreams really do come true. Do you believe that? I do, with all my heart."

She peered deep into his eyes, pondering his words.

"But on the flip side, if you lie and treat others badly... then bad karma will catch up to you. You are setting yourself up for disaster."

Chapter 24

Mitch buried his face in his hands, rubbing his temples to alleviate the pressure. He hated having to depend on others, especially the whack jobs on the far left and far right. He chugged his glass of seltzer, hoping to cool the inferno that was smoldering inside. The record high temperatures had him clamoring for relief, along with the rising unemployment numbers, his drop in the polls, and the ever present protesters who were inventing new ways to annoy him. He squirmed in his seat, trying to find a comfortable position, his skin feeling clammy inside his air conditioned office.

He spun his chair toward the window, peering down at the protesters who splattered red paint all over his SUV. Why didn't the building have a garage entrance? Who was the imbecile who designed a government building without a VIP entrance?

What he needed was a long vacation—a break from the idiot council members who didn't know their right side from their back side.

He reclined in his chair, closing his eyes, and trying desperately to clear his mind. He inhaled several deep breaths, channeling his thoughts to a faraway Caribbean island— complete with long stretches of sugar sand beaches and tropical blue water. He could feel the golden sunshine, a light breeze spraying off the crashing waves. He smelled the ocean air, tasted the salt water on his lips. Even the angry birds seemed to be happy, chirping overhead, and soaking in the sun. He stretched out beneath a shaded palm, slurping a frozen Mai Tai, then drifting off to sleep.

Suddenly, Jester plunked a stack of documents onto his desk, snapping him out of his Paradise getaway.

"Don't you knock?" he snipped.

"Taking a cat nap?" Jester smirked.

"Power nap."

"Dreaming about the White House?"

"Something a little more tropical."

His assistant, Bernice, poked her head in, further disrupting his beach excursion.

"What is it, Bernice?" he rubbed his eyes.

"I just spoke to Balinda's people about your request to do a show on autism…"

"And…"

"And…, they said they have to respectfully decline."

"What?" he clenched his jaw, his blood pressure shooting through the roof.

"Their executive producer sends his apologies, and said they're completely booked."

"Booked my ass!" Jester blurted out. "They're playing politics. They weren't too booked for the Tony Chambers show!"

"Thank you, Bernice," Mitch replied, his voice calm, but his eyes brooding.

He sank into his chair, heaving a heavy sigh, a sharp pain cramping inside his stomach.

"Oh, well," Jester scoffed. "You can't win 'em all."

Mitch sat very still, his anger swelling like a hot air balloon. He was tired of being Wall Street's underling, giving tax breaks to corporate bigwigs. How dare they say no to him; how dare they say no to the children.

"So what are you buying me for lunch?" Jester smirked.

Staring straight ahead, Mitch could taste the bile on his tongue, his cool exterior straining to harness the wild beast.

"Mitch?"

"Shut her down," he fumed beneath his breath.

"What?" Jester raised his eyebrows in shock.

"Shut her down." His voice was measured, but his eyes were spewing fire.

"Mitch, I was just joking."

He crossed to the mini bar to refill his glass of seltzer. "Call Anderson at the network and tell him I want her off the air."

"But she's been on for like…?"

"Just do it!" he thundered. "I don't care who she is! If she wants to play games…!" he closed his eyes, fighting to control his temper. "Let me explain something to you. Don't underestimate her influence over voters. If she's backing Chambers, then we have to pull the plug right now."

"I don't know, Mitch." Jester shook his head.

"Call Richard Anderson at the network and tell him I want her gone A.S.A.P. Then call Charlie down in legal and tell him to squeeze."

"All right." Jester conceded, dialing his cell, and walking toward the media center.

Mitch's mind swirled like a blender. "Next year…" he scoffed, "you won't be around next year!"

The intercom buzzed, slicing through the tension.

"What is it, Bernice?" he snapped.

"The interns are here for your luncheon."

He inhaled deeply, tempering his rage and searching for an inner calm. "Give me a few minutes." He closed his eyes, clenching his fists.

He stared out the window, gazing at the storm clouds gathering in the distance. He hated to lose more than anything, and his tolerance level had sunk to zero.

"Okay," Jester chimed in, "I called Charlie down in legal…, but he's out to lunch."

"And Anderson?"

"Are you sure you want to do this?" Jester wavered.

"Let me enlighten you my mentally challenged compadre. 'Speed is the essence of war.' Have you never read Sun Tzu's *The Art of War*? 'Opportunities multiply as they are seized.' Our real battle is not against Chambers...it's against her. He may be the face on the poster, but she is his backbone—she is his confidence right now. If it weren't for her, we would've buried him last week."

"I'm just saying...it may not be easy...she's been on the air for nearly twenty years."

"You call Anderson, and tell him to handle his business or he's gonna be sweeping the streets and picking up garbage!"

"All right, I'll make the call." Jester cowered in surrender.

He exhaled a heavy sigh, then sipped his seltzer. Was he making the right decision? The redness in his face began to subside.

He dabbed his forehead with a cocktail napkin, semi-satisfied with his plan of action. As his heart rate receded, he flicked the intercom. Maybe a lunch break was just what he needed.

"Bernice, go ahead and send them in."

He slumped in his chair, inhaling several deep breaths, then flashing a confident smile at his jittery assistant.

"What's the matter Jester..., this is the exciting part." He stroked his chin, his swagger back in full effect.

The door creaked open, and three bashful interns staggered in single file. He paid them no attention, returning to his paperwork—skimming over the final stack of legal contracts.

"Come on in," he greeted them. He snuck a peek at the visitors, flashing a generic yet engaging smile.

"I'll be right with you," his eyes dropped back to his work, scratching out a few more signatures. He stacked the papers into separate piles, then nodded to Jester to pick them up.

The interns wavered like wallflowers near the door, overwhelmed by the grandeur of the stately office. Their eyes were like saucers, marveling at the lavish décor; their mouths gaping in awe at the view of the city skyline.

He handed the documents to Jester, who was still flustered over the Balinda ordeal. He grabbed Jester's arm and escorted him to the door.

"If you have any problems, let me know."

Jester half-nodded, then stumbled out the door.

"So who's hungry?" His energy perked up, as he addressed his guests.

All three smiled bashfully, raising their hands halfway, and giggling beneath their breath. Mitch's eyes darted immediately to a single intern—a statuesque blond whose blue eyes and bright smile sent a jolt of electricity to his heart. He cracked a smile, unable to hide his enthusiasm. He averted his glance, being careful not to let his eagerness or his eyes linger too long.

"What's your name?" he extended his hand to the first student.

"Michael," the young man stuttered.

"Nice tie...very sharp."

"Thanks." Michael blushed, relishing the favorable impression.

Michael stood straight and tall, a clean cut yuppie, dressed in a light gray, two-piece suit. He seemed to be an intelligent guy, a little nerdy—more engineer than politician.

Mitch's eyes dropped down to Michael's shoes. "Are those Hush Puppies?" he chuckled.

The two girls giggled at the beige shoes with the oversized buckle.

"Yeah, my dad said they're making a comeback and... um..."

"Wow... okay." Mitch grinned, then offered a friendly wink, assuring him that he was only poking fun. "Anyway, what are you in the mood for?"

Michael flushed red, shrinking from embarrassment. His tongue was paralyzed, his courage shredded to pieces.

"That's okay, we'll..., we'll come back to you." Mitch moved on. "Ladies? Hi, what's your name?"

"Bridget."

"It's a pleasure to meet you, Bridget."

"Thank you," she blushed.

"And what's your favorite food?"

"I'm fine with anything." She averted her glance—biting her bottom lip to keep from giggling.

She flashed a toothy smile that still bore the shape of teenage braces. She had the look of a typical band geek, somewhat artsy, probably spoke a little French. She leaned awkwardly in her heels, her posture not matching the professionalism of her navy skirt suit.

"Bridget, the lovely Bridget is undecided," he smiled, shaking her hand again and following it with a friendly wink.

"Italian?" Michael chimed in having regained his composure.

"Pizza man," Mitch joked. "Okay, good. Nice recovery, Michael."

Michael breathed a sigh of relief, then settled back into place.

The wait was over. Mitch had arrived at the vision of beauty that captured his attention. His breathing grew heavy, the air thickening all around him. He loosened his necktie, careful not to betray his inner stirrings.

"And what's your name?" he asked with an innocent smile, looking deep into her light blue eyes.

"Tiffany," she blushed.

"I love your jewelry," he teased.

"I'm not wearing any," she smiled, brushing her hair from her face.

"I'm sorry..., don't you own that little boutique on Madison Avenue, near diamond row?"

"I wish," she giggled.

He winked, invigorated by her playful spirit.

She was dressed in a snug, black mini dress—not too revealing, but very chic. At first glance, she superseded all the qualifications of a supermodel—an infectious smile, a curvaceous body, and a golden tan.

"What do you like, Tiffany?" their eyes were locked in an embrace.

"How about Sushi?"

"Wow, exotic."

"I could eat sushi for breakfast, lunch and dinner."

"Classic," he smiled. "Sushi actually sounds perfect." He reached over and brushed her arm lightly, in a nonchalant way. She smiled at his touch, biting her bottom lip and playing with her hair.

"And what else do you like besides sushi?" he asked.

As she spoke, his mind blurred into a cloudy haze. The sound of her voice flowed like honey from her lips. She was both articulate and intelligent, displaying a maturity far beyond her years. He noticed a twinkle in her eye that sparked a youthful vigor within him—a playful passion he had not felt since college.

Suddenly, a beeping sound from Michael's scientific watch snapped him out of his fantasy and back to reality.

"Okay, nice," he stuttered. "Um…any other requests?"

They shook their heads, eager to be dining at an elite restaurant.

"Okay, how about sushi today, and tomorrow we'll have Italian?"

"Sounds good." Tiffany applauded, as they shared a quick smile.

He grabbed his suit jacket, then waved everyone toward the door. He was hungrier than he realized, maybe today would be an extended lunch.

"So Michael…" he said, sliding his arm around his shoulder, "Life lesson number one: You need to know that women pay attention to your shoes…that's all I'm gonna say.

And lesson number two: Always treat women well..., and they'll treat you well. But..., and this is important... you gotta keep it fun," he winked.

Chapter 25

B alinda's eyes glazed over, as she pressed her face against the backstage door. Was this really happening? She strolled through the crowd during her usual fanfare introduction— going through the motions as she had done a thousand times before. But this time something was different—something was very wrong. She climbed onstage, offering a few cursory waves; the crowd's applause ringing in her ears.

"Thank you. Please, be seated. Thank you." She smiled casually, her enthusiasm waning.

"You 'all are wonderful." Her eyes grew misty, laboring to hold a smile.

"If you don't mind, I'm gonna grab a seat. It's been one of those sit-down type days," she laughed nervously, sinking into her chair.

The audience looked on in bewilderment; the air emitting a sudden chill.

"I've always been honest with you...," she hesitated. "Sometimes there are too many cooks in the kitchen, and you can't get much done..., and right now, our network is doing a lot of cooking behind the scenes."

The audience listened with puzzled expressions.

"I'm sorry," she laughed nervously. "I know I'm not making much sense," she turned aside, trying to regain her composure. "Well, let me just come right out and say it. After this week, the Balinda Show will be taking a hiatus, indefinitely…, the show's first extended break in twenty years."

The crowd moaned in disbelief, shaking their heads and grumbling to one another. What was going on? Her words made no sense, and the audience was jumping to conclusions. The commotion grew louder, the speculation rolling like ripples across a lake.

She raised her voice to calm the crowd, waving her hands, trying to wield damage control. Her thoughts were jumbled, her temperature rising from the stress. It's not that she was keeping secrets from them; she was just as confused as they were.

"I'm sorry I can't tell you more," her voice quickened. "But let me say this, we are working through contractual issues…network obligations that I don't fully understand," she scoffed, "but our lawyers are on it, and I promise…, we are not going away!"

A few audience members applauded halfheartedly, still confused, and trying to make sense of it all.

"I am always here for you," she choked back tears. "Always here for you…, because you 'all are my family."

The crowd rose to their feet and chanted "Balinda, Balinda!" They clapped in rhythm, showing their loyalty and support.

Her eyes turned glassy, overwhelmed by their outpouring of love.

"Thank you. Please, thank you." She waved her hands, signaling for them to take their seats. "See, you made me smear my mascara," she chuckled, wiping the mist from her eyes.

"Now you 'all have known me for a long time, and you know I don't dwell on the past. So what do you say we keep this train moving…is anybody with me?"

"Yes," a scattered few replied.

"Alright then, moving right along," she cleared the lump in her throat. "Remember, I don't do this for me, I do this for you… and today, we have an unbelievable show for you. Are you ready?"

"Yes," the semi-subdued audience replied.

"I can't hear you?" she yelled.

"Yes!" they shouted.

She flashed a smile, satisfied with their response.

"Now, let me ask you…there's a saying that I'm sure you've all heard that says, 'It is better to give than to receive.' You've all heard that, right?"

The audience nodded.

"Well I've always believed it is better to give *and* receive," she continued. "What do I mean? Here's what I mean. These are challenging economic times, aren't they? Not just here at the Balinda Summers show… but all over. I mean, there are some weeks when bills seem to roll in nonstop, don't they? You turn around, and there's another bill—mortgage, rent, car payment, credit card bill, phone, cable, it's always something, isn't it?"

"Yes, it is," they replied.

"Anybody here like to shop for new clothes?"

The audience laughed, raising their hands.

"You know I do," she chuckled. "But there are times when I go to a boutique or a department store, and I look at the prices and think… you want how much for these shoes…? You're joking, right?" she grinned. He heart fluttered just thinking about shoe shopping—it was by far her number one guilty pleasure.

"And it's not just clothing…, but food prices are going up too. And even eating at restaurants is more expensive. Times are not what they used to be," she shook her head.

"By a show of hands, how many of you know someone who has been hit hard by this economy… I mean, really struggling just to make ends meet?"

Everyone reached for the ceiling, some mumbling under their breath.

"All of us know at least one person who has lost their

job, is unemployed, or can't find a job, right? It could be a family member, a friend, a neighbor…it could be you?"

"Right here!" a woman called out.

"See that," she laughed, waving to the woman. "All over the country," she continued, "people are drowning in debt. Hard working Americans, people losing their homes, grandmas, grandpas, aunts, uncles, and poor people…." she sighed.

"When you see people hurting, like single moms who can't pay their bills, being crushed by debt…. don't you wish you could…, first, give them a hug, and let them know you care…, and, second,… make their problems go away?"

"All right now!" a woman called out.

"Don't you wish you could say, 'Hey, it's gonna be okay,'" she nodded. "But don't you wish you could say it, and actually mean it?"

"I know that's right," the same woman cried out, as the audience began to buzz.

"Well I've got good news for you," she spoke above the chatter. "Each of you is going to make a difference in someone's life… today. How's that sound? Exciting?"

"Yes." They stirred in their seats.

"Now pay attention," she giggled, "Because here's how it's gonna work. Are you ready?"

"We're ready!" they screamed, bubbling with excitement.

"Each one of you will be given a small amount of money, a few dollars… and you need to pass it on to someone who is truly in need. Okay?" she peered around, making sure everyone was onboard. "So first, take a few seconds and think of someone in need other than yourself," she smiled, "Other than yourself."

The audience laughed.

"I know what you're thinking," she grinned, "but let's think of others first. So think about someone else who could use a helping hand right about now. Do you have someone in mind?"

A hush fell over the audience, their eyes wandering about

as they pondered deeply. After a few seconds, the widespread smiles affirmed that they had chosen someone.

"Good. Now here's what we're gonna do," she said. "I'm gonna give each of you a small amount of money…, it's just a small amount… but to a struggling person or a poor person, fifty dollars, a hundred dollars, or two hundred dollars is a lot of money, isn't it?

"Yes, it is," they agreed.

"Well, I'm gonna give you this small amount…, and you're gonna contact this person or persons, call, visit, email, text, carrier pigeon, whatever… and then you're gonna give them this gift. You think you can handle that?" she grinned.

"Yes," they replied in unison.

"Now the amount of money that you must give away…," she scanned the back row quickly, "Are you ready?"

"Yes!" they roared.

"The amount that you must give away is… ten thousand dollars!"

Mouths dropped all over the studio, the air was sucked out of the room. Some of the ladies grabbed their hearts, shaking their heads in a state of shock.

"But wait…," Balinda continued, "I'm also going to give each of you… an additional ten thousand dollars for you!"

The audience erupted. The crowd leapt to their feet in disbelief. Women jumped up and down, hugging and screaming; grabbing hold of anyone within reach. The studio risers shuddered beneath their feet like a rolling earthquake. The room exploded with emotion—rumblings vibrating from front to back, as cries of happiness flooded the studio. Everyone yelled, pulling at each other's clothes, flailing their arms—in every direction. Some of the women rushed the stage, bowling Balinda over with their affection. She burst into tears, caught up in the elation, her body trembling with waves of joy. She threw her arms around the ladies, jumping up and down, and embracing their outpouring of love.

"If we're going out, we're going out with a bang!" she

shouted above the mayhem, "We're not done yet! You mark my words, we're not done yet!"

Chapter 26

"All right, settle down," Mitch waved his hands, calling for order. "Anything else? Any other pressing matters…, lawsuits…, constipation?"

The bigwigs in the room grew restless, eager to bring the meeting to a close. Driven by hunger pangs, the local leaders and attorneys stuffed papers into their brief cases. Some were already discussing lunch plans, checking their phones for nearby restaurants. Along the side windows, the interns observed in silence. They were peons in the bureaucratic pecking order—strictly seen and not heard.

"Anything else, anybody… going once, going twice…?" Mitch's stomach growled.

Heads swiveled from side to side, but no one said a word.

Before he adjourned the meeting, he peered around— relishing his role as puppet master. He drank a satisfying swig of water, pleased with how the meeting went; he got everything he wanted, with very little compromise. It was good to be king.

"Oh, and one more thing …don't forget," he added, "Fund raiser, two weeks from tomorrow, so mark your calendars. And by the way, our theme for the event has not been finalized. Does anyone have any additional ideas?"

Everyone glared back and forth, shuffling papers and

leaning toward the doors. One assistant poked his hand up as if to speak; however, he quickly recanted, feeling pressure from the hungry masses.

"Hey, what am I paying you people for?" he joked, "Just kidding."

He noticed the interns in their bright colored outfits. He chuckled, when he saw Michael shuffling around in his lime green pair of pants. There was something refreshing about having spritely college students around, infusing fresh air into the stagnant meetings.

"How about the interns?" he grinned. "Any fresh ideas?"

The students squirmed in their seats, averting their eyes, and fidgeting with their clothes. Every eye in the room was on them—glaring like spotlights, exposing every hair out of place. Mitch smirked at their bashfulness, deciding to prod them a bit.

"Anything, any potential fundraiser themes?" he asked. "Michael, not to put you on the spot?"

Michael stammered, his face turning ghost white. His voice quivered, but he choked out a few syllables. "Um, wine tasting?"

Mitch raised his eyebrows, pleasantly surprised, "That's good," he nodded. "That's actually a very good idea. Is everyone over twenty-one?"

The room spattered a few laughs.

"Wine tasting... all right, we'll call that plan B," he grinned.

"Anyone else?" he asked. "Ladies?"

Bridget cowered behind Michael, relegated to biting her nails. Tiffany surrendered a pageant smile, then sheepishly raised her hand halfway.

"Tiffany?" He acknowledged with surprising delight.

"How about a masquerade ball?"

"Ah, Tiffany likes to play dress up," he teased.

Tiffany blushed, biting her lower lip, then quickly regaining her self-confidence.

"I like it." He affirmed. "We'll save that for the future as well."

He closed his portfolio, signaling that the meeting was adjourned.

"Thank you, everyone. Play nice, and enjoy your lunches."

The crowd separated into mini cliques, shedding their business etiquette for casual conversation.

Mitch snuck a smile at Tiffany who caught his eye, then quickly looked away. His lunch appetite faded, as he fantasized about a different kind of entrée.

He tarried near the head of the table, shaking hands with various leaders. A few brownnosers handed him business cards, eager to set appointments—trying to swing deals. As the masses trickled out, the interns pushed in chairs, gathered drinking glasses and straightened the buffet area—part of their menial responsibilities.

Mitch cut short his meet-and-greet, grabbing his glass and meandering to the buffet table. He brushed by the breakfast section, skipping over the bagels and croissants, then made his way to the exotic fruit spread, grabbing a few strawberries to go. He set down his glass, then nonchalantly bumped elbows with Tiffany.

"Hey," he smiled. "Great idea, very creative."

"Thanks," she beamed, "I thought it'd be fun."

"Ever been to a masquerade ball?"

"Never, but I'll try anything once." She grinned, locking eyes for just a moment.

He was intrigued by her sense of style, impressed with her poise and confidence. If she harbored any nervousness from being around state leaders and VIPs, it didn't show.

She smirked at his subtle advances, sliding to the next table to gather glasses. He sensed a playful cunning beneath her youthful veneer, a hypnotic charm—an allure that went beyond her physical beauty.

He slid up beside her, grabbing the water pitcher to refill his glass. This was an enticing game to him, and he always played to win.

"If we hosted a masquerade ball, what would the theme be?" He bit into a fresh strawberry, savoring the juices.

"Maybe something medieval," she grinned.

"Any particular costume?"

"Hmm. Something playful..., something mischievous," she brushed a strand of hair from her face.

"Sounds more exciting than wine tasting," he teased.

"Wine tasting is pretentious... it's for old people..., and Michael." She rolled her eyes.

"Why you hating on Michael?"

"I'm not hating on Michael..."

"What, you mean he hasn't swept you off your feet with his Hush Puppies?"

"No," she smiled, shaking her head.

"Why not?"

"Well, because... Michael's just a boy," she sipped her water, lifting her eyes to meet his gaze.

"I see," he nodded.

She looked deep into his eyes, taking pleasure in the playful tension. He blushed, exhilarated by the connection, but cautious of the public setting. He could sense the eyes around him; but in his mind, that only raised the stakes. The more he got to know her, the more he wanted to know.

"What department are you working in?" he asked.

"Mostly the mailroom, and occasionally banquet services." her face soured.

"How would you like to work with event planners?"

"I'd love it!" she beamed.

"I think they could use some fresh ideas..., maybe infuse a little style into the events."

"Oh my gosh, I would love it," she squealed.

"Okay, I'll talk to the boss," he smiled. "Oh, wait, that's me."

She leaned in to hug him, then stopped herself, aware of the curious spectators. A smile spread across his face, amused by her hesitation. He peeked over his shoulder, surveying the remaining stragglers; he couldn't tell if anyone was watching, but a part of him really didn't care.

"It's okay," he touched her arm, "And hey, if anyone gives you trouble, you come to me personally, okay?"

"I will." She raised her eyebrows, acknowledging the underlying invitation.

They stared into each other's eyes, enjoying the subtle flirtation. The sparks began to catch fire, turning up the heat in an already hot summer. He knew he was being drawn into a risky game of cat and mouse; but he relished the danger—he was up for the challenge. After all, wasn't life about taking risks? Even as a little boy, he enjoyed playing with matches.

"Do you have plans for lunch?" he asked.

Chapter 27

"Governor, I tried to call you," his secretary called out. "Senator Greene is furious…. You missed your two o'clock meeting."

As he walked by her desk, he picked up the mail. He was more relaxed than usual, still savoring the chocolate mousse that capped off his late lunch.

"I'm sorry, Bernice, I was detained, and I turned my phone off, accidently."

"Well, he waited for nearly half an hour…, he was not happy."

"He'll get over it, he's looking for contributions."

She smirked at his nonchalant attitude.

"Please send him my apologies, and see if we can reschedule for next week," he winked.

He bounced into his office, his adrenaline pumping, feeling invincible, untouchable. He tossed his briefcase on the couch, then paused to admire the city skyline—the breadth of his domain. He inhaled deeply, reveling in the vastness of his success—anything he wanted, his every desire was within reach.

Jester paced anxiously in front of the TV screens, engrossed in the up-to-the-minute political happenings.

"I can smell the finish line, Jester!" he boasted.

"Oh yeah, what's it smell like?"

"Pennsylvania Avenue."

"Well, not to pass gas on your parade..." Jester chimed in. "But I've got good news and... some other news."

"Don't play with me." His daydream trailed off.

He plunked down in his chair, kicked his heels on the desk, then stretched his arms overhead. An afternoon siesta sounded good right about now, but lunch break had to end sometime, so he clicked on his computer.

"What do you have?" he asked matter-of-factly.

"Well, the good news is, the Balinda Show is on its last legs." Jester smirked.

"Of course it is," he bragged. "She can't run with the big dogs."

"Yeah, well, I heard there were major fireworks at the network." Jester snickered.

"Anderson and I go way back, I knew he'd make it happen."

"Frat brothers?"

"Let's just say, he and my paddle were well acquainted," he chuckled. "What else you got?"

"And on another note," Jester hesitated, "the latest polls are out, and I don't think you're gonna like them."

"You know I don't care about polls," he snipped.

He crossed to the mini bar and poured himself a drink, convinced that the polls were as fickle as the weather. His mind wavered, curiosity gnawing at his ego. Maybe the race was closer than he thought.

"What are the polls saying?" he relented, staring out the window.

Jester's voice wavered. "Chambers' numbers are up."

"I knew they would be," he scoffed.

"Really?"

"No," he grinned sarcastically.

"Balinda's show... he got a sympathy bounce."

"Incredible," he scoffed. "He gets to spend the night with a gorgeous masseuse *and* his numbers are up.... Next time, tell that masseuse to slip him a Viagra, then let's see if he can resist!"

Jester smirked, shaking his head.

"Gimme the numbers, what's the damage?" he barked.

"He closed the gap..., your lead is down to five."

He sighed, sinking into his chair. "What's the next move?" he thought. He reclined as far as the chair would allow, staring up at the high ceiling. "Time to take him out," he surmised. He spun his chair one hundred and eighty degrees, and stared pensively at the spattering of rain clouds in the distance.

"Chambers has got nothing on me," he surmised. "He's nothing but a street urchin. Head to head, he can't match my education, my experience or my wits. He's gonna slip up, if he hasn't already."

"What do you wanna do?" Jester pressed.

He spun back around, starring Jester in the eye. "What else do we have on him?"

Jester shook his head, clueless.

"Come on, Jester, I thought you were the best!"

Jester buckled, his face crumpling from the pressure. "I hear he spends time at some homeless shelter on the lower East side.

"Is that where he lives?" he smirked.

"Yeah, right," he scoffed. "No, he actually lives uptown, overlooking the river. But he has some sort of history or ties to this shelter.

"Then shut it down," he blurted, without skipping a beat.

"What?" Jester scoffed.

"Shut it down. Health inspector, drug enforcement, pest control, fashion police..., whatever."

"These are homeless people."

"And who's gonna miss them, you?"

Jester shook his head, "But what good is that gonna do?"

"Hey..., the fresh air will do them good."

Jester smirked.

"I see you haven't gotten to chapter six yet in *The Art of War*, 'Strengths and Weaknesses,'" he crossed to Jester, leaning back on his desk. "First you flood his mind with distractions, then sooner or later, he's gonna slip."

Jester listened intently.

"Use your head, man." He tapped Jester on the noggin as if he were a child. "If this is what he loves, then we cut his heart out. Sure, I feel bad for the bums, but hey…, collateral damage. And then we make both Chambers and his family suffer. We hit him with tax evasion, mortgage default, raise the interest rates on his credit cards, and then we bring pain to his family. Why aren't you writing this down?"

Jester scrambled to the media center to grab a notepad.

Mitch's mind churned in attack mode, the pressure feeding his adrenaline. He actually preferred a tight race, because now he could unleash his arsenal. He was never satisfied with simply winning. The alpha male code was clear and unequivocal—to annihilate the opposition, and make them suffer.

"Find out his wife's old lovers, his children's school report cards, and a complete record of his charitable giving. I want this guy so paranoid that he'll be afraid to step out of his house; and then we'll squeeze the life out of him. I want a complete background check—girls who rejected him, class detention, lateness… Even if he picked his nose in kindergarten, I wanna know about it. And then we run him into the ground."

Jester shook his head in amazement—part shock, and part admiration.

"Everybody's got skeletons, the trick is to dig until you find them," he snickered. "Information is power. You press the right buttons, you torment his family, and he'll collapse like a house of cards."

"I'm on it." Jester nodded.

Satisfied with his plan of action, he crossed to the sofa and grabbed his jacket. He slid over to the mirror for a quick hair check, then licked his lips, he could already taste the late afternoon beer. He relished the stiff challenge—it forced him to get a little creative.

"Oh, and this time, no more slinky senoritas, got it? We need the fat lady. No one ever lets the fat lady sing anymore."

"Ah, I miss the fat lady," Jester mourned.

Just as he stuffed a few folders into his briefcase, the intercom buzzed.

"What is it, Bernice?"

"Senator Greene is on the line and wants to speak with you."

"Sure, put him through."

He picked up the phone. "Richard, how are you?"

He listened.

"Glad to hear it. First let me apologize for the mix up, today. I had an emergency meeting..., an issue that's close to my heart." He pulled his cell from his breast pocket, glancing at a picture of Tiffany, from the restaurant.

He listened as the senator pacified the situation, assuring him that rescheduling was no big deal.

"Well good, I was hoping you'd understand. And I also wanted to mention another issue... a serious issue that you may not be aware of...," he sighed, "I've been tracking the unsanitary living conditions in the homeless shelters..., and I'm hearing reports of criminal activity..., drug deals, extortion, and prostitution." He winked at Jester.

Chapter 28

The air reeked of body odor, the sidewalk teeming with homeless people. Dozens of vagrants were sprawled out on cardboard boxes, some dressed in winter coats in the heat of summer.

Dr. Chambers cringed when he stepped out of the car, the stench burning his nostrils, causing his eyes to water. He handed a dollar to one of one vagabonds who was mumbling under his breath, and scratching every conceivable part of his body.

A news van pulled up, and a TV crew hopped out with press passes dangling around their necks.

"It's supposed to hit ninety-eight today." The reporter complained. The cameraman shook his head, cringing in disbelief.

"Hey, you made it." He called to the crew.

"Whoa...!" The reporter gasped, the odor smacking him in the face.

"Don't breathe through your mouth, and you'll be okay," he winked.

The crew stepped over a sleeping vagrant, then followed him into the shelter.

As they walked through the front door, the doctor was greeted by an impromptu applause. Rows of homeless people—seated around cafeteria tables—cheered with their scratchy voices and pounded on the tables.

"Hey everybody!" He waved, smiling from ear to ear.

Homeless folks of all ages were scattered around the cramped quarters, surrounded by shopping bags overflowing with bottles and cans. The stench in the room smelled like rotten cheese, exacerbated by poor ventilation, and the ninety-five degree heat.

The news crew clung to the doctor, tiptoeing cautiously around the vagrants in the main room.

"How 'bout we get some video of you milling amongst the guests." The reporter suggested.

"Sure, I don't think they're camera shy," he grinned.

He weaved his way around the room, shaking hands with staff members and homeless folks alike. The guests were busy eating lunch, but paused to chat, especially when the camera was on them. As they approached the kitchen, an elderly man rushed from behind the counter—catching the doctor by surprise, a huge grin on his face.

"Hey doc," the old man laughed heartily, his gold teeth shimmering in the light. "Welcome back."

"Marvin, my man. How are you?" He chuckled, embracing him in a man hug.

"I'm good, I'm good, can't complain. You 'all picked a great day to stop by, I baked my famous cornbread this morning."

Dr. Chambers turned to the reporter, "Marvin is the shelter director, and an incredible cook."

"It's a pleasure." Marvin shook his hand.

"What I wouldn't give to smell your cornbread right about now." The reporter smirked.

"Yeah, sorry about that." Marvin sighed. "I think I've developed iron nostrils over the years."

"Marvin's been running this place for forty three years."

"I don't think we gonna make it to fifty," Marvin grumbled.

"Yes, you will. You're still open aren't you?"

He slung his arm around Marvin's shoulder, reminiscing about the good ole days. Marvin was the one who gave him a job when he was struggling to get back on his feet. He had known him for over thirty years, like the father he never knew.

"So how you holdin' up, Marv?"

"I still got my health," he patted his pot belly, "But I'm not gonna lie to you, Doc, it don't look good."

"Well, that's why I'm here. You gotta hang in there, you gotta keep fighting," he squeezed his shoulder. He turned to the reporter. "I'm sure you've heard, the governor cut social services two days ago, and this shelter may not survive the week," he sighed.

"Hey, Doc! Remember me?" a homeless man cried out from the corner. "I was in the clink with you last week?"

"Hey," he waved, trying to suppress the memory.

"It's like a reunion," the reporter joked.

"How was the food in the joint?" someone shouted.

"Awful, don't take your girl there," he smiled.

"What were you in for, Doc?" an old man asked.

He hesitated, choosing his words carefully in the presence of the reporter. "Me and the governor…we, uh…had a little disagreement."

"Take him down, Doc!" A homeless man yelled.

"So let's eat," he laughed, eager to change the subject. "I could use a little cornbread right about now."

"Then, come on in." Marvin led them toward the food line.

He waved to the food servers, "Hey, how's it going?" Feelings of nostalgia swept over him as he peered around the room. He recalled spending endless days in the kitchen, peeling vegetables, and scrubbing pots.

"Hey, Pops…, good to see you." He waved to an elderly man who was sweeping the pantry.

He shook hands with one of the servers, a woman in her fifties; she was missing a few teeth, but her smile was genuine.

He wondered what her story was—drug addiction, alcohol, or maybe just down on her luck.

The reporter stood in line with him, scribbling observations, and jotting down names.

"This used to be my home back in the day," he said.

"Hey, Doc." A man yelled from the back, while pushing a mop.

"Hey, Chief!" He thrust a fist pump in the air. "These are my brothers and sisters," he laughed.

"Do you really think you can save this place?" the reporter asked, digging for a hard news angle.

"I have to try," he sighed. "Somebody has to try."

"How do you feel about the governor's cutbacks?"

He glared at the reporter. "I've said it on record and I'll say it again, the governor is a coward and an opportunist. But my biggest concern right now is raising support for this shelter."

The reporter sighed. "Come on Doc, give me something fresh…, something juicy…?"

"You tell the governor that he needs to get off his ass, restore the money for social services, and fight for what's right for once! You tell him to come down here…, I challenge him to come down from his plush office, and debate me like a man." He wavered, restraining his anger—biting his tongue. As much as he wanted to bash the governor, his main priority was to save the shelter.

"Outside of this place, who cares about these people? Anyone?" he scoffed. "The bankers… nope. How about the Pope, or the Governor, or the President? Nope. Nobody cares. These people are being swept aside. They are somebody else's problem. Unwed mothers, crack addicts…"

"Hey, who you calling a crack addict?" a straggler yelled. He winked at the heckler, then continued his plea.

"These folks aren't perfect, we know that. But they need a place to live and eat just like everybody else. They have feelings… they laugh and they love just like you and me. But when they're thrown out in the street…who's gonna fight for them?"

"Hey, Dr. Tony for president!" a woman squawked in her smoker's voice.

A loud cheer went up from the common area, the crowd whooping it up, like a gathering storm.

"Tony, Tony!" they chanted. He joined the revelry, waving his arms like a conductor.

"Look at these people. Are you nobodies?" he shouted.

"Screw the governor!" someone yelled.

As the interview continued, dozens of homeless folks streamed through the front door. They squeezed in from every direction, some jumping in front of the camera—trying to get their fifteen minutes of fame.

"Tony, Tony!" they yelled at the top of their lungs.

The crew cowered from the commotion, the cameraman wheezing from the toxic stench.

Suddenly, two older residents began pushing and shoving. They started screaming at one another, fighting over a bag of personal belongings. Punches were thrown, hair was pulled, and the plastic bag was ripped to shreds.

Instigators along the wall started throwing food and utensils, followed by anything else they could get their hands on.

"Stop it! Hey! Everybody back up!" Dr. Chambers shouted, waving his hands, trying to stop the melee.

The room exploded into full blown chaos, with vagrants throwing cans, bottles and lunch trays across the room. Fists were flying, people were yelling, and the vagrants were stealing one another's possessions. Dr. Chambers grabbed the news crew, and shoved them into the kitchen. Three burly staff members leapt into the fracas, then separated the main combatants—dragging them through the crowd and out the front door. After a chaotic fifteen minutes, order was finally restored. The room was hotter than a sauna, the temperature skyrocketing due to the frenzied activity. Residents climbed over one another, gagging in retreat, doing whatever they had to do to escape the bedlam.

"Sorry about that," Dr. Chambers shook his head. "Down deep, these folks have good hearts, they just need a little patience." He wiped the sweat from his brow, trying to catch his breath.

"How about we continue the interview here in the kitchen?"

He peeked around for Marvin. "Can we open a window or something?" He was desperate to change the tone of the interview, get some fresh air in the room, and get back on message.

"Please don't show the skirmish in your piece..., I'm begging you. You see what little these people have."

The reporter tucked his notebook in his pocket, looking over at the cameraman who was coughing incessantly. Dr. Chambers knew the interview was going nowhere. He had no recourse, but to make a final plea.

"Look, let's do one last take. Let me at least appeal to the public for help."

The reporter conferred with the cameraman, who looked like he was about to faint. The cameraman nodded, seemingly relieved that the whole thing was almost over.

They fired up the lights, as the doctor cleared his throat.

"We desperately need help." He spoke directly into the camera.

"We are looking for people with heart..., corporations, small businesses and food banks to step up and help these people," he appealed.

"Do you realize that some of these people have no families?" he asked. "Some of them have been on the streets since they were children. They have nobody. Can you imagine what it would be like to have no family?" his throat tightened. "Can you imagine going through life...and never having a place to call home?"

Chapter 29

The walls rattled like a mild earthquake, the foundation of the home shaking from the party music. Christy could feel the electricity in the air, as she and her boyfriend squeezed through the bodies blocking the front door. They weaved through the dark living room hoping to see a familiar face and possibly grab a drink.

She covered her ears as she sidestepped the speakers, exhilarated by the throbbing base—her body quivered from the vibrations.

"Great party!" She shouted, her voice drowned out by the music. "Do you see anyone you know?"

"What?" Tereek screamed back.

She shook her head, realizing that talking was useless.

Nudging their way through the middle of the room, they hit a wall of bodies, unable to push through the sweaty crowd. She fidgeted with the cotton blouse clinging to her skin; the jam-packed space was a virtual steam bath.

The air thickened from the sexually driven rap music and the stench of marijuana billowing overhead. She looked at Tereek and caught him eyeballing a couple of scantily clad girls, dancing on top of the bar. They couldn't have been more than fifteen years old, carousing shamelessly, giggling and spilling beer on the crowd. She slapped him on the arm, pushing him toward the kitchen doorway; she was anxious to get to another room—the smoke was burning her eyes.

As they inched their way through the thicket of bodies, she avoided eye contact with guys who were ogling her—dozens of teenage boys leering at her, whispering and blowing kisses.

Her boyfriend shouted across the room, calling someone's name, and waving his hand; it gave her a sliver of comfort—apparently they were not totally alone. Tereek peered back at her, squeezing her hand and pulling her along. She forced a half smile, her eyes darting around the room with apprehension. Her nerves teetered toward paranoia—she knew that if her dad ever found out, she would be grounded forever.

"Do you want a beer?" He shouted in her ear.

"I'll share whatever you're having." She stroked his arm.

Suddenly, a tennis ball flew screaming by her ear, nearly plunking her on the forehead. Two shirtless jocks cackled like hyenas, whipping the ball across the room—howling like stereotypical frat boys. It was hard to tell whether they were actually drunk or simply acting like jerks—pumping their fists and cursing at the top of their lungs. The two buzz-cut rabble rousers sprayed the crowd with beer, soaking everyone within a five foot radius. She threw her arms up trying to shield herself from the deluge, but it was too late—her hair caught the brunt of the beer spritzer.

One of the thugs on the bar spotted her, then began barking and panting like a dog. He leapt into the crowd, body surfing in her direction. He managed to squirm in behind her, and then spun her around.

"Yo. What up, ma?" he shouted, slurring his rap.

She was startled by his loud voice and forceful aggression; he clamped onto her, then started rapping in her ear. His breath reeked of beer and tuna fish, causing her to cringe and twist away. She grabbed her boyfriend by the t-shirt, and wrapped her arms around his waist; she trudged in lockstep with his every move, hoping the thug would disappear. Tereek was unaware of the drama behind him, the music blaring in his ears. The thug was unrelenting, placing his paws on her hips, and grinding to the beat.

"Yo. Show me what you got!" he yelped in her ear.

Her body recoiled from his slimy touch—his hot beer breath was making her nauseous. She spun her boyfriend around, then pointed at the thug's fingers clawing at her waist. Tereek slapped his hands away, pulling her behind him, then confronted the brute nose to nose. Fire blazed in Tereek's eyes.

"Yo. Back off!" He yelled in a jealous rage. The two squared off bumping chests, their noses only a few inches apart.

"What you got? What you got?" the thug barked in his face, stuttering from the alcohol.

Tereek's face turned beet red, as they stared each other down as much as they could in the dark. The football player appeared to be a few inches taller and twenty pounds heavier, but Tereek didn't back down. The pounding music added to the growing tension, as the crowd started chanting, "Fight, fight, fight, fight."

Christy's heart stopped beating; she was terrified by the confrontation. She shivered in the heat, her hair dripping, her clothes soaked with sweat and alcohol. She tugged on her boyfriend's arm, pleading for him to walk away.

"Please, let's just leave!" she begged.

Tereek and the thug fired death glances at one another, waiting for the other to throw the first punch.

"Tereek, come on!" she cried.

She finally managed to pry him away, as the thug continued cursing and threatening her boyfriend. She dragged him through the agitated crowd, squeezing past the potheads, and backtracking toward the front door.

The jock snickered, stirring the crowd into a mocking laughter.

"Yo, you better run!" he taunted.

Tereek ignored him.

"Come back when you want to be with a real man, instead of that lil punk!" he cackled.

Tereek snapped like a crazed boar and charged the drunken thug. He lunged shoulder first into the football player's chest, sending them both crashing into the crowd.

"Tereek, no! Tereek!" she cried in desperation.

Both swung wildly. The scuffle was a whirlwind of arms and fists flailing through the air. The crowd scattered like roaches, shouting and cursing, as nearby victims were struck by erratic punches. Christy gasped in horror, her body shuddering—her legs paralyzed by fear.

"Tereek!" she screamed, watching helplessly as the crowd closed in around her. The thunderous music fed the chaos like gasoline on a fire. Beer bottles were hurled across the room as instigators began trashing the place. Mirrors were shattered, furniture was smashed and alcohol was spilled all over the carpet. Some of the jocks sprayed beer on the girls, running around groping whoever they could grab. Girls were shrieking, lights were flickering, and people were crashing into one another.

Within minutes, police sirens blared outside the home. Christy panicked when she saw the flashing red lights. She was trapped inside the living room—pinned in the corner with a hoard of other frantic girls. The music was killed abruptly, but the cursing and crying persisted—everyone was gasping for oxygen in the stifling heat.

The officers stormed the front door sending party goers into a panic. Some teenagers dove out the windows, while others bull-rushed the backdoor, trying to escape any way they could.

Christy strained her eyes, trying to focus in the darkness, but all she could see were red lights flashing through the haze. She started coughing uncontrollably, choking from the heat and cigarette smoke.

Officers dragged the teens outside, frisking them, and detaining them along the curb. Christy rubbed her eyes, causing them to water even more, because of the alcohol residue on her fingers. She was one of the last girls to be ushered out, corralled like cattle, and separated by the side of the house. She peered across the yard, searching for her boyfriend amongst the guys being detained near the patrol cars.

"Tereek!" she shouted.

"Sit down!" An officer yelled.

She plopped onto the ground, exasperated, but grateful to be out of the sweat box. Her skin felt clammy beneath her wet clothes, and her stomach was nauseous—the girls around her reeked of marijuana and cigarettes.

She thought for a moment about calling her dad, but that notion was quickly squelched, when an officer confiscated her cell.

"Wait, can I call…?"

"Sit down and be quiet, and don't make me tell you again." The officer snapped.

"Please let me call my dad," she begged.

"You'll get your phone call at the station, now zip it."

Two paddy wagons screeched to a halt in front of the house, sending the already stir-crazy teenagers into a panic. She closed her eyes in disbelief. How could this be happening? The thought of being arrested terrified her to her very core. The officer slapped plastic riot cuffs on her wrists, as the nightmare worsened.

Two news crews pulled up in vans, and began videotaping the party aftermath. The camera operators shined lights in people's eyes which enflamed the situation even further.

Christy was ordered to move, as officers began herding groups into the vans. Feeling desperate and alone, she cried out to one of the officers.

"Can someone call my dad, please?" she panicked.

"I told you, no phone calls."

"But you don't understand," she pleaded.

"You'll get your chance at the station."

"But my father is the governor." She broke down in tears.

The officer froze, staring at her for a long moment. He walked over to a senior officer, leaving her in limbo beside the paddy wagon.

As the news hour approached, a reporter scrambled to set up for her live report. She positioned herself in front of the camera, shuffling her notes, and touching up her makeup.

"They're coming to us next, here we go!" the cameraman shouted.

Christy ducked away from the lights, slouching behind the girl next to her. The last thing she needed was to have her face splashed across the evening news.

"We are live in North Shore County," the reporter began, "where police have arrested dozens of teenagers, mostly high school students. The big story here tonight involves Governor Mitch Jameson's teenage daughter. Officials tell us that the sixteen-year-old has been taken into custody, and is being detained in one of the police vans which you can see behind me. Officials say they've seized crack cocaine and marijuana from some of the suspects, and that many of the teens are suspected of underage drinking. Also, witnesses tell us that police officers were called onto the scene after a fight broke out inside the home, and one witness claimed she heard gunfire."

The officer in charge returned to the paddy wagon, then loaded the remaining girls into the overcrowded van, including Christy.

"But wait!" She protested.

"Get in." The officer pushed her along. "No special treatment."

Inside the van, she shook involuntarily, scrunched between dozens of girls who were cursing and crying. She closed her eyes, her lungs convulsing inside her chest; she was pressed on all sides by half a dozen strangers, yet she felt totally alone.

As the van door shut, she burst into tears. She began

hyperventilating—wheezing from a sickening sense of guilt. What was her father going to say? She didn't want to think about it, she just wanted to die.

Chapter 30

Mitch burst through the front door, throwing his keys down, and rushing toward the kitchen.

Christy lingered through the door, her face smudged with eyeliner, and her hair knotted in a bird's nest. She stormed toward the staircase; her face glowing beet red from the nonstop shouting match.

"This is a nightmare!" He reemerged from the kitchen, shaking his head at his wife who just entered the house. "We give your daughter everything she could possibly want, let her date whoever she wants, and this is the thanks we get?"

"I said I was sorry!" Christy screamed without turning around. She climbed halfway up the stairs, kicking off her beer drenched shoes.

"Tell me, what part of your genius brain thought that going to a keg party was a good idea?"

"I told you, I wasn't drinking," she turned, rolling her eyes.

"Oh, that's right, you only drank water with a little lemon in it, I forgot. So let me reward you for going to a drunken soiree filled with underage drug addicts and potheads, and not drinking from the pig trough. Congratulations, Mother Teresa, should I bump up your allowance to…, I don't know, a billion dollars a week?"

His wife nudged him toward the kitchen, "Come on, honey, let's let her go to bed."

"Or do you know what's even better?" he continued, "I think I should receive the Father of the Millennium award, for allowing my sixteen-year-old daughter to date Pinhead-the-loser, get locked in the slammer, and then come home covered in dried puke and other people's body odor. Hooray for me!" He clapped heartily.

His wife chuckled under her breath, shaking her head, as she disappeared into the kitchen.

Christy rolled her eyes, "Why do you always get to go out, but I can't hang out with my friends?"

"You can hang out with your friends, just not at beer parties with a bunch of criminals," he roared. "And I forbid you from seeing that thug ever again."

"What? Why, we didn't do anything wrong," she protested.

"Oh no, you didn't do anything wrong." He snickered. "You lie to us, you run off to some stranger's house and then you end up in the slammer. Let me see, which one of us here smells like the sewer?" He calls to his wife in the kitchen, "Honey, are you covered with beer? Cause I'm pretty sure it's not me."

"I don't care what you say, you can't keep me from seeing my boyfriend," she barked defiantly.

"Go to your room!" He snapped. "You're grounded forever!" He marched into the kitchen seething with anger.

His daughter growled in anguish, storming up the stairs.

"I hope you die!" she yelled from the top of the stairs. She stomped into her room and slammed the door.

He burst back into the foyer, with his emotions running rampant, shouting up into the darkness.

"It's bad enough you lied to us. But you could have been killed, you know that? Bunch of animals!"

His blood pressure was shooting through the roof. His controlled world was unraveling—and he knew it.

Chapter 31

Balinda peeked through the crack, her heart racing like a giddy school girl. She felt like a five-year-old walking into kindergarten for the first day of class. The lights flickered causing her heart to jump, then she heard a booming voice thunder through the loudspeaker.

"Ladies and gentlemen... she's back and she's better than ever!" the producer announced. "Here she is, put your hands together for... Balinda Summers!"

She burst through the studio doors, the lights flashing to full capacity and the crowd erupting into boisterous applause.

"Balinda, Balinda!" they screamed, as she started down the aisle.

The atmosphere was electric as fans showered her with love—reaching out to touch her, hug her, and tell her how much they missed her. Her eyes welled up with joy—overwhelmed by the crowd's affection. She drank it all in—their energy, their loyalty, their adoration. Being appreciated never got old, and she vowed never to take it for granted. She strolled to center stage, feeling like a queen in her golden silk dress, waving her hands unabashedly, and blowing kisses all around.

After the endless ovation, she gestured for everyone to take their seats.

"Wow, you'd think the president just walked in." She chuckled.

The audience laughed, then resumed chanting her name, "Balinda, Balinda." Once again, they leapt to their feet.

"Please, thank you. Please, have a seat," her eyes glimmered with gratitude.

They settled reluctantly into their chairs—still antsy with excitement.

"Welcome back! You can't keep a good woman down!" she shouted.

The audience whooped and hollered as she smiled from ear to ear.

"I know it's only been three weeks, but did you miss me?" she giggled, her eyes getting a bit misty.

"Yes!" they roared.

"Wow, what a month it's been." She exhaled, trying to find her bearings. "I've always said that when you are generous, karma will always reward you. And we've always tried to live generously here at the Balinda Show. And it doesn't hurt to have a few high powered attorneys either." She chuckled.

"I want to be very honest with you..." her demeanor changed to a serious tone, "There are some folks who don't want us on the air."

The audience groaned, waving the thumbs down sign—a chill of animosity sweeping through the room.

"Oh, if only you were a fly on the wall at our network... Your head would be spinning right now." She rolled her eyes, chuckling sarcastically.

The crowd buzzed with speculation.

"Pending litigation prohibits me from disclosing any more details," she hesitated, "but if I've learned anything from my good friend, Dr. Tony Chambers, it's that we are here to fight! And the good news is, we are here to stay! We're not going anywhere!" She threw her hands up, declaring victory.

The audience erupted once again, rising to a standing ovation, and chanting her name, "Balinda, Balinda!"

The studio shook like a rock concert—the show's theme song blaring through the speakers, and the audience clapping to the beat.

She shouted above the jubilation, "And for those cowards who hide in the shadows, they're gonna get theirs, you wait and see!"

Chapter 32

Mitch choked down two aspirin, the chalky pills scratching his throat, getting stuck momentarily.

"Gotta get some gel caps," he sighed.

He mused alone in his office, an eerie tension sweeping through his mind as he peered out at the storm clouds brewing over the horizon. The clouds thickened, concealing the sun and casting foreboding shadows between the steel skyscrapers. He closed his eyes and massaged his temples. He was exhausted from his third sleepless night—still smarting about his daughter dragging his name through the tabloids. He kicked off his shoes, sinking his feet deep in the carpet.

He stared at the media center, his mind floating in a daze. He looked at the news channels which were generating their usual irrelevant breaking news. And the bottom row featured the fluff entertainment, sports and weather channels. Balinda's show was broadcast on the lower left screen—which he noticed, but dismissed as a rerun.

He reclined in his chair, his back muscles clenching from fatigue. He picked up the newspaper, then flipped mindlessly through the sports section; all his favorite teams lost last night, even the sports world provided no relief. He loosened his tie, hoping to release the nagging tension in his neck—and his world.

Crashing through the door unannounced was an agitated Jester.

"What's wrong with you?" Mitch flinched, snapping his head toward the door.

"My apologies Mitch, but this couldn't wait."

Jester streaked to the media center, then muted every TV set except for Balinda's show. Mitch stood up, creeping toward the screen, dumbfounded as to what was vexing him.

"It's a rerun, right?" He furrowed his brow.

"Nope." Jester shook his head, emphatically.

"Are you sure?"

"I checked with the local affiliate before I came in." Jester confirmed.

Mitch's face burned bright red, the vein in his neck was about to burst. "What's going on?"

"I don't know." Jester shrugged. "Maybe your boy cracked under pressure."

He rushed to his desk, sweeping the newspaper onto the floor, then punching the intercom.

"Bernice, get me Anderson at the network, immediately."

He stared at the TV, a sharp pain twisting in his stomach. After a long impatient moment, the intercom finally buzzed.

"Mr. Anderson's assistant is on the line, Governor, if you'd like to speak with her," Bernice stammered.

"Put her through, Bernice." He closed his eyes, straining to compose himself.

"Hello, Governor?" the assistant answered.

"This is Governor Jameson," he forced out a superficial greeting.

"I'm sorry, Governor, but Mr. Anderson was called out of the country unexpectedly, on personal business."

Mitch could feel his body clenching as he glared at the phone. She apologized profusely, then droned on about how her boss was on emergency leave and gave instructions not to be disturbed under any circumstances. His blood boiled as he listened to her flimsy excuse.

"Where is he?" he barked. "He knows why I'm calling, so you tell him I want it taken care of now!"

He squinted his eyes, peering at the TV screen. He caught a glimpse of Balinda laughing which enraged him even more.

"But, Governor...," she stammered.

"Look," he interrupted, snatching up the phone receiver. "I don't care if he's attending his own funeral, you tell him to call me or so help me, I will bust him so low the mail room will look like a penthouse." He rolled his eyes, then lashed out again. "Hey, I don't care where he is, you tell him to call me!"

He slammed the phone down. Shaking his head, and looking around for something to throw.

"Ahh!" he growled.

"He'd better hide!" he screamed, staring at Jester with wild eyes. "How hard is it to run a network?" He seethed. "He's a dead man!"

Chapter 33

An elderly African woman groveled in the mud, her threadbare clothes hanging from her emaciated body. She sobbed, as a child's coffin was hoisted into the air. Mourners wailed in despair, the crowd chanting—begging for an end to the violence.

"Countries like these were thriving a short ten-twenty years ago," Balinda narrated, wincing as she watched the news footage. "But witnesses now say that whole villages are being wiped out...that men and women are being slaughtered at the hands of government raiders."

The audience cringed at the carnage—averting their eyes when they saw victims who had been maimed.

The villagers cried incessantly, begging for food to give to their babies. Children scurried about, cradling their bloated stomachs, moaning from hunger—their rice bowls infested with insects.

The audience squirmed in their seats; shielding their eyes from the horror.

"Tragic. Unspeakable." Balinda shook her head, her voice asphyxiated from the savagery. "We will continue to track these developments and keep you updated with the very latest."

The news video faded to black.

"When we come back, we'll be shifting gears slightly,

bringing you a story that hits a little closer to home." She closed her eyes, trying to settle her emotions.

The video tease for the upcoming segment flashed onto the plasma screen. A wild teenage party showed young people binge drinking, smoking crack pipes, and engaging in lascivious behavior. The faces of the minors were blacked out, but the nature of the salacious frolicking was explicit. The ensuing video transitioned to teens that were ransacking a wealthy home—smashing lamps against walls, and throwing furniture through the windows.

"If you think this type of violence and recklessness is exclusive only to poor countries and impoverished cities..." Balinda commented, "Think again. We'll be right back."

The director counted down to the commercial break. The network faded to black.

Balinda ducked backstage during the break, sipping her water and collecting her thoughts. She forced herself to breathe evenly, still agonizing over the plight of the elderly woman. A makeup girl touched up her powder, covering any visible signs of anguish. After a two minute emotional respite, the director called for places.

"In our last segment," She narrated, "We brought you updates on the unconscionable violence erupting along some of Africa's border nations. But if you think brazen violence is exclusive only to third world nations or even impoverished inner city neighborhoods here in the U.S., think again. Take a look at this."

The plasma screen lit up with Youtube-ish video showing upscale teens roughhousing around a swimming pool at a wealthy suburban mansion. The adolescents were horsing around, sucking down beer shots and pouring drinks into the mouths of preteen girls. The faces of the kids were blurred; however, the youthful ages of the party goers were undeniable. The video turned violent as fights broke out with guys and girls punching one another, pulling hair and scratching each other's eyes out. Groups of kids ganged up on helpless individuals, beating and kicking them, while others stood by laughing.

"These are not shirtless trailer park juveniles like the ones we often see on TV," she narrated. "These are wealthy suburban teenagers—sons and daughters of doctors, lawyers, and Wall Street executives."

A second video flashed on the screen showing another party in a well-to-do neighborhood. The wealthy home was surrounded by expensive cars including a Mercedes, BMWs and a Maserati. Police officers swarmed the premises, arresting hordes of teenagers who were climbing over fences and diving into bushes.

"This is not a crack house party in the inner-city crawling with street thugs and hood rats," Balinda continued. "This is an upscale suburban home being raided by police. Officials say that at this particular party, dozens were charged with underage drinking..., and the air reeked of marijuana. They say fights broke out all night long and one teenager was charged with illegal gun possession."

"Now let's be honest...," she continued, as the plasma screen faded to black, "Does this type of behavior...in some of our country's wealthiest neighborhoods...surprise anyone?"

The audience shook their heads.

"Has the problem gotten better or worse?"

"Worse," they mumbled.

"That's right. Teen violence has been on the rise every year for the past ten years," she sighed. "And not just violence. Reports show that high school dropout numbers are up and test scores are down. In fact, the list is endless..., drug addiction, binge drinking, teen pregnancy, sexting, salacious internet videos and wild parties... What is happening to our society? Lower class, upper class... it doesn't matter. It's everywhere. Recently, a governor's sixteen-year-old daughter was arrested at one of these parties and her face was plastered all over the tabloids. Now the question I want to ask is this: What is happening to our country? And where are the parents..., should the children take *all* the blame? What does this say about their parents?"

Chapter 34

Sifting through a handful of mail, Mitch's face soured, plucking out a single envelope that caught his attention. As he walked through the foyer toward the kitchen, he wiggled his fingernail inside the crease, but couldn't rip it open—the adhesive was sealed tight.

"Hi, honey." His wife greeted him as he entered the kitchen. "How was your day?"

He shook his head, exhausted. "I'm just glad it's Friday." He was looking forward to kicking back in his recliner and not waking up until Monday morning.

He gave her a peck on the lips. "Mm... smells good, what's for dinner?" the aroma filling his nostrils.

"Lasagna, buttery corn on the cob, and Caesar salad." she smiled.

"Amazing," he kissed her cheek. His tongue could already taste the tangy tomato sauce, his taste buds salivating with anticipation.

He flung the stack of mail onto the table, still clinging to the single letter. The pile landed in front of Christy, who was pouting with her head down; she was grounded until further notice.

"How was school today?" He grabbed a letter opener from the pencil jar on the counter.

"I don't want to talk about it," she rolled her eyes, stuffing her mouth with Oreo cookies. She leaned her head against the wall, dying from boredom without her cell, computer, TV, and iPod.

"You're going to spoil your dinner." he snickered.

"There's nothing for me to do," she whined. "What am I supposed to do, you took everything away from me."

"Help your mother make dinner."

"Whatever," she sighed loudly, grabbing her Cosmopolitan magazine and bolting to the family room.

Just as he was about to open the letter, his phone rang.

"Hey, Bernice."

"Hi, Mitch," she answered, "Your lawyer, Todd has been trying to reach you. He wants you to call him immediately."

"Did he say what he wanted?" he scowled with concern.

"No, but he said it was urgent."

"Okay, thanks, Bernice," he exhaled. "Great," he murmured, as he hung up.

"What is it?" Rachel looked over her shoulder, as she washed the lettuce.

"Todd called, said it was urgent. Anytime he says that, it's never good."

As the dial tone rang in his ear, he jabbed the letter opener inside the envelope, and ripped it open. He yanked the single page letter out—his curiosity quivering through his fingertips.

"Hey, it's Governor Jameson, can I speak to Todd? Thank you."

He flattened the two fold creases, turning the letter right-side up.

"Hey Todd, what's the word?" He listened intently. His face crumpled in distress.

"Freaking animals." He shook his head. "What's our next step?"

"All right, keep me posted." He sighed, as he hung up.

"Incredible," he mumbled.

He glanced at the letter in his hand, skimming over it briefly, his face twisting into a deeper scowl.

"Unbelievable. Shoot me, shoot me now." He scoffed.

"What is it?" Rachel asked, turning off the faucet.

"In light of recent events...," his voice broke.

"Honey, what happened?" Her face flushed with concern.

"Christy, get in here!" he called.

"Honey, what is it, what did Todd say?"

His inner rage churned; he grit his teeth to keep his emotions from exploding. He forced a smile at his wife. "Well, what would you like first, the bad news, or the bad news?"

Christy appeared in the doorway.

"What?" She grumbled.

"You just keep spreading the sunshine, don't you?" He mocked, crossing to the refrigerator to retrieve a beer.

"Whatever." She turned to leave.

"My attorney just called, and according to two of the girls who were arrested with you at your little drunken soiree..., they claim the crack and marijuana they were busted with..., came from you."

"What?" She pivoted to face him, her eyes wide with shock.

"Wait, it gets better, listen to this." He straightened out the letter. "In light of recent events, we here at Legacy Gold Magazine want to respect your family's privacy due to the sensitive nature of the current circumstances. Therefore, we have decided to withdrawal your name as a finalist for Person of the Year."

He held his beer up to propose a toast. "So thanks to our daughter and her little boyfriend, I am the father of a teen drug dealer, and I just lost my shot at the presidency. My day just keeps getting better and better!"

"What are you talking about?" Christy shouted, "I never gave anyone drugs."

"Well, according to your two BFFs, you are their drug

kingpin."

"Whatever, I didn't give anybody anything." She growled defiantly.

"Oh, and thanks for throwing our whole family under the bus and ruining my chance at becoming president.

"What are you talking about? So what, so you won't get your face on another stupid magazine." She sneered.

"Another stupid magazine? You just don't get it do you?" his tone blistered with rage.

"Get what... a dumb title? Big deal."

"Big deal?" He nearly choked on his beer. "Your reputation, our family's reputation?"

"Is that all you care about, your precious reputation?" she scoffed.

"How can you be so selfish?" he shouted.

"Selfish?" She snapped, whipping her head around and staring straight into his eyes. "I'm not the one who wants to be president. And I never asked to be in the stupid spotlight."

He froze, startled by his daughter's zealous rebuke. He raised his eyebrows, calling off the dogs momentarily; her words resonated in his mind—concealing a modicum of truth. He stared back at her, musing for a moment, drinking a swig of beer and gathering his thoughts. Had he been hypocritical, condemning his daughter while pursuing his own selfish ambitions? He inhaled deeply, sizing up her demeanor.

"Wow, you know, honey, you're right." his acrimony tapered off. "You never asked for the spotlight. But your mother and I have bent over backwards for you all your life. When you turned sixteen and wanted to date, we said, 'You know what, let's let her go out with whoever she wants,' because we trusted you. And now, look how you've treated us. You lie to us... you run halfway across town to some crazy drunken party filled with drugs and guns and God knows what else... and you end up in the slammer. Was Rickety Rick, or whatever the hell his name is... was he there to bail you out? Huh?"

"What do you want from me?" her voice cracked from frustration. "I said I was sorry like a million times."

He bit his lip, grasping for words that were not forthcoming. He wasn't sure what he wanted from her; the damage had been done. He closed his eyes, rubbing his temples. His mind raced, searching for answers—something, anything to stop the hemorrhaging. His world was collapsing—and he knew it. Forget the presidential elections in a few years, and forget the Person of the Year nomination—his state re-election was now in jeopardy. His poll numbers were bound to dip once these drug charges came out.

"You know what, I don't even care anymore," he sighed. "You want to wreck your life, be my guest. You act like saying 'you're sorry' makes everything better. Well, you keep telling yourself that."

"Hey, nobody's perfect," she sniped.

"Unbelievable," he grumbled, heading toward the door.

"Oh, and what…, like you and mom had such perfect childhoods?" Christy rolled her eyes.

"Don't try and change the subject… that's not the point," he winced, tired of the bickering.

"Yes it is. It's been like two freakin weeks…, and you're still making such a big deal. The truth is, you're just mad because of that stupid award, that Person of the Month thing or whatever. Nobody cares."

"Nobody cares? Let me clue you in Miss I-know-everything-there-is-to-know. For your information, this award was important, not for me and another title, and not for your mother. Do you know why it was important? Huh?"

She crossed her arms, pouting, and staring at the floor.

"It was important for your sister. That's right. This award came with a million dollar prize that is now gone. Do you realize what one million dollars would have meant to the Autism foundation? Do you realize how much it would've benefited her if I would have been elected president? Huh? Of course you don't. Maybe you could stop being so damn selfish for once, and stop and think about your sister."

He stormed out of the kitchen, his mind reeling with anger and confusion. For the first time in his life, he was losing control—his dream was slipping away. Desperate times called for desperate measures.

Chapter 35

Night descended on the governor's home like a tempestuous storm, casting a shadow over the troubled paradise. Mitch escaped to his study where he scrutinized his next course of action—in politics and in life. Reclining in his Lazyboy, he tossed his head back, then kicked his feet as high as the chair would allow. His thoughts twisted inside his head, agitated by the unknowable future. He squirmed in his seat, shifting back and forth—his body languishing for a comfortable position.

His memory was stuck on repeat—replaying his recent failures over and over. The Balinda snub was merely a personal brush-off, not fatal—a minor cosmetic rejection that could have enhanced his presidential chances, but in hindsight, was a mere bump in the road. His opponent's rising poll numbers were a more immediate concern; if he was to lose reelection, it could set him back to square one. His daughter's pending drug charge was a nuisance more than anything. After working a plea deal behind the scenes, the incident could be relegated to an image problem, reparable in a few years. But the Legacy Gold rejection cut deepest of all. Winning the most prestigious award in America could have catapulted him into the national spotlight, making him a potential frontrunner in his presidential bid.

He sighed, fidgeting with uncertainty. He racked his brain for answers from past experiences, searching for anything that might steer him back on track. The tension mounted in his mind, the internal clock was ticking, and no answers were forthcoming. His tenacity drove him forward—he had no reverse gear—going full speed ahead was all he ever knew. He peered out the window in frustration, staring into the darkness—searching desperately for any type of relief—a bright spot, hope, satisfaction, anything.

With sweat beading on his forehead, he pulled out his cell and started scrolling through his pictures. His pulse suddenly quickened, as he paused on a particular photo. His mind streaked to the one person who excited his senses, and triggered feelings of power and pleasure. It was not his familiar trophy wife—his faithful spouse and cushion of dependability. And it was certainly not his rebellious teenage daughter or energy draining four-year-old; fatherhood had its joys, but it also had its share of aggravation. Instead, his fantasies flowed to a certain forbidden pleasure, the company of a college coed, a provocative and playful blonde with whom he had shared undeniable electricity. After all, life was about being happy, right? And Tiffany was his ray of sunshine in the midst of the darkness. Forsaking all others, his imagination ran wild—his thoughts reveling in the tantalizing possibilities, indulging in an illicit masquerade.

He hesitated, then dialed a number.

"Hey…" a smile spread across his face.

Meanwhile, Rachel curled up on the couch, unwinding in the family room—her nighttime sanctuary for nesting. She wrapped her grandmother's afghan around her shoulders, tucked her legs beneath her, and cozied up to her favorite fiction writer. She relished her quiet evenings, sipping on a smooth cappuccino. She peeked over at Cindy—who was playing with Goldie on the carpet—teasing the little pup with a ball of yarn and a bag of doggie treats.

Rachel turned on the plasma TV, then dialed the volume down low; she liked having the big screen on, insisting it gave the large room a serene ambiance.

She settled in beneath the reading lamp, anxious to put the family squabble out of her mind and escape into a literary reality.

She peered over at Cindy who was yanking the puppy's tail, determined to make her fetch the ball of yarn on command.

"Fetch, fetch!" Cindy ordered.

Goldie tilted her head in bewilderment, more interested in the jerky treats that were lying on the table. Cindy tossed the ball across the room again, but the puppy simply wagged her tail with indifference. Cindy groaned, exasperated. She ran around the room, diving recklessly onto the yarn ball, hoping to incite the puppy into action.

"Be careful, honey." Rachel warned, peeking over her book.

As Cindy zigzagged from corner to corner, the puppy paid no attention.

"Bad doggie," she chastised her.

"Honey, what did I tell you? Be nice."

Cindy pouted, then flung the ball across the room and into the kitchen. When Goldie refused to play along, Cindy held the treats above her head, then started jumping, and spinning in circles. While twirling with reckless abandon, she tripped over the jittery puppy, lost her balance, and tumbled into a wooden end table. Her head smacked against the solid oak edge with a thud—sending her sprawling to the floor.

Rachel jumped when she heard the bang, a chill flashing up her spine. She dropped her book, then ran to her daughter who was holding her head and writhing in pain. Cindy burst into tears, her cries echoing throughout the house.

"Shh, it's okay, honey." She threw her arms around her—cradling her, and rocking back and forth.

She ran her fingers along Cindy's head, searching for bumps or any visible contusions. With no sign of bleeding, it appeared that the bump was above the left ear—the spot that Cindy was rubbing. The wailing grew louder and more painful, so she scooped her up and carried her to the couch. She tried her best to console her, stroking her hair, and whispering in her ear. The tears continued to gush, the screaming was endless, and getting louder.

Rachel's face turned ghost white, her daughter's cries triggering a sudden panic attack. She felt her lungs seize up— gasping for oxygen—her vision blurring as if she was going to pass out. Her mind flashed back to the grocery store with bottles crashing and people staring.

"Just breathe," she kept telling herself, "Just breathe."

After a long minute of hyperventilating, her dizziness finally abated, her focus returning back to her daughter. She doubled her efforts to comfort her, wrapping the afghan around her shoulders—embracing her in calmness.

"It's okay, honey. Mommy's here. Shh, it's okay."

Eventually, Cindy's crying subsided, and she curled into the fetal position and closed her eyes. Rachel cooed her to sleep, rocking her gently, and whispering in her ear.

Her own pulse returned to normal, as she rested her chin on her daughter's head. She peered up at the TV, and noticed that the Faith Healer program was on. She squinted through the darkness, watching as people were streaming toward the stage. The volume was low, so she increased it slightly. Rocking back and forth, she inclined her ear to the program, listening intently to what the televangelist had to say.

"Isn't it true…," David Connolly asked, "when our little ones hurt, we hurt? When our children cry, we cry on the inside…, don't we? For those of you who are hurting, please don't give up hope. Sometimes you've seen every doctor, every specialist… you've tried every form of therapy, every natural remedy…"

Rachel looked down at her daughter, brushing her bangs

aside—her face so peaceful, so still. She couldn't help but wonder what the future held. Would she ever have a normal life? Would she marry or have a family? Who would take care of her later in life?

Feelings of guilt flooded her mind, wondering what more she could've done as a mother. If there was the slightest chance that this guy could help her, wouldn't it be worth a visit? What kind of mother would she be to deny her daughter even the remote possibility?

"You've said every prayer in the book," David Connolly appealed, "Day after day, week after week after month after year. Well, maybe your miracle is here, waiting for you. Cancer, epilepsy, arthritis, autism… You'll never know, unless you come join us…"

Her mind stirred, her heart beating faster and faster, conflicted about what to do. Her husband's adamant objections resonated clearly in her mind. But wouldn't the chance to help her daughter be worth the risk? She closed her eyes—torn by indecision. Did she even believe in miracles? This was a once in a lifetime opportunity that would cost her nothing, but could mean everything to her daughter. She glanced down at Cindy, wiping the tears from her cheeks. As a mother, what was the right thing to do? What was her heart telling her to do?

Chapter 36

"We believe, we believe!" the crowd chanted, the air buzzing with electricity.

Dr. Chambers beamed with pride as he stepped to the podium, soaking in the adulation, and waving to the thousands of supporters.

"We believe!" he yelled out, sending the masses into a frenzy.

The crowd cheered, waving their placards high, and dancing to the music.

He pointed to the large banner stretched across the rear of the stage which read 'Fighting For You,' printed in fiery red letters.

"We're almost home!" he shouted. "Almost home! Who's coming with me?"

He pumped his fists in the air, then turned and hugged the celebrities who joined him on stage. The crowd chanted his name, clapping along, and celebrating like it was a rock concert.

TV crews scurried into place as one of the major networks began broadcasting live. The correspondent shouted above the crowd, his voice being drowned out by the celebration.

"Here at City Hall," the reporter yelled into the microphone, "the unthinkable has happened. Life long civil rights activist, Dr. Tony Chambers, who has never held a political office, has arisen out of nowhere. He is currently tied for the lead in the governor's race and some polls have him slightly ahead. Dr. Chambers took to the podium a few seconds ago—and was greeted by a thunderous ovation. Let's listen in."

"They said it couldn't be done," he shouted, as the crowd began to settle. "They said it was foolish to even try. They said that the current administration was too popular, had too much money, had too many supporters…"

"Boo!" the audience jeered.

"And they said if we challenged the status quo, it would be a waste of time. But you are proving them wrong, and I have heard the call, and I am here today, fighting for you!"

The crowd erupted into a thunderous applause, bouncing up and down—rolling like waves in the ocean—as the music blared once again. The air was supercharged; the streets were flooded with thousands of people stretching as far as the eye could see. A small army of supporters from the doctor's soup kitchen were clustered down front dressed in matching red t-shirts, jumping around—whirling towels, flags, and anything else they could wave.

He waved to his friends from the shelter, then blew kisses to the elderly women who were wearing t-shirts bearing his face. He showed off a few dance moves, getting caught up in the festivities, and feeding off the crowd's energy.

After a long minute, he gestured for the music to be cut, waving his arms for everyone's attention.

"I don't know about you, but I could do this all day!" he laughed. "This is just the beginning. Your destiny is in your own hands, no one can decide it for you. Like the popular songwriter wrote, 'I did it my way,' and now, it's time for you to do it your way, it's time for us to do it our way. Are you going to just sit back and let someone else tell you how you should live, sit back and let someone steal the happiness that you deserve?"

"No!" the crowd shouted.

"You could do that, you could let others call the shots, let them use your money for their own pleasure, use your money to make them rich, you could do that..., or you can create your own destiny, forge a path that's right for you and for your children, and the people you love."

"We have come a long way," he called out, "But we have a long way to go. All my life I've seen the rich get richer and the poor suffer needlessly. This current administration..., do you think they care about you?"

The crowd booed, screaming obscenities. A few rowdy supporters raised the single finger salute.

"They don't care about you," he scoffed. "Don't let anyone else tell you what's right for you, or how you should spend your money. It's time for you to take back your own happiness, what you deserve. No one is going to hand you anything in this world, you've got to fight for it. The question is, are you a fighter? Anyone who knows me, knows that I've been fighting for justice my whole life. Who will fight for the outcast, the homeless, the mentally ill, and the broken hearted? I am a soldier who fights on your behalf. We are one big family, brothers and sisters. Family fights for family, and I will never leave your side. We will fight. Government is broken. We will fight. Society is broken..."

"We will fight!" the audience joined in.

"Corporate greed is stealing from you."

"We will fight!"

"I will never leave your side and together..."

"We will fight!"

"We will fight till the day I die!" He raised his hands skyward like a prize fighter celebrating a victorious knockout.

Music filled the air as the multitudes bounced up and down with hearts overflowing with joy. The rally erupted into a full-fledged dance party with people singing and dancing, then chanting the doctor's name.

"Tony, Tony, Tony!" They clapped in rhythm.

He waved to the crowd one last time, joining hands with

the celebrities onstage and raising their arms in victory. He stepped forward and gave a final shout-out.

"Together, we will fight for your happiness!" he roared. "We will fight! We will fight till the day I die!"

Chapter 37

Sirens blared as ambulances and fire trucks inched their way down the street. Balinda peered at the spectators gathering along the sidewalk—craning their necks, and jostling for a better view. She waved to fans from atop her decorated float, smiling and cherishing her role as the parade's grand marshal. The emergency vehicles were the centerpieces of the parade, followed by marching bands, children's dance troupes, and little league teams.

She waved to the grandmothers, and threw lollipops to the kids. Whenever someone yelled her name, she struck a pose, as fans held up their cells—snapping photos and recording video.

Joining her on the float was a Caribbean band that energized the crowd with their sultry island sounds. Balinda swayed her hips to the salsa rhythms, joining the other dancers—getting caught up in the festive flavor. The floating party enlivened the crowd, launching a beach party in the middle of the city.

In between songs, she blew kisses to the fans, as the procession rolled down Main Street; the crowd thickening, eight to ten people deep. When they approached the main stage, her jaw dropped in disbelief; the crowed extended as far as the eye could see—thousands upon thousands, all cheering her arrival.

She looked up and saw her name painted high above the stage. A fifty foot banner that read: the 'Balinda Summers Hospital & Medical Center Grand Opening'. She was amazed at the grandeur and stateliness of the event—military officers were lined in formation, giving the celebration both prominence and prestige.

When her float reached the platform, her feet were still dancing to the music. She was caught up in the bongo beats, shuffling along to the hypnotic rhythm. When the song finally ended, she exhaled a sigh of joy—exhausted, in a good way. She hugged the musicians and dancers, then made her way into the crowd. The mayor escorted her through the masses, where she signed autographs and shook a few hands.

"Balinda, Balinda!" her fans chanted, stretching out and trying to touch her.

She climbed onto the platform, waving both hands above her head. She shaded her eyes from the noonday sun, drinking in the affection from her adoring fans.

As the formal ceremony got underway, Balinda took her seat beside the medical staff. She was easy to spot in her red designer dress, surrounded by doctors dressed in white jackets, and nurses in their scrubs.

The mayor stepped to the podium, wiping his forehead, and pulling out his notes. He gave an introductory speech, which tarried much too long—thanking every politician on earth, and all his relatives including his dog. The crowd grew restless, talking and laughing amongst themselves.

"This community will never be the same," the mayor wrapped up, "and we are forever indebted to Balinda for her overwhelming generosity. Her gracious gift will continue to touch thousands of lives for generations to come."

The crowd cheered as she rose from her seat, their patience was about to be rewarded.

"We've asked Balinda to christen this glorious facility which bears her name, and to offer both an invocation and a prayer of dedication. So without further adieu... I give you... Balinda Summers."

The audience erupted with wild enthusiasm, whistling and cheering, as a local marching band played an anthem in her honor. Her heart pounded in her chest, astonished by the crowd's outpouring of affection. As she stepped to the podium, she accepted a kiss from the mayor, then waved to her fans, reciprocating her love for them.

"Thank you, and thank you, Mr. Mayor. Wow, how exciting is this? Is this a great day or what?"

The audience roared in response, the children jumping up and down in front. She blew kisses to the kids and to the wheelchair patients who were cheering along the side.

"This day and this hospital are not about me..." she spoke with humility. "It's about you, and it's about this great city. And it's about the hard working doctors and nurses, the medical staff and volunteers who help save lives and treat sick patients day and night." She turned and applauded the doctors and nurses who were seated behind her. They rose to their feet, flashing modest smiles and waving to the audience.

"I was asked to offer a prayer of dedication for this grand opening," she continued, "an honor which I eagerly accepted. Many of you know that I'm a spiritual person, and that I support and embrace all the different faiths—many of which are represented here today." She turned and acknowledged the clergy and spiritual leaders who were standing off to the side. "I do not elevate any one religion over another, but instead, I believe in the sanctity and beauty of the human spirit. Amen?"

"Amen," the crowd responded.

"So for this joyous occasion, let us offer up a prayer of gratitude for this wonderful new beginning. And in the quietness of your own heart, let us have a moment of silence... and feel free to offer up a prayer of thanksgiving to your god... whoever he or she may be."

She bowed her head reverently and offered spiritual good thoughts, sending positive vibes out into the universe.

Chapter 38

Rachel hurried through the main entrance, still smarting about being late. Her eyes darted back and forth behind her sunglasses, as she weaved through the masses, towing her daughter close behind. Doubts gnawed at her conscience, so she tried to push all fears to the back of her mind. The soft guitar harmonies wafting from inside the arena did little to soothe her anxieties.

"Honey, we have to hurry," she urged, "Do you want mommy to carry you?"

Cindy shook her head.

"Then we need to hurry."

They scurried up the escalator, then pressed through a crowded tunnel, and into the open arena. Her jaw dropped when she saw the thousands of people crammed into the huge complex. The dome was packed to the rafters with parents, grandparents, mothers with their babies, everybody—she began to feel self-conscious. "Someone is going to recognize me," she fretted. She swallowed hard—her confidence caught in her throat. Ducking beneath her baseball cap, she drifted into line with the other late comers, heading up to the upper decks.

After climbing a dozen steps, she felt Cindy pulling on her arm.

"I'm sorry, honey, we're almost there."

She spotted two seats halfway up, so she picked her up and carried her—anxious to get seated without being identified.

When she reached the open row, she shuffled to the middle.

"Excuse me, I'm sorry, excuse me."

She pushed down on the seat, but it didn't move; it was tied into place with a wire.

"Oh, yeah, these seats are broken." The lady on the other side offered an apologetic smile.

Anger welled up in her mind, "Well, why didn't you tell me that before I climbed over all these people," she thought.

She shook her head, exasperated, then scooted back into the aisle. They continued climbing toward the nose bleed section, her leg muscles burning with every step.

"Come on, honey, we're almost there." She labored to sound upbeat, her energy waning by the second. "Why aren't there escalators here?" she moaned.

When they reached the open area, the couple seated on the end scooted into the center allowing them to sit on the aisle.

"Thank you so much." She smiled, relieved to see a friendly face.

"You sit here, honey, and let mommy sit on the end."

She settled into her seat, her legs aching for a rest.

She peered around the arena, noticing people from every walk of life—young, old, blue collar types, and every ethnicity under the sun. Near the front of the stage were the hospice patients—a boy on crutches, a dozen wheelchair patrons, and senior citizens toting oxygen tanks.

She snuck a peek over her shoulder, cautious to avoid all eye contact. Her nerves were still on edge, so she took a quick survey of the people around her. A woman across the aisle smiled at her, so she averted her eyes, and faked a half smile.

"So far, so good," she thought, convinced that her anonymity was intact. She pulled her baseball cap low on her forehead, then removed her sunglasses—afraid they might draw unwanted attention. Cindy squirmed in the hard-plastic seat, pulling off her cap, and throwing it to the ground.

"Honey, you need to leave your hat on."

She handed Cindy some candy to keep her occupied.

A woman climbing up the stairs suddenly stopped, and peered over at her. She felt the woman's eyes on her, so she tilted her head down and began rummaging through her purse. She whipped out her cell phone, and pretended to answer a call.

"Hello..., hey Julie, how are you?" she listened. "Girl, you are not going to believe what happened to me today..."

She carried on the conversation, hiding beneath her ball cap, her eyes fixed on the woman's feet.

After a few tense moments, the woman finally left, continuing up the stairs and disappearing into the crowd.

When the coast was clear, she tucked her phone away—then exhaled a huge sigh of relief.

People around her began to stir, craning their necks and whispering to one another. She looked toward the stage and saw a groundswell of activity, so she scooted to the edge of her seat, but couldn't see what was going on.

"I think that's him." A lady speculated.

"Can you see him?" Someone asked.

"No, but it's got to be him."

The entire arena buzzed with curiosity as the person up front was shaking hands with the wheelchair patrons.

When the musicians wrapped up their final song, the unannounced gentleman walked onstage, then took his place behind the podium. The crowd erupted into a standing ovation.

"Please, have a seat." He downplayed the attention, gesturing for everyone to be seated.

"There are a few open seats in the back. Hopefully we can get you all in." His tone was warm and sincere.

Onstage, a massive fifty foot screen flashed to life—the camera zooming in on the face of the unannounced speaker. A hush fell over the crowd.

Rachel knew immediately that this was David Connolly. She had recognized him from the TV interviews and his televised crusades.

She felt butterflies in her stomach, sensing that something wonderful was about to happen. She squeezed her daughter's hand, trying to temper her excitement.

David stepped from behind the podium, smiling at the elderly folks down front. He had a warm aura about him— dressed in jeans and a brown tweed jacket. With a microphone in hand, he leaned toward the audience, and spoke informally, as if conversing with a friend.

"You know, every other day I pick up a newspaper," he began, "and I read that this person or that person is making fun of me—late night comedians mocking me. I am here to tell you..., its okay. It's okay to laugh. It's true what they say, 'Laughter is the best medicine,'" he chuckled.

Rachel smiled, feeling at ease with this home grown, salt of the earth, gentleman. Whatever reservations she had, were but a distant memory.

"It's good to laugh at ourselves sometimes, isn't it?" he asked. "So please don't let it bother you, because it doesn't matter to me. What matters to me... is that miracles are happening. Amen?"

"Amen," the crowd replied in unison. Rachel felt chills— the good kind. She breathed easy, feeling like she was amongst family.

"I want to thank you all for coming, we're glad you're here," he continued. "You may be suffering from cancer, diabetes, HIV, autism, arthritis, brain tumors, bad hearts, bad lungs... but I'm here to tell you, that I believe in miracles. Miracles happen to good people. Do you believe you are a good person and deserve a miracle?"

"Yes," they replied.

"Well, I believe you do. So if you believe you've been living right and you deserve a miracle, I want you to get out of your seat right now, and start making your way down front.

You step forward and believe and we will believe together."

Rachel's heart pounded inside her chest, her legs were glued to the seat. She hesitated for a moment, there was no way she was going down front.

"Excuse me." A lady and her son climbed over her, brushing against her knees, and sliding into the aisle.

Rachel cowered, her eyes shifting back and forth while audience members passed by on both sides. She watched as people were streaming down the aisles from every corner of the arena.

"What am I doing here?" she thought, sneaking a peek at her daughter, "Maybe Mitch was right."

She closed her eyes, desperate to find her bearings—her husband's objections echoing in her head. The whole event seemed surreal.

"Come on, honey, we're leaving," she grabbed Cindy's hand. They scooted into the aisle, then made their way down the stairs. About halfway down, they were halted by a wall of people.

"This is crazy." She moaned.

The musicians played a soft ballad on their guitars, the warm melody putting everyone's mind at ease.

"Many of you have suffered needlessly for so long," he spoke above the music. "Some of you have endured chronic diseases for years, or you're stuck on medication—taking five, ten, fifteen pills a day. And some of you are parents, and your children have been suffering from incurable conditions since the day they were born. Well the good news is, today is a new day. You come join us, because you deserve good things in life, you deserve happiness, in fact, no one is more deserving than you."

Rachel finally reached the exit tunnel at the bottom of the stairs, her heart thumping inside her chest, her conscience pulling her in opposite directions. She stepped into the tunnel, then hesitated. "What do I have to lose?" she sighed. "Who cares if people know I'm here." She leaned against the wall, trapped in a fog of indecision. She tried to think of excuses to leave—her mind flip-flopping as she stared over the crowd.

"Could all these people be crazy?" she thought. "There are thousands of people here."

She looked at her daughter who was fiddling with shoestrings that she couldn't even tie. She felt that she deserved happiness, and her daughter deserved happiness. Perhaps tonight could be a special night, an evening that could change their lives forever. What did she have to lose?

"I believe in the golden rule," David said. "Do unto others as you would have them do unto you. I believe in karma. No matter what your religious beliefs, or how you were raised… you put goodness out there and goodness will be paid back to you. You bring joy and happiness to others and the universe will fill your life with happiness in return. If you truly believe that you deserve happiness, then now is the time, and this is the place. All you have to do is reach out and embrace it.

Mitch shuffled backwards through the doorway, nearly tripping in the dark. The moonlight streamed through the panoramic window, casting a glow over the shadowy silence. He wobbled, feeling tipsy—then giggled, reaching out for something—or perhaps someone. He was not alone. Dangling a champagne flute in one hand, he escorted his guest through the moonbeams and toward the scenic vista. His lady friend hopped onto his feet—nearly knocking him over as he waddled backwards. He put his arm around her waist to steady himself, pulling her body close to his. They laughed as he struggled to navigate through the darkness. They tripped over each other's feet, nearly tumbling to the floor; then bumping into his desk, he spilled champagne on his pants.

"Uh oh, that's gonna leave a stain," he grumbled.

"So just cut them off, and wear them as shorts." She suggested.

They both started laughing.

She jumped back onto his feet—clinging to one another—and continuing on with their penguin waddle. They squealed like little children, somehow managing to stay upright all the way to the window panes. He held her close as they gazed out over the city skyline.

The full moon was casting its spell on them—piercing the secrecy of the governor's lair. The intern's blond hair shimmered in the moonlight, reflecting the radiance of the golden rays. Mitch's heart was giddy like a love struck schoolboy, relishing the fact that they were finally alone. There were no prying eyes or ears around—the masks were off, and they were free to throw caution to the wind.

Tiffany spun around, wobbling from her fifth glass of champagne, giggling and nearly spilling her drink.

Mitch kicked off his shoes, sinking his toes deep into the plush carpet. The tension drained from his body, down through the floor, his heart fluttering with anticipation.

She reached down and peeled off her heels, then stood on her tiptoes, her eyes rising up to meet his gaze. The moonlight twinkled in her eyes; a soft halo glowed around her face. She loosened the knot on his tie and unbuttoned his collar; he smelled a whiff of her perfume—her scent was smooth and fresh—heavenly.

He stroked her arm lightly, her body reacting to the sudden chill. He brushed the tip of his finger against her lips, caressing them ever so gently; the passion between them was undeniable. Her smile was radiant in the moonlight, her giggle—music to his ears. He gazed deep into her eyes; their emotions were entwined in a grapevine of intimacy. The silhouette of the two became one.

Chapter 39

A chill lingered in the air. Rachel stared through the darkness with empty eyes, the heart machine flickering in the background. Her mind stirred with apprehension. She tried to suppress the doubts that were creeping in—refusing to consider what life would be like without her husband. She watched the oxygen meter rise and fall—the single lifeline that was keeping Mitch alive. His face was lifeless, white as a sheet, wrapped in hospital gauze that concealed his forehead. His chin was tracked with stitches; his cheeks striped with bandages—masking the cuts that he received from the shattered windshield.

She suddenly realized that the last conversation they had together was the fight on the dance floor. Would that be her lasting memory? A twinge of guilt swept through her mind, as she recalled the fateful night: the chase down the stairs, the confrontation in the ballroom, the angry outburst that ensued—that was the last time she heard his voice. It couldn't end like this—how could she live with such an insufferable memory?

Her eyes traced the tubes protruding from his mouth, and the IV lines dangling off the bed. The sound from the life support machine echoed in her ear—beeping rhythmically like a ticking time bomb. She sank into a chair beside the bed, exasperated—the beeping was grinding on her nerves.

"This is a nightmare," she moaned. Her thoughts ran wild, her mind fluctuating between empathy and anger. She wiped the scornful tears from her eyes, struggling to suppress the bitterness. She was weary of the rage that was eating away at her insides; tired of living a lie, and tired of posing as the perfect wife.

"Damn you, Mitch, how could you do this to me... to us?" she seethed, not caring that he couldn't answer.

The door cracked open and a beam of light crept across the floor. She heard nervous footsteps behind her, as someone stepped inside the door. When the door clicked shut, she heaved a heavy sigh, prompting the unwanted guest to speak.

"Rachel, I'm sorry to bother you," a man's voice apologized.

She froze in silence; her stare cemented on her husband's lifeless face. She processed the semi familiar voice in her mind, quickly dismissing it as being unfamiliar. She drifted into numbness, wishing there was a lock on the door, or at the very least, a 'do not disturb' sign. A long minute passed. She released a sigh of exasperation, prompting the visitor to reopen the door.

"Just wanted to pass along a note from your sister, Jennifer," he said quietly. "Your girls are fine."

"Thank you," she whispered, turning her head slightly and offering a half smile. She peeked up and confirmed her initial suspicions. It was the local pastor, a clergyman she would see twice a year—at Christmas and Easter.

The momentary thought of her two daughters beamed like sunshine in her darkness, a much needed breath of fresh air.

"How are they?" she asked.

"You sister says they're good. They're worried about you. We're all worried about you."

Her eyes grew misty, thinking about her girls. If there

was a bright spot in her life, it was her daughters. She wished with all her heart that she could shield them from this misery. She cringed, recalling their recent visit—wailing incessantly—their cries resonating in her memory. She shook her head, wishing the pain would go away.

The pastor released the door handle, then crossed to her side. She felt a consoling hand on her shoulder, a gentle touch of compassion. She inhaled deeply, her body absorbing the gesture of kindness.

She was grateful for his concern and the news about her daughters; however, she refused to be a victim—pity was the last thing she wanted. Who could possibly understand the betrayal she was going through?

She patted his hand. "I'll be okay, thank you," she insisted. Her body tensed once again.

Sensing her resolve, he retraced his steps to the door.

"If you need anything," he added. "My wife and I are just a phone call away. Please feel free to call, day or night."

After he left, she sat alone in the shadows, her thoughts descending back into despondency. Her mind jostled back and forth, trying to come up with a way out of this nightmare.

A zillion questions raced through her mind, questions she wasn't sure she wanted answered. Would he live or die? What could she have done differently? And the ultimate question of *why*? She needed answers, but feared they might never come.

She stared straight ahead through bleary eyes, cowering alone in the dark. Was she not living right? Was the universe teaching her a lesson?

Chapter 40

The fuselage still smoldered the next morning following the fiery crash. The flames gutted the metal carcass completely, the stench of burning steel lingered in the air. An entertainment reporter for *Hollywood True* covered her nose with a towel, nearly gagging from the nauseating odor. She sidestepped a patch of thorn bushes, then cringed when her slacks got snagged in one of the thickets.

"I knew I should have worn jeans," she grumbled.

She shook her head in disbelief as she stared at the splintered hull—the fifty foot plane was wedged between a boulder and an oak tree the size of a garage. Debris was scattered everywhere, with search crews sifting through the dense foliage trying to locate every little fragment.

"Make sure you get a shot of that." She told the cameraman, pointing to the inspectors who were crawling inside the burned cockpit.

She scribbled on her notepad, jotting down meticulous observations about the cleanup investigation. She smirked when she saw a looter being lead away in handcuffs; apparently some scavengers had no shame. She also noticed colleagues from other TV stations; she couldn't remember the last time she saw so many entertainment reporters show up to cover a disaster.

Aviation inspectors removed large sections of the charred instrument panel—presumably searching for the plane's black box recording device. She wished she could hear what they were saying—any news about the cause of the crash would be huge.

She leaned over the 'Do Not Cross' police tape which encircled the crash site, hoping to get a better look. A federal agent with a German shepherd patrolled the zone, eyeballing her with a menacing look, then approaching as if to yell at her.

She scurried away—tracking through the mud—in search of first responders to try to get some answers. She spotted a member of the local coroner's office, tagging pieces of debris that were scattered inside the 'no trespass zone.' The worker sealed a plastic bag, then documented the piece of evidence. She shouted to the man, "Sir, can you comment on what you've found." The crew member ignored her, carrying on with his duties, and sifting through the charred rubble. He photographed what appeared to be a piece of luggage and some personal belongings.

"Excuse me, ma'am, but you're going to have to move back." A fire captain chastised her.

"Oh, I'm sorry. Can you tell me anything about…?"

"No comment." He said abruptly.

She knew the policy, but thought she'd ask anyway.

Fire fighters streamed past her, rolling up hoses, and packing away oxygen tanks and utility equipment. She tried to get out of the way, but was nearly run over by recovery workers hauling huge spotlights and generators.

She sighed as she peered around. Everywhere she turned, investigators and forensic photographers were scouring for evidence, but everyone was tight lipped. She didn't feel like a total failure, she noticed that the other reporters weren't getting much information either.

She met up with her cameraman and producer as the broadcast hour drew near. She positioned herself in front of the 'no trespass zone,' with the wreckage situated just over her shoulder. She realized she didn't have many details; however, the camera shots they had were quite explicit.

As the crew fired up the lights, she peeked into her compact mirror to brush on some last second powder, then counted down to the live broadcast.

"There is no greater loss in life then the tragic death of someone you love," she spoke with solemn respect, "... a wife or husband, a child, son or daughter, an intimate family member. For we the fans, these larger than life celebrities were like family. But for the cherished relatives of Balinda Summers, David Connolly and Dr. Tony Chambers, this is a pain that will never go away. May they rest in peace."

Chapter 41

Tears welled up in her eyes, as she pulled in front of the funeral home. Dr. Chambers' sister, Stephanie, closed her eyes and then opened them again—a tear spilling onto her cheek. As she stepped out of the limousine, the sun felt warm against her face—the bright sunshine, a stark contrast to the darkness that festered inside. She peered around the parking lot and saw rows of cars as far as the eye could see. Hundreds of mourners streamed toward the funeral home—a sea of black suits and dresses.

She barely recognized people she had known for years, struggling to match faces with names. She extended her arm to her brother's widow, Mrs. Chambers, then escorted her into the chapel, to a private waiting room, reserved for family members only. Inside the parlor, she busied herself, primping the grandchildren's clothes and waiting for the ceremony to begin. Everyone fumbled for things to talk about—chatting about the little girls' dresses, and the boys' new shoes.

The funeral director walked in, informing them that it was time to begin the service. Stephanie forced herself to take a deep breath, dreading this so-called celebration of life. She escorted her sister-in-law toward the sanctuary, her mind floating in a state of numbness.

When they entered through the rear doors, her jaw

dropped, astonished by the thousands of mourners and the sheer size of the chapel. She looked toward the stage and saw a large tribute photo of her brother—displayed in the center—bringing a smile to her face. Her heart thumped with pride as she stared at his picture, soaking in the warmth of his eyes. Draped above the photo was a sweeping banner which read 'Forever the People's Champion' in bold magenta letters.

As she continued down the aisle, she could feel every eye watching her—a wave of love and support flowing all around her. Her spirit was lifted as she listened to the soprano singing a soulful ballad—setting a regal tone for the ceremony. The stage was decorated with multi-level arrangements of white lilies, which brightened the chapel—giving the room an aura of new life.

When they reached the front, she noticed her sister-in-law's eyes tearing up, as she stared at the tribute photo. She handed her a tissue, wrapping her arms around her, and holding her close.

"It's okay," she whispered.

The organist played a traditional Southern anthem, and then the moderator raised his hands, signaling for everyone to stand. The mourners turned toward the door, as the pall bearers carried the coffin down the aisle. Stephanie's heart was heavy, her eyes following the slow march—her lungs shuddering with each passing step. The room felt a little darker, a little colder, the music invoking a somber, melancholy mood. When the coffin passed in front of the family, Mrs. Chambers kissed her hand, then reached out and touched the casket. The pall bearers set the coffin to rest in the middle of the platform—beneath the large tribute photo.

Celebrity singers and musicians sang inspirational songs, offering tributes of gratitude—of recognition and remembrance. A series of guest speakers, including local politicians and even Marvin—the shelter director—eulogized him, sharing personal stories of the difference he made in their lives.

Stephanie beamed with pride as they reminisced of her brother's love for people, and passion for human rights. She was anxious to speak, and share from her heart, because no one knew him better than her.

When Marvin wrapped up his tribute, it was her turn to speak. She took a deep breath and walked onstage, her heart brimming with mixed emotions.

She blinked twice, trying to focus her thoughts, suddenly realizing that she was more nervous than she thought she'd be. She peered out at the thousands of faces, and noticed people from every walk of life. It warmed her heart to see celebrities and homeless people both paying homage to her brother.

"Wow, the first thing I want to say is, Tony would've been proud of all of you," she laughed. "Thank you all for coming, and carrying on the work that he loved."

The audience applauded.

"The world knew him as Dr. Anthony Chambers," she continued, "Our family knew him as Tony, Tone-tone. He was our brother, husband, daddy, pap pap. But he will always be remembered as the People's Champion."

The audience rose to their feet, erupting into a rousing ovation.

"He was a fighter to the end," she recalled, "I'll never forget...," she smiled, "Back when I was in fifth grade and Tone was in third, I ran home crying after school one day, and I was sitting on my bed bawling my eyes out because my first boyfriend, Ricky, had broken up with me. Well, Tony overheard me blubbering to my girlfriend on the phone..., and then the next thing I knew, there was Tony, tearing out the front door. I found out later that he ran to Ricky's apartment, and punched him in the nose."

The audience chuckled.

"Well Ricky, who was a sixth grader at the time—and twice Tony's size—beat the living tar out of him. He came home with a bloody lip, scrapes on the side of his face—his shirt was shredded and his pants were covered with mud. And when he stumbled through the door, Daddy said, 'Son, what happened?'

And Tony said, 'Nothing.'"

The audience chuckled.

"'Don't lie to me.' Daddy eyed him down. Then Tony begged, 'Daddy, can I take karate lessons?'

'What did I tell you about fighting?' Daddy yelled.

'It was Ricky.'

'Why were you fighting with Ricky?' he asked.

'Because he broke up with Stephie and made her cry.'

Daddy smirked and said, 'Well, I'm proud of you for standing up for your sister, but, unless karate lessons are free, it ain't gonna happen.'"

She smiled, tickled by the story.

"He was my little protector." She turned and looked up at his photo, her face flush with pride. "I think he got into a fight every other week in elementary school...,"

The audience laughed.

"But after a few bloody lips, he learned his lesson. He eventually learned to fight with his mind, and nobody fought harder."

"If there was one thing true about Tony, it was this, he always loved the underdog." Her eyes glazed over. "If you were out of work, out of luck, out of love, even out of your mind—strung out on drugs, he always treated you as if you were somebody. If you had no job, no cash, no clothes, no hope, no home, no family, and not a prayer in the world, he would smile and say, 'Snap out of it! There's always hope.' And he didn't care who he fought, you could be the CEO of World Bank International or the President of the Universe—sitting high and mighty and peering down your nose at everybody—he didn't care. He wasn't impressed by Wall Street billionaires, big cars and fancy titles—in fact, the bigger the challenge, the harder he fought."

During the eulogy, a video montage of her brother was being broadcast to the TV audience, featuring high points in his life. The highlights showed him speaking in front of large crowds in all the major cities—leading protests, and stirring thousands into action. His smile lit up the screen as he shared meals with street people and embraced the poor—the neighborhood rejects, drug addicts and runaways. Ensuing video showed him being roughed up by police, handcuffed to fellow protesters, and conducting sit-ins at civil rights marches. He was arrested, loaded into a police van, and hauled off to jail.

Stephanie hesitated, swallowing hard, as she pondered some of the harsh treatment that he endured.

"He confided in me during dinner one day—just a few weeks ago—when he said, 'Stephie, people in Washington are getting nervous.' And I asked, 'Why?' And he said, 'Because they know I'm coming for them. I'm coming to clean house.' He always said, 'Power and greed flowed from the same bottle, and if you were in a position of power..., then he came to fight.' No one fought harder or with more passion than Tony, fighting for the nobodies, fighting for the outcasts and the misfits, fighting for your rights and mine... that's what he lived for."

Chapter 42

Patricia's friend was wrong—a good night's rest did not make her feel better. Her mind was plagued by loneliness all morning, her eyes hollow as she stared at her husband's coffin. The large suburban church was packed to the gills; much like it had been for one of David's rallies a short two months earlier. She knew this was going to be hard, but didn't realize it would be this hard. She reached by the armrest and grabbed the hand of her four-year-old daughter—yearning for a familiar touch.

Onstage, a mammoth video screen flashed a portrait photo of her husband, which stirred mixed emotions deep within her. Her eyes welled up with tears, as memories began to flood her mind. She closed her eyes and wrapped her arms even tighter around her body, hoping to feel a sense of his presence. A part of him was still with her, and always would be.

She peered down at his closed coffin which was nestled in the middle of the stage. The casket was surrounded by dozens of his favorite flowers—exotic breeze orchids, lavender daisies, and roses of every color and style—including red fuchsia, peach, magenta, yellow and white calla lily. She wondered how she could be staring at such beauty and yet be feeling so much pain.

The guitarists strummed a folk melody—a ceremonial

prelude, casting a hypnotic aura over the thousands of mourners. She closed her eyes, losing herself in the rhythm, relishing the momentary solitude as the lights in the sanctuary were dimmed.

A video tribute flashed onto the big screen with the subtitle: 'A Heart for People.'

David's smile sent waves of joy through the otherwise somber auditorium. Patricia's face brightened as soon as she heard his voice and sensed his spirit. A sprightly montage of behind-the-scenes outtakes was shown, showcasing David's lighter side. He joked with musicians and staff members— acting silly, laughing and carrying on. He made faces at the camera as he commenced with his pre-rally warm-ups— stretching his arms and legs, twisting and turning—a routine he practiced before stepping onto the stage.

She laughed along with the audience, and for a few lighthearted moments, the long faces were transformed into smiles of joyful remembrance. She peeked down at her daughter, Bethany, and her two sons who joined in the laughter; it warmed her heart to see her kids' reminiscing and celebrating their father's memory.

Following the video tribute, several family members stepped onstage to eulogize David's life, including his eighty-nine-year-old grandmother.

"I remember when Davey was only three-years-old," she recalled in her slow, deliberate tone, "He was so funny. I said, 'Davey, what do you wanna be when you grow up?' And he said, in his squeaky voice, 'I wanna be like you, grandma.' And I said, 'You wanna be a grandma?' And he said, 'Uh-huh.' And I said, 'Why?' And he said, 'Cause you bake the best apple pies, and you always give me money and stuff.'"

The audience laughed.

"And I said, 'Well don't you wanna be like grandpa?' And he said, 'Nope.'' And I said, 'Well, why not?' And he said, "Because all grandpa does is talk about his hip and spends all day in the bathroom.'"

The crowd chuckled.

"And I said, 'But Davey, you can't be a grandma, it's impossible.' And he crumpled his little face and looked at me, and said, 'Yes, I can, grandma. You said I can be anything I want.'"

The audience laughed along with grandma.

Patricia wiped tears of joy from her eyes, listening to aunts and uncles tell stories of her husband's embarrassing childhood moments, the one time, he locked himself out of the house in his underwear, then wrapped himself in a plastic trash bag, and asked the neighbors if he could borrow their phone.

After a few home grown stories, the service continued with another video subtitled: 'Family Man,' showing private moments of David's last Christmas with the family. The children hopped around the living room, ripping open presents, and screaming with unbridled excitement. Eight-year-old, Cody, yelled hysterically, hoisting a new video game above his head. The parents plugged their ears, watching the boys thrash about the room—jumping on the couches, and rolling on the floor. Not to be outdone, little Bethany tore the wrapping paper off of her present, a new piano keyboard, causing her to squeal with delight. She lunged into the laps of mom and dad, then smothered them with hugs and kisses.

The ensuing video included cousins and grandparents, as the whole family frolicked during a summer beach weekend. David chased the kids along the shoreline, drenching them with bucketfuls of water. He grabbed hold of them, one at a time—carried them into the surf, and hoisted them on his shoulders where they jumped into the crashing waves. The kids laughed hysterically, belly flopping into the whitewater, then begging to do it again.

The video concluded with a tribute of David's healing rallies. Excerpts showed him welcoming crowds and assisting audience members onto the stage—this was the David that the public knew best. As Patricia watched the footage, her face shifted from a smile of lighthearted levity to a glazed look of fond remembrance.

Her husband reached out to the masses, hugging and greeting the attendees who were weeping with joy. He was mobbed from every side by elderly folks, wheelchair patients, parents and children alike, all clamoring to touch him, their faces filled with expressions of hope.

When the video faded, Patricia made her way onstage, her hand quivering—clinging to a two-page prepared statement.

"I'm a little nervous," she leaned into the microphone, "so please forgive me." She hesitated, taking a deep breath. "I can't begin to tell you how much I miss my David. He was my husband, my lover, my confidant, the father of our children, and my best friend. To have your soul mate ripped from your life is inexplicable—a pain that cuts deeper than anything in this world."

She looked up, chuckling nervously, "I bet he's looking down right now and saying, 'What's all the fuss about?'"

The audience laughed.

"I'd like to tell you a story, that I bet many of you have never heard…, about how David's crusades began…and the night that changed our lives." She inhaled deeply. "I will never forget the night he came home after visiting one of our college friends in the hospital. Our friend, Jocelyn, was dying from heart failure—having suffered from coronary artery disease—and was told she only had a few weeks to live. Her name was buried near the bottom of the donor's list and she had given up hope. David held her hand that night, and told her how wonderful she was, and how she deserved so much better in life. When she broke down in tears, David wrapped his arms around her and told her that the universe owed her so much more. He sat with her for a while, encouraging her, and telling her not to give up, to never give up. Well, two weeks later we got a phone call from Jocelyn, a healthy Jocelyn—who never received a transplant—but was somehow one hundred percent healed.

We couldn't believe it...we thought she was kidding. But when she showed up at our door, we were speechless. The doctors couldn't explain it, the experts couldn't explain it, and from that day forward, our lives were never the same. We had no idea what had happened, but then again, we didn't need an explanation. Our friend Jocelyn was alive and happy, and that's all that mattered to us. There are a lot of things we don't know about the human brain and it's connection to the human spirit, but somehow David was able to tap into that 'never-give-up power'—that energy that sits stagnate inside all of us—and was able to energize people's hope.

He was the ultimate optimist, a hero, a deeply spiritual man. His life could be summed up in one simple phrase... the golden rule. Do unto others as you would have them do unto you. He lived a life of good karma and deserved good karma in return."

She shook her head, "Why was he taken from us...? Only the universe knows."

She folded her prepared statement, then tucked it into her pocket. She peered out over the thousands of mourners, feeling their positive energy, their sympathy and support.

She lifted her eyes heavenward, "I love you, David, with all my heart."

She looked down at the front row, and saw her daughter burst into tears. "Daddy loves you, Bethany." She blurted out. "He's looking down right now and smiling on you and saying how proud he is of you. And you too, Cody and Jeremy."

Bethany jumped out of her seat, with tears streaming down her face, then ran up, and leapt into her arms. She held her close, stroking her hair and trying to console her.

"It's okay, honey. It's okay." She whispered. "He's watching right now, and he loves you so much."

Chapter 43

A mournful dirge rang out above the cemetery as bagpipe musicians marched along the cobblestone walkway. Balinda's sister, Tara, was escorted through the front gates, past a makeshift memorial that was set up by grieving fans. She thought about stopping to sign one of the posters, but resisted, not wanting to draw attention to herself. The shrine overflowed with cards, candles, balloons, teddy bears—and countless bouquets of wildflowers.

She felt her lungs laboring for breath, as she drew closer to the gravesite.

"We love you, Tara!" A little girl called out.

She looked in the child's direction, and offered a half wave. Accompanied by two bodyguards, she trudged through the crowd of onlookers who were sprawled out along the hillsides in every direction. She knew the turnout was going to be large, but never expected the response to be this big.

She hurried past several news reporters and cameramen who were preparing to broadcast the funeral service worldwide. She ducked behind her sunglasses, sidestepping the paparazzi, as one correspondent was already reporting live on the air.

"Tens of thousands have flooded this intimate community," the reporter said, "paying tribute to this international icon. As a well-known national talk show host,

Balinda was honored recently at a Presidential banquet, and was referred to as an ambassador to the world. She will be remembered for generations to come because of her countless humanitarian efforts, both here, and in some of the poorest countries in the world."

Tara felt nauseous, as she approached the gravesite; her heart was heavy with grief. She couldn't remember a time when she and Balinda were not together; they were more than sisters—they were best friends. Her sister was the only family she had left, following the death of her mom back in high school. Her mind floated as she reminisced, then settled into her seat beside a group of faceless Hollywood VIPs.

The white clouds overhead began to thicken—a light breeze sweeping through the valley.

She stared straight ahead—almost in a state of shock. The silver plated casket was suspended above the grave, and surrounded by a plenitude of yellow and white roses. The shiny casket sparkled amidst the ocean of black suits and dresses, glowing like a beacon of light amongst the headstones.

She closed her eyes and listened to the bag pipe musicians as they finished their somber ballad. The dire sounds of the pipes evoked deep sorrow within her soul, sending shivers down her spine. She tried to think of something positive to ease the pain, but her mind kept flashing back to her sister—pulling her back to the painful reality.

A hush fell over the masses, as the ceremony was about to begin. A new age spiritualist stepped to the podium beside the casket, and opened the service by reciting an original poem. She thanked the universe for the generous soul who was taken to the great beyond, celebrating the triumphant journey of the human spirit.

Tara took a deep breath. Her throat tightened, as she stepped to the microphone, painfully aware that the eyes of the nation—and the world—were on her.

"Words cannot express," she began, "the gratitude and love I feel from everyone here today. You are all family... we are all one big family. In Balinda's world, she was a sister, a mother, and a daughter to everyone... everywhere. It didn't matter what your background was, or what your name was, because to Balinda, you were all family. It's amazing that you can travel to almost any place in the world—whether in this country, or to some remote areas that most of us have never heard of—and even there you will find people whose lives have been touched by Balinda."

She hesitated for a moment, recalling one of her fondest memories. She smiled, set her speech aside, then let her heart lead the way.

"Once, I traveled with Balinda," she beamed, "to a small Caribbean nation that had been devastated by a hurricane. Everywhere we went, we were swarmed by hundreds of villagers who were begging for food and clean water. Mothers were crying hysterically..., pleading for anything we could give them to feed their starving babies. And I remember Balinda not eating for five straight days, drinking only water, because what little food she had..., she gave away."

The home viewing audience listened to the stirring tribute, while watching video of Balinda's visit to one of the poor countries. She walked through a village that was reduced to rubble—passing out blankets and shoes to the homeless. She hugged many of the women who were crying, sharing their grief and offering words of hope. She distributed water bottles to the children, and handed out burlap sacks full of rice to starving villagers who were frantic for something to eat.

"It's only been a little over a week," Tara continued, "and I still can't believe it. I walk into her office, and I still feel her presence there. It's like I'm expecting her to walk into the studio at any minute to discuss the show's topic for the day. It doesn't seem real, it certainly doesn't seem fair." She paused to catch her breath. "What made Balinda different? Why did she give away so much? She didn't belong to any particular religion, in fact she embraced them all. The reason she was so generous..., is because she was a kind soul, and because she cared."

Chapter 44

"Man is destined to die once, and after that the judgment. The question for us is this... what happens the second you die?"

The pastor's words hung in the air. He watched as the congregants pondered in silence.

"Now, I know what some of you are thinking... 'Gee, I'm so glad I came today," he smiled.

The audience laughed.

"You may be thinking, 'I guess that's right, but do we really need to think about it? I was hoping for something a little lighter..., maybe a little 'Be kind to your neighbor..., blah, blah, blah..., or maybe a clever story before lunch.'"

The congregation smiled.

"The truth is, we all think about our existence. Sure, we try to avoid it with distractions, entertainment, and the latest electronic gadgets. But down deep, we know that the clock is ticking."

"Every time we watch the news or read the newspaper..., it seems another famous person has died, or is battling some terminal illness... superstar singers, Hollywood actors, national personalities. I bet everyone here could name a dozen famous people who have passed away in the last few years. It doesn't matter how rich or famous they were, or how young or old..., the sad reality is, that some of them are no longer with us."

The room grew quiet, as the listeners reflected.

"The question is, where are they now? What happens when you die? At the end of each of our lives, there is a doorway through which we all must pass. A door that is unavoidable, a door that is inescapable, a doorway that waits for all of us..., and there are no exceptions."

He inhaled deeply, wiping the sweat from his brow.

"Think back with me if you will... to a happier time. Do you remember when you were young..., and there were certain celebrities that you absolutely loved? I mean really loved...singers, actors...?"

A few audience members blushed.

"We watched them on TV, danced to their music, talked to our friends about them..., followed their personal lives..."

People smiled and nodded.

"You remember," he grinned.

"But the sad truth is...," he sighed, "that some of them are no longer with us."

He paused, reminiscing about his own personal loss. As he peered around the sanctuary, he noticed an elderly woman sitting near the window, her eyes listening intensely to every word.

"Has anyone here ever lost someone really close to them? A loved one... a mother, father, sister, brother, spouse, friend, child?"

The woman's eyes welled up, her face revealing deep emotional pain; she pulled a tissue from her sweater pocket, then dabbed her eyes.

The temperature in the sanctuary rose slightly, still comfortable, but noticeably warmer. Electric fans oscillated along the sides, while some congregants fanned themselves with their bulletins.

The pastor loosened his collar, pondering whether he should mention his personal story. He stepped around the podium, then leaned toward the listeners—his face taking on a softer tone.

"Losing someone is never easy. Most of you know my personal history, that I lost my first wife, my college sweetheart, when she was killed by a drunk driver. The emotional pain of losing someone close to you is devastating… to have them torn away from you is indescribable.

"I could tell you true stories of a little girl…whose mother died when she was only nine-years-old. Of a father who lost his daughter when she was seven-years-old. Of a sister who lost her little brother to cancer when he was only twelve.

"I could tell you stories…, and I bet you could too.

"You know, some people try to sugarcoat death and say, 'Hey, death is just a part of life…, it's natural.'

"Well, if anyone believes that, let me ask you this:

"What do you say to a mother whose newborn baby is clinging to life after being born with a hole in her heart? Do you say, 'It's okay… suffering and death is natural.'

"Or what do you say to the four-year-old girl whose mother is dying from breast cancer and is undergoing grueling chemotherapy treatments? Do you say, 'Honey, don't worry about it, suffering and death is natural.

"Well, I respectfully disagree. The Bible respectfully disagrees, because death is a travesty, an abomination, an affront to the living God. Death is unnatural, because according to the Bible, you and I were created to live forever.

"When Jesus approached the tomb of Lazarus—his friend who had been dead for four days—the Gospel of John says that Jesus was furious at death. Jesus was angry, because the people he loved were being tormented by death.

"The truth is…, death looms for all of us. It is inescapable. And to this day, it continues to torment you, it torments me, and it torments those we love.

"According to the Bible, suffering and death are definitely not natural."

He circled back to the podium, letting his thoughts catch up to his emotions.

"Now, I don't know what tomorrow holds for you or for me, we just never know. But I do know this for certain, Hebrews nine verse twenty-seven says, 'It is appointed unto men once to die, but after this the judgment.'"

He hesitated, looking out over the congregants—some shifting in their seats, but everyone's eyes locked on him.

"When we leave this world, and pass through the door that we all must go through..., what will happen, exactly?" he asked. "What will your eyes see, what will your ears hear, and what will you feel?"

Chapter 45

D r. Chambers' eyes flew open wide with amazement, gazing at the radiance that surrounded him. The heavenly brilliance was more dazzling than anything he had ever seen. His imagination surged into hyper real, marveling at the rich colors and fragrances that enveloped him. His skin tingled with excitement, sensing that he was about to be honored in the presence of millions, to be rewarded for his unwavering courage. As he anticipated the cheers of the multitudes, he heard trumpets blaring around him, filling his soul with triumph and satisfaction.

Surrounded by unimaginable beauty, his eyes were riveted on the man standing before him. The jagged nail scars in the man's hands confirmed that this was Jesus.

Jesus' face shined with radiant glory, and yet his soft humanity emitted a gentleness and compassion. His eyes embodied the power of the mighty oceans, the richness of wisdom, and the innocence of a newborn baby. His clothes beamed brighter than the noonday sun, whiter than the brightest fluorescent light—yet welcoming and irresistible.

Meanwhile, inside the funeral home, Dr. Chambers' sister, Stephanie, reminisced about her brother's compassion for the poor. She spoke with pride, knowing that his legacy of strength and perseverance would live on in posterity. Family members wiped the sadness from their eyes, lifting their heads high, and basking in his heroic achievements.

"He was one of a kind!" Stephanie beamed. "He will be remembered for fighting against injustice in all its ugly forms. He fought against corrupt government, standing up for what was right, even if it meant being locked in jail. He fought against corporate greed and corrupt politicians. He stood up for the poor and the outcast when society threw them in the gutter. And when nobody else cared... Tony cared!"

The audience erupted into applause, getting swept up in the moment.

"No one fought harder or with more passion than Tony. Because Tony was a fighter!"

The crowd sprang to their feet, applauding furiously in honor of 'The People's Champion.'

Up in heaven, Dr. Chambers stood tall and confident, glowing with self-assurance before Jesus. He thought to himself, 'It was all worth it, all the pain and sacrifice... and I'd do it all again.' He lifted his chin high, thinking about the homeless people he fought for, the endless years of volunteer work, and the persecutions he endured, all in the name of justice. The smile on his face enlarged by the second, convinced that his record was selfless and honorable. He smiled with expectation as he looked at Jesus, eager for the celebration to begin—to finally receive his just reward.

Meanwhile, in the small inner city church, the pastor shaded his eyes, as the sun peeked through the front of the sanctuary. He stepped forward to the platform's edge and spoke to the congregation like a confidant talking to a friend.

"The Bible says, 'If I surrender my body to the flames…', in other words, if I fight for the greatest causes in the world, with everything I have… but do not have the love of Jesus inside of me, I gain nothing."

In an instant, like a crash of lightning, Dr. Chambers' smile contorted into a ghastly scowl. His face twisted in agony, disfiguring from the torment convulsing within him. Fiery torture swept through every fiber of his being. His designer suit curdled blood red from the heat—his garments bursting into a raging inferno. He spun out of control as if being sucked through a vacuum, swept to eternal damnation.

"No! Ahhh! Ahhh!" he shrieked.

Consumed by darkness, he plummeted into the blazing abyss. He was devoured by a skin-crawling nightmare, twisting helplessly through a violent whirlwind. His blood curdling scream ripped through the silence—thrashing about in excruciating pain. His screech hissed, then exploded like a trail of lightning. A deafening clank came crashing down—a thunderous sound—like a metal chamber door slamming and sealing shut.

Chapter 46

Patricia choked back tears, struggling to tell the story of David's last Christmas. Her mind couldn't move past the sorrow, his smile and laughter were so vivid in her memory. She lowered her head, and closed her eyes, demoralized by the painful reality. Her four-year-old daughter squeezed her hand and looked up with teary eyes.

"Can I say something about daddy?"

"Sure, honey," she smiled. "Bethany would like to share a few things, if you don't mind."

She kneeled beside her and held the microphone.

"Go ahead, honey."

"I miss …" her daughter mumbled.

"It's okay, speak a little louder."

"I miss my daddy."

"Aww," the audience sighed.

Her daughter nestled against her—shying away from the crowd. She whispered into Bethany's ear, "It's okay, honey…Daddy's watching."

Bethany smiled, then fixed her eyes on the microphone.

"And Daddy loved Christmas…, it was his favorite day of the year… because we went to grandma's house. And we went sled riding, and played in the snow, and made snow angels…and we got lots of presents," her smile beamed with innocence. "And when we drove home from grandma's…, I fell asleep…, and Daddy carried me into the house and tucked me in." She froze, not knowing what else to say.

"Anything else, honey?" Mom asked.

"I miss you, Daddy, and I wish you didn't have to go."

Up in heaven, David's face lit up with wonder, marveling at the beauty that surrounded him. He inhaled deeply, breathing in the rich floral aroma. He caught a whiff of a fresh ocean breeze, the sweetness of strawberries, peppermint and cinnamon—a different fragrance wherever he turned. A waterfall of serenity washed over him—causing his skin to tingle, as he gazed at the picturesque grandeur all around. The rapturous joy he felt was light years above any happiness he had ever dreamed of.

But it was the glorious presence standing before him that captivated his attention. The radiance emanating from Jesus was transcendent—his face was illuminating. David stood mesmerized, his adrenaline pulsing through his veins. The sight of Jesus evoked feelings too wonderful for words. Jesus was more majestic than the greatest wonders in the world, and more enthralling than any floral landscape he had ever seen.

However, the nail scars in Jesus' hands told a different story—a human story, a tragic story. David cringed at the scars of imperfection. What was going on? The blemishes didn't make sense. The torture markings appeared out of step with one so brilliant and magnificent. David averted his eyes from Jesus' hands, recoiling from the signs of weakness. Instead he chose to fix his gaze on the glorious face of the Holy One—full of beauty, and love.

Meanwhile, back inside the funeral, his wife, Patricia, regained her composure, and continued pouring her heart out.

"He was the perfect husband, the prince charming I

dreamt about as a little girl. He was quirky in his own way," she smiled, "but he always made me laugh..., and every day was special. Each morning, I would wake up and find a fresh rose resting beside my pillow. And every morning he would tell me how much he loved me. When I looked in his eyes..., I felt beautiful, I felt safe, and I felt our hearts being woven closer together every day." She took a slow breath. "And he also gave the best Valentine's Day gifts," she laughed. "But that will always be our secret."

The audience chuckled.

"He was an amazing father to the children. He spent time with each of them—playing baseball with the boys, and building a tree house in our backyard. And the boys loved to beat daddy at video games, which was a big deal at our house," she smiled. "And he always made time to play 'house' with Bethany, and always let her paint his toenails."

The audience laughed, as she reached down and stroked her daughter's hair.

"To our friends across this great nation, he gave everything he had..., bringing hope to the hurting, and spreading joy to the sick and broken hearted. His motto was simple, 'Live the golden rule, do unto others,' and he put forth good karma wherever he went, always putting others before himself. Let me close with this," she raised her eyes toward heaven. "I love you, David, you are my heart..., and I miss you."

"He was right when he said that healing begins in the heart, and if your soul is pure, and your motives are right, then miracles can happen. And because of David..., a greater karma still lives on."

Up in heaven, David's heart raced with eager anticipation. He stood speechless before Jesus, basking in the splendor that surrounded him. He smiled with confidence, anxious to be commended for his compassion toward others.

He felt he lived a good life, practicing the golden rule, and always showing kindness to those in need. He was faithful to his wife and a good father to his children, and promoted the message of good karma every day. But the thing he was most proud of was the miracles he performed. Was it possible to perform miracles without divine favor? Of course not. He was a shoe-in for heaven. His whole life was about good karma, and he was ready for his reward.

Meanwhile, down in the sun-filled inner city church, the pastor shuffled through the pages in his Bible. He squinted his eyes, flipping back and forth until he reached the passage highlighted in yellow.

"The Bible says, "Many will say to me on that day, Lord, Lord, did we not prophesy in your name, and in your name drive out demons and perform many miracles? Then I will tell them plainly, I never knew you. Away from me, you evil doer."

"Aaahhhhh!" a high-pitched shriek rang out.

At that moment, an explosion detonated inside David's soul like a volcanic eruption. His conscience convulsed, shuddering uncontrollably, ripping apart his insides, sending shockwaves through his entire being. His face melted in horror, twisting in unsightly anguish; his clothes igniting into a raging fire. His body contorted, tossed about like a splinter in a whirlwind, then consumed like a vacuum into a fiery abyss.

"No! Ahhh! Noo!" his blood curdling screech trailed in horror.

His soul was engulfed by flames, swept up in an unquenchable inferno. A toxic stench spewed from within him, an odor of nauseating excrement more wretched than a rotting corpse. Screams of desperation shrieked from inside the bottomless chasm, until a thunderous clank came crashing down, silencing the grisly cries like a cast iron closure, sealing shut its lid for all eternity.

Chapter 47

"Mourners are filling the cemetery," the reporter said, "fans from all over the world who have come to pay their final respects to Balinda Summers. As you can see behind me, folks are carrying candles and flowers, and they've created a memorial filled with cards and mementos. Fans are crying and hugging one another...each person expressing their sorrow in a different way. We read one sign by the gate that simply said 'Thank you.'"

The reporter approached a woman near the shrine. "Let's see if one of the mourners will speak with us. Excuse me, ma'am, can you tell us what you're feeling... and why you came?"

"I had to come." The middle aged woman looked up with swollen eyes.

"Did you bring something for the memorial?"

"I did, I brought flowers and I signed a few of the posters...," she dabbed her eye with a tissue. "I'm sorry..., I just had to be here."

"What did Balinda mean to you?"

"She meant everything. She was my hero, and there's never been anyone like her. I've watched her show for the last ten to twelve years, and the things she did for people... unbelievable...she was a special person, she was an angel."

Up in heaven, Balinda threw her arms open wide, soaking in the celestial beauty that surrounded her. She marveled at the luminous colors—a tapestry of dazzling yellows, rich ocean blues, romantic incandescent reds, pure whites, and brilliant shades that she couldn't even describe. She felt like dancing, spreading her arms and soaring through the boundless utopia.

Her desire to fly was preempted only by the captivating presence standing before her. The man in front of her was ravishing—incomparable to anyone she had ever seen. She knew this was Jesus. His eyes were filled with compassion—a wellspring of kindness and wisdom. She stared at his face, her soul leaping within her—ecstatic just to be near him. She yearned to be embraced by him, and wrapped in his loving arms.

As the sun nestled behind the clouds, the mourners at the cemetery stared blankly at the coffin, listening reverently as Balinda's sister gave the final eulogy. Tara stammered briefly, fighting back tears, laboring to breathe. She felt the heaviness of the moment—sensing the eyes of the world upon her; but more importantly, she knew her sister was watching, and was determined to make her proud.

"I love you Balinda," she looked skyward, "and wherever you are, whether its heaven, or paradise, or whatever's out there, I know that you are taking charge, and bringing joy to everyone there. And I can't wait to see you again."

Her voice faded, as she struggled to finish. "My sister traveled all over the world, pouring her heart out, with one goal in mind…to make people happy. If she could put a smile on your face, then her job was done." She looked up one last time. "Smile, Balinda, you've done your job."

In the splendor of heaven, Balinda stared at Jesus, her heart fluttering with uncontrollable excitement. She was eager to get the party started—anxious to move into her luxury palace, and start mingling with heaven's finest. She smiled at Jesus and thought, "Wow, we are so made for each other, good, fun loving people who just want to spread happiness."

She was slightly miffed that no one was around to witness her big moment—her coronation—as she was about to be ushered into paradise. She envisioned an angelic parade singing her praises, much like the parades she had attended for the hospital grand openings—only on a much larger scale.

Her heart danced with anticipation, proud of the fact that she had opened fifteen new medical centers in the past few years—all bearing her name—to help the poor in some of the most impoverished countries. A wave of eagerness lit up her face. She was giddy with confidence, for surely her generosity deserved a reward fit for a queen.

Meanwhile, in the storefront church, the pastor drew his message to a conclusion. He looked up at the attentive listeners, and referred to a simple verse speaking about love.

"The Bible says, if I give all I possess to the poor, but if I do not have the love of Jesus inside of me, I gain nothing."

Without warning, Balinda's face contorted violently as if an earthquake imploded within her soul. Her eyes ruptured in horror, her body thrashing uncontrollably—being whipped about by a vicious whirlwind. Her garments flashed into flames, covered in feces and diseased ridden rags. She cried out in anguish as she was swept up like a tornado and thrown into the filthiness of hell.

"Noo! Ahhh! Ahh!" she shrieked.

She was consumed by an eerie darkness, her mind igniting from searing heat. The stench of stomach-turning sulfur spewed from her insides, as she flailed helplessly in the horrid nightmare. She was cast into a dungeon of excruciating torment, and condemned to inescapable suffering for all eternity. Ear piercing shrieks screamed out in terror, as she tumbled through the raging inferno of the bottomless oblivion.

Instantly, the blood curdling cries were silenced when an ominous crashing sound was heard, like the sound of an iron chamber door the size of a mountain slamming shut.

Chapter 48

Rachel flinched awake in the corner chair, startled by a loud, angry buzz. She rubbed the sleep from her eyes, then scanned the room—blinded momentarily by the emergency lights bouncing off the walls.

She gasped in horror when she saw Mitch's lifeless body convulsing in the bed, thrashing as if a tremor was quaking inside his chest. She inhaled an anxious breath, then ran to the door, screaming at the top of her lungs.

"Help! Please... somebody. Help!"

A team of nurses rushed into the room, snapping on the lights—nearly trampling one another. They shouted lifesaving procedures back and forth as Rachel shrunk into the corner. She couldn't swallow her mouth was so dry, biting down on her bottom lip and trying to stay calm.

A nurse ripped her husband's gown open, then began flipping switches haphazardly on the monitors. His body shook violently from side to side, and the cast on his leg was banging against the railing. A second nurse scurried, screaming for doctors to rush to the governor's room immediately.

In an instant, the room was filled with a team of white coats.

Rachel forced herself to breathe, reeling from the sudden commotion—hunched over and feeling nauseous. Was this the end? She grabbed a pillow from a nearby chair, clutching it tight across her chest—trying to steady her nerves, and hold herself together.

Mitch's convulsions lasted only a few seconds.

Zzzzzzz! The heart monitor flat-lined. His body stiffened, then fell limp.

"No!" she screamed.

"Quick, we're losing him!" a doctor shouted. "Emergency procedures!"

The doctor ordered a nurse to ready the heart defibrillator—and to commence when ready.

Precious seconds ticked away. Rachel began crying hysterically, slinking into the recliner against the window—a cold shiver running down her spine.

She shifted her eyes back and forth—straining to follow the frenzied activity—desperate for any sign of hope. She bristled at the sight of the shock paddles, clutching her stomach and bracing for the worst.

"Clear!" a nurse shouted. She thrust the metal paddles against his chest, sending shock waves through his limp body. His torso buckled, his body jerking from the sporadic charge. Everyone stared at the monitor, watching and hoping for a heartbeat. No response. The ominous buzz grew louder—his chances of survival were slipping away.

The air thickened by the second, intensifying every sound, and every sudden movement. This was not the way things were supposed to be. Was this really the end? Rachel couldn't imagine her life without him.

She stood to her feet, craning her neck to see what was going on, but her view was blocked by the wall of white coats. What was happening? Why weren't they saving him? She clasped her hands together in a prayer position, then elevated onto her tiptoes, anxious for any sign of life. She steadied herself against the wall, nearly falling over when her knees gave way. She shook her head, exasperated, then stumbled back into the chair. She had no other recourse but to cover her eyes and listen.

"Give me more!" the doctor shouted, demanding a higher voltage. Time was running out.

"Again!" he ordered.

The nurse thrust the paddles onto his chest once again, causing his body to twitch like a rag doll.

Beep! Beeeppp!

The heart monitor jumped to life. Green lines flickered across the screen, and a rhythmic heart beat reverberated above the chaos. Everyone held their breath, their eyes staring at the monitor.

The doctor scowled with painful concern.

"It looks like cardiac arrhythmia..., an irregular heartbeat," the doctor frowned. "Even if he pulls through," he sighed, "something's not right here. We're going have to wait and see."

"Come on, Governor," he urged.

The tension mounted in the room, the seconds ticking by.

Rachel huddled in her chair, clammed up, with a cold sweat beading on her forehead. Her hands were ice cold, and visibly shaking; she rubbed them together, then blew on her finger tips—her warm breath making little difference. Her eyes darted back and forth, listening intently and trying to decipher the medical jargon being bandied about.

As she stared at the blur of white coats, her mind melded into a pseudo-hypnotic state. The doctors and nurses appeared to drift in slow motion. The lights in the room brightened to a soft haze, and their voices slurred as if they were speaking underwater.

After a long thirty seconds, a doctor cried out, "I think he's back. We got him back." The nurses exhaled heavy sighs of relief.

Rachel swallowed hard, still frozen in the chair—terrified to move lest she upset the balance in the room.

"We'll have to run some tests," the doctor speculated,

"to check for brain damage."

"It was nearly forty-five seconds," a nurse sighed.

"And run a report on his family history, something doesn't seem right."

One by one the hospital staff trickled out of the room, shaking their heads, but relieved that he was still alive.

Rachel's hands shook involuntarily, her mind tangled in a web of confusion. What just happened? Was he better or worse? She took a deep breath, then wrapped her arms tightly around her body—uncertain what to do next.

A single nurse stayed behind, cleaning up, and reordering the chaos. She checked his vital signs, scribbled on her clipboard, then pulled the sheet up across his chest. She did a final check of the fluid levels, and then headed toward the door.

"It's okay, we got him back." The nurse sighed, opening the door halfway.

Rachel felt compelled to run over and embrace her husband, but was afraid to get too close.

"Can I get you anything Mrs. Jameson, coffee, or an extra pillow?" the nurse asked.

"Is he going to make it?" she whispered.

"He's still in critical condition." The nurse averted her eyes, her tone was less than optimistic.

Rachel stared at the floor, praying that the worst was over, and struggling to sort out her frazzled emotions. She buried her face in her hands—racking her brain for a way out of this nightmare.

"Would you like me to leave the light on?" the nurse asked.

Without looking up, she shook her head.

The nurse switched off the light, then exited—the door clicking behind her.

Rachel was alone, cloaked in darkness, listening to the static hum from the oxygen machine. She didn't mind the darkness; somehow it seemed more peaceful—easier to breathe.

She wrapped a sweater around her shoulders, shielding herself from the air conditioner. Her skin felt clammy. The ordeal left an icy mist on the back of her neck.

Yearning to be near him, she stood, and stepped slowly between the shadows. The moonlight was casting a soft glow on his face.

She stopped about a foot from the bed, then leaned over and fixed her eyes on his lifeless yet peaceful face. His eyelids were closed concealing any hint of life. She stared at his lips, the only part of his face that retained any color.

She felt the urge to speak, but when she opened her mouth, no words came out. She sighed, shaking her head. She wasn't sure what she felt anymore.

Tiny beads of sweat formed around his eyes, so she pulled a tissue from her pocket, then gently dabbed the skin below his lashes. She stared at his face for what seemed like an eternity.

The beeping noise from the life support machine grew louder by the second, creating a cadence in her mind—casting a hypnotic spell. The steady rhythm triggered flashbacks in her mind, conjuring up memories from the night of the accident. Images from the VIP fund raiser poured into her thoughts—the festive music, the party atmosphere, and the vision of her husband embracing another woman. The haunting image was etched in her brain, stirring up feelings of bitterness and rage. She closed her eyes, tired of wrestling with the past. Why should she feel guilty, what had she done to deserve such a horrific betrayal? She opened her eyes, searching the room for a much needed distraction—tired of reliving the same nightmare over and over.

With a heavy heart and equally heavy body, she pulled a chair beside the bed, then collapsed in the seat from exhaustion. She reached out instinctively and grabbed his swollen hand. His fingers felt cold to the touch, causing her to wince—she felt no connection, no sense of life. She squeezed his hand, caressing the familiar shape of his palm, hoping to transfer feelings of warmth and compassion.

As the night wore on, the darkness weighed heavy on her mind—draining her of hope, and pulling her deeper into the cold reality. She leaned back, exhausted from the emotional rollercoaster. Her eyelids grew heavy. The night closed in around her.

Chapter 49

Mitch clenched his jaw, grimacing from the fiery pain. He tried to scream, but his vocal chords were muffled, barely forcing out a stifled groan. He gasped for air—his lungs laboring to inflate, until finally, he sucked in a few sustained breaths—bringing a moment of anxious relief.

He opened his eyes, glaring into the black emptiness. Paranoia swept over him as he tried to make sense of what his brain was telling him. Where am I? An ominous chill quivered through his mind. Am I alive?

The stagnate air felt dry inside his nostrils as though he was buried in a coffin—breathing the same air over and over. His ears perked up, listening for any signs of life. Nothing, only dead silence.

He shifted his eyes from side to side, searching frantically for something tangible. He strained his eyes downward as far as they could move, and noticed a hazy glow—a kind of shifting shadow. What was going on? Nothing made sense.

His mind drifted in and out of consciousness—trapped between exhaustion and anxiety. He felt pulsing sensations in his extremities, but couldn't move his arms or legs; his body felt like it weighed a thousand pounds. His head was groggy, freefalling into a vacuum of claustrophobia.

He flinched awake when he felt an excruciating pain

throbbing behind his eyes. He inhaled several quick breaths, then gnashed his teeth, trying to fight the stabbing irritation with the force of his will power. The pain flared up without rhyme or reason, fueling his anxiety and compounding the misery. There had to be a way out of this cycle of torment.

From the corner of his eye, he saw a tiny sparkle—a faint glimmer that was shining down by his side. The gleaming speck looked like a chunk of broken glass or perhaps a small diamond.

He stretched his fingers toward the sparkle—then bumped into something that felt like a person's hand. He tilted his neck, and squinted into the gray glow, discovering what looked like the top of a person's head. He gasped with anticipation, a surge of adrenaline pulsing through his veins.

He stretched his fingers with what little strength he could muster, and nudged the person's hand, trying desperately to get their attention. No response. Maybe the person was dead. He flicked their hand vigorously, until finally the person shifted and raised their head up into the darkness. They disappeared into the shadows for a tense moment, then reappeared in the hazy glow.

Mitch squinted into the smoky beam of light, focusing hard on the person's face, when suddenly, he gasped, exhaling a sigh of joy. He recognized those soft green eyes. It was his wife, Rachel. Was this a dream? It had to be, everything felt surreal—except the pain.

She rubbed her eyes—blinking repeatedly, and trying to clear her head. Her eyes popped wide with shock, her mouth dropping when she realized he was awake.

"Mitch," she gasped.

She squinted with a look of doubt, then jumped from her seat and clicked on a small lamp, giving the room a soft glow.

"Oh, Mitch," she smiled, kissing his cheek and peering deep into his eyes.

He labored to speak, groaning, and clenching his jaw. His chest heaved with excitement—but when he opened his mouth, he started gagging—choking on a lump that was caught in his throat. His vocal chords seized up, cramping, as if he was being strangled from the inside. He managed a few stifled moans, but the sobs felt like sandpaper—grating against his windpipe—until the burning became unbearable.

His mind scrambled for answers, tangled in fear and uncertainty. What was going on? He tried to sit up, but his back muscles spasmed, sending ripples of pain shooting along his spine. Blood rushed to his face, as he let out a silent scream; his heart thumped against his rib cage, his body collapsing in surrender. Was this nightmare ever going to end?

"Stay still, honey," she whispered.

She wiped his eyes with a damp cloth, allowing him to see the room more clearly.

He squinted at the ceiling, gritting his teeth until the pain subsided. His memory was scattered—a blur of images, and nameless faces; he recognized his wife, but nothing else seemed to make sense. Why was he in the hospital? And how long had he been here?

Rachel's phone rang, which she glanced at, then promptly tucked back into her purse. The high-pitched ring triggered images in his mind—an array of dark visions that made no sense. He saw a rain covered highway and headlights flashing in his eyes. He saw windshield wipers whipping back and forth, and blinking red lights; he heard the sound of screeching tires.

He glanced over at Rachel, who looked back at him with a half-smile. Her eyes glazed over with a mist of sadness, her expression revealing something other than joy.

The fog suddenly lifted, and the despicable truth came flooding into his mind. The blood drained from his face when he realized why he was there, and what he had done. A shooting pain pierced his conscience as he recalled the car chase, the party, and the look on his wife's face when she caught him on the balcony with the other woman. His eyes welled up with shame, recoiling from the sting of reality. He wished he was dead.

He averted his eyes, as the guilt began to crush him. He turned away, ashamed to look into her knowing eyes—a tear trickling down the side of his face.

Rachel leaned in and kissed his cheek, wiping away his tears.

As she caressed his face, he sensed her compassion—which caused his eyes to well up even more. He wanted to crawl in a hole and die. His conscience squirmed from humiliation, crying out in desperation—but there was nowhere to hide.

Straining with all his might, he agonized to produce words that were lodged in his throat. His raspy voice cracked, his words slurring into a heap of inaudible groans. The ashen look on his face flushed crimson red, as he fought through the excruciating pain. There was no holding back, he was determined to speak.

He inhaled as deeply as his pain-ravaged body would allow, then pushed out a choked whisper.

"Please…, please forgive me…." He wept bitterly.

Chapter 50

Mitch flinched when the glass of juice tipped over, banging off the side of the tray. He squirmed to avoid the spill, his gown clinging to his skin.

"Damn," he cringed, flipping the glass right side up. A nurse rushed over with a towel and sponged up the majority of the apple juice, opening his gown and wiping along the side of his stomach.

"Great, I'm going to enjoy that sticky feeling all day," he winced.

The wet towel gave him chills, the cold water seeping into the sheets.

"Is there no warm water in those faucets?" he smirked.

"Sorry about that," she sighed.

He winked at the elderly nurse, poking fun, and flashing a smile. He was actually relieved that all his senses were working again. Most of all, he was loving the morphine drip.

As he spooned the lemon jello squares into his mouth, three doctors filed into the room, grabbing his attention, and lifting his mood. He was hoping for good news.

"Ah, tres amigos... can I offer you some jello?" he asked. They grinned.

"How are you feeling, today, Governor?" a doctor asked.

"I think I'll be ready for that triathlon, tomorrow."

"Well it's good to see you've gotten your appetite back."

The doctor glanced at the patient's report, showing no emotion—good or bad.

"Hey, Doc, what's this I hear about no restaurant deliveries?" he grinned, scooping up his fruit cocktail.

"What, our menu doesn't do it for you?" the doctor smiled, crossing his arms.

"I've been craving sushi for like two days."

"Well, you're going to have watch your sodium intake from now on."

"Why, what's wrong?" He set the spoon down.

The doctor's face turned somber, swallowing hard and averting his eyes. Mitch took a quick sip of water, troubled by the doctor's non response. The hairs on the back of his neck stood up, as he waited in the silence.

"Governor, I'd like you to meet Dr. Jorgenson and Dr. Rhodes."

Mitch shook hands with each of them. "Nice to meet you." He offered a courteous smile, anxious to get past the pleasantries.

"Dr. Jorgenson is the leading Cardiothoracic Surgeon on the east coast, and we brought him in to review your test results. And Dr. Rhodes is a Pulmonologist who's going to be examining your lungs to make sure they're healthy."

"What's wrong with my lungs, do I need more surgery?" His eyes widened with concern.

The doctor stuttered, "Um, we were hoping your wife would be here..., but we couldn't get a hold of her. We left several messages."

"What is it?" He shifted his eyes, bracing for the worst.

"One of your heart valves was damaged during the accident, probably when you hit the steering wheel."

Mitch sunk his head into the pillow, staring up at the ceiling—dreading the sound of what was coming next. He wanted to cover his ears, but dealing with fear was an anomaly for him.

"We could perform open heart surgery," the doctor continued, "and replace the leaky valve, but I'm afraid it's more serious than that. You're suffering from a rare genetic disease called Hypertrophic Cardiomyopathy. In other words, your heart muscle is thickening, and it's obstructing the blood flow. We could replace the leaky valve, but that wouldn't fix the problem long term."

Mitch's eyes glazed over, as he peered out the window, desperate to make light of this demoralizing news. Surely they had a pill for whatever he needed. Isn't this the twenty-first century? He glared at the rain clouds rolling in, staring blankly at the impending storm and searching for a way out.

"Ultimately, you're going to need a heart transplant," the doctor said.

His eyes snapped shut. The words 'heart transplant' came crashing down like a bolt of lightning.

The room fell silent.

"How much time do I have?" he whispered.

"We can't be sure."

He pulled the sheet tightly around his shoulders, hoping the doctors would disappear; hoping this was all a bad dream.

The doctor broke the tension with a loud exhale, then continued, "Governor, I'm sorry, there's something else I need to mention. If a donor does become available, they would need to match your blood type exactly, or come as close as possible," he sighed. "And I'm sure you already know that you're AB negative…, one of the rarest."

The blood drained from Mitch's face, and a chill shot through his body. Was this the end? He clammed up, wishing he had died in the accident.

'The game's over,' he surmised, no more rabbits left in the hat. He retreated into the recesses of his mind, searching for a place to hide, cowering in the dark.

Chapter 51

The crowd stirred with anticipation, as Mitch propped himself up behind the podium. His cheeks flushed red when he noticed the TV cameras—the bright lights glaring, there was no place to hide.

His critics stood off to the side, eager to lambaste him, and watch him squirm in front of a national audience. The humidity was unusually high; the storm clouds overhead were threatening to open up at any second.

The white gauze wrapped around his forehead was dripping with anxiety. He dabbed his face with a tissue, blotting between the thick scabs that were striped across his cheek. He never thought this day would come—his mind still wrestling through every misstep that led to him to this point. How did he get so close, then let it slip away?

He wobbled in place on his good leg, then steadied his broken body with a crutch under each arm.

The electricity in the crowd was palpable, igniting his competitive fire and revving up his ego. His mind flashed back to previous campaign rallies—images of political debates, and memories of victory celebrations. For a brief moment, he felt like he was in control—hovering over the commoners like a dominant chess master.

He peered down at the media without actually seeing

them—hordes of reporters jockeying for position and bickering like adolescents.

He tapped the microphone with his finger, then listened for the return echo. He shook his head in frustration, when he realized that the sound system wasn't working. Maybe this was a sign. Maybe the universe was telling him to walk away.

He lingered helplessly on the vacant stage with no dignitaries there to support him—no police chief, local politicians, or close personal assistants. Most notably absent was his wife who was not by his side. He was all alone.

A knot the size of a fist twisted inside his stomach as he peered anxiously over the crowd. "This is ridiculous," he groaned. He knew he should've held the presser in his office.

He sifted through his thoughts, struggling to simplify his message, knowing that the piranhas were hungry for details of his relationship with the intern.

He feigned a smile at a familiar reporter in the crowd, then grinned at a spattering of staff members who were lined along the side of the building. His competitive fire flickered just beneath the surface. He smirked under his breath, "Maybe this isn't the end."

Standing above the multitudes—with camera shutters clicking away—his chest swelled, and a rush of defiance surged through his veins. Why not rally his team once again and fight to the end? What did he have to lose?

A shrill buzz pierced the air, causing the crowd to wince. The PA system crackled, sending a shiver down his spine. It was game time.

He tapped the microphone with his finger, relieved that something was going right today. He cleared his throat, then waited for the masses to settle. The blood rushed to his face as his emotions flip flopped back and forth. He stared at the silver mic, shaking his head and debating whether he had anything left in the tank. What do I have to lose? And what am I living for?

He peeked over his shoulder at the empty stage, when a

curl of nausea suddenly flummoxed inside his stomach. Loneliness swept over him, rocking him back on his heels. His bravado was caught in his throat. He knew what he had to do.

"I am resigning my position as governor effective immediately. I have been unfaithful to my wife. I have asked her to forgive me."

He bowed his head in defeat, bracing for the backlash from the hecklers and critics.

"Are you kidding..., that's it?" a reporter yelled.

He hobbled away like a wounded animal.

The crowd roared in anger, hissing profanities and demanding answers.

"Governor, did you have an affair with the college intern?" someone shouted."

"Where's your wife, Jameson... is it true that she dumped you?" a tabloid reporter scoffed.

He ignored the insults as best he could, hopping down the stairs, and exhaling a quiet sigh of relief. The thousand pound albatross tumbled from his shoulders. He wanted to smile, but the pain shooting up his leg quickly quashed his urge to celebrate. His conscience breathed a little easier—the pain in his leg served as a mini blessing, creating a mental shield, and distracting his thoughts from the verbal attacks.

He stumbled toward the lobby entrance, hanging his head, and avoiding eye contact with everyone. The crowd pressed him from every side, his security guards fighting to clear a path through the taunters and cynics. He hobbled through the masses, anxious to put this all behind him.

"You're a loser, Jameson!" a heckler yelled. "Nothing but a quitter. You're getting what you deserve, you coward. I hope your wife does leave you... maybe she'll find a real man!"

Chapter 52

Mitch squeezed between the church pews, wishing he had stayed in bed. Being cooped up in a church was the last place he wanted to be, but he complied, at the insistence of his estranged wife. For the first time in his life, he had no idea where he was going or what he was doing—floating aimlessly at the whim of the universe.

As he navigated his leg cast in the narrow space, he banged his knee off the wooden bench. He clenched his teeth, stifling a curse word before it slipped out of his mouth. He rocked back and forth, anxious to find a comfortable position, then glanced at his watch—counting down the minutes until lunchtime. He pretended to be enthused about being there, anything to make the wife happy and salvage what time he had left with his family. His daughters plopped beside him, being careful not to brush up against him. His wife crossed to the other end of the pew, choosing to maintain a discreet distance, keeping the girls nestled between them.

He stared straight ahead—his eyes drooping with dark circles from another sleepless night. The pain killers had lost their potency, and the sleep medicine was nothing more than syrup with a kick. His eyes glazed over in a fog, hiding behind a necessary masquerade. He glanced up at the vacant pulpit, then let out an audible sigh. He rolled his eyes and thought, "Great, this is a fantastic waste of time."

He remained seated through the first half of the service, listening to the songs and nodding along. When the offering plate passed by, he dropped a crisp one dollar bill into the dish, chalking it up as his good deed for the week.

When the pastor stepped onto the platform, Mitch tried his best to look attentive, but in his mind he sulked, "Here we go again. This is where he tells us to 'Love thy neighbor,' and be a good person, three points and a poem..., the same stuff everybody already knows." He pasted on a compliant smile, hoping to win brownie points with his wife.

The room fell silent as the sound of oscillating fans buzzed along the sides of the sanctuary.

"I want everyone to close your eyes," the pastor began, "and think about the one person in your life that you love more than anyone else. Go ahead, close your eyes. I'll wait," he smiled. "Can you picture that person? Look into their eyes, listen to their voice, and feel the touch of their hand. Can you see them? Now, picture the two of you playing on the beach, soaking in the warm sunshine..., or sharing a meal together, or whispering your deepest secrets to one another. You're connecting with them on a heart level. Do you see them, and feel their presence?" He waited. "Then suddenly...," he clapped, "...they're gone."

"Now open your eyes." He peered around the room, waiting for everyone to look up. "There is nothing more devastating in life, than losing someone you love to death.

"In the news recently, we learned of the tragic plane crash that claimed the lives of three beloved national figures. Some of you may have known them personally, for they were certainly a part of the American fabric. First and foremost, we pray that our compassionate Heavenly Father will comfort their families, especially their grieving spouses and children. The sad truth is that death is never an easy thing to face—or to even think about at any time. But the stark reality is that in this existence, which we call life, there is a doorway that waits for all of us, a doorway that we all must pass through someday, it is unavoidable.

"For some of us, that time could be fifty years from now, or maybe twenty, for some it could be tomorrow—you just never know, but there is a doorway at the end of each of our lives.

"The big question is, 'What happens to your loved ones the second they pass through that door? And what will happen to you and me? What's on the other side?'" The question lingered for a moment in the silence.

Mitch sighed in dismay—his mind reverting back to his hospital bed and the doctor's dire prognosis which was emblazoned in his memory, 'Governor, you're going to need a heart transplant...' His lungs tightened inside his chest, the recollection sending chills up his spine.

He shot a panicky glance at his daughter, then averted his eyes quickly, trying to hide his anxiety. Questions swirled in his mind, pondering the tentative time he had left. Will I even make it to my little girl's graduation? Or will I be there to escort her down the aisle, or get to play with my grandchildren?

"Tomorrow is guaranteed for no one," the pastor continued. "Are you ready for what awaits you on the other side?

"It seems that every week we turn on the news and hear reports of earthquakes, hurricanes, tsunamis or massive floods that are ravaging entire nations—homes being swept away, cars and bodies disappearing in the flood waters.

"The Bible says, the very second you die, you will stand before a man with scars in His hands, and you will be judged.

"Hebrews 9:27 says, 'Man is destined to die once, and after that the judgment.'

"But how will we be judged..., what's the criteria? If you asked the average person, they would say, 'Well, *good* people get into heaven. It depends on whether you're good or not.'

"Do you consider yourself a good person? Think about it for a moment. Most people tend to compare themselves with their neighbors, people they work with, or criminals they see on the evening news…Am I a better person then those people? Be honest…most people would say, 'Yes,' right? Or maybe we're all about the same…, you know, we're all good in a general sense. Right?"

"According to the Bible, there are a lot of good people in this world, people far better than me and perhaps better than you…people who make more money and give away more money, are more successful, more charitable, better role models… good people, nice people, millions… who the Bible says… will unfortunately be cast into hell. 'Now, wait a minute,' someone says…, 'how can good people be cast into hell? That can't be right, can it? It sounds unfair. How can people who have done good things in their lives be cast into eternal torment?'

"The Bible says, your eternal destiny, either heaven or hell—either being welcomed into God's presence, or cast out of His presence—is not determined by how good you are, but instead it will be determined by a single question, the most important question of your life. One question… does anyone know what that question is?"

Mitch's eyes were glued on the pastor, waiting anxiously for what would come next.

"The answer is found in one of the most chilling passages in the Bible. In Matthew seven, Jesus says, 'Many will say to me on that day…, Judgment Day, 'Lord, Lord, did we not prophesy in your name and in your name drive out demons and in your name perform many miracles?' Then I will tell them plainly, 'I never knew you. Away from me, you evildoers.'"

"I never knew you."

"The one question that will determine your eternal destiny, either heaven or hell is this…'Does Jesus know you?'" He repeated, "'Does Jesus know you?'

"Let's be clear about what is says, and also about what it does not say. It does not say that I must know Jesus. A lot of people are going to stand before Him and say, "Jesus, I know you." And Jesus will say to them, 'Depart from me, I never knew you.'

"But instead, what does it say? It raises the question, 'Does Jesus...know...you?'"

"Judgment is not based on whether you've been good most of your life, it has nothing to do with karma... the universe doesn't owe you anything. It has nothing to do with how well your behavior compares to others. We might try to reason, 'Well, I was better than those criminals I see on the news, those bad people.'

"No, judgment is based on one thing and one thing only... 'Does Jesus actually know you...personally.'

"Let's switch gears for a minute, because I'm sure many of you are thinking, 'Wow, this is kind of heavy, Pastor. Death, judgment, goodness, heaven, being known by Jesus, personally.'

"Well, what I'd like to do is..., I'd like to talk about these issues in a way that I bet you've never heard before. In fact, I would like to tie all our subjects into a single issue...the one issue that excites people more than anything else. There is one issue that people think about more than anything else. It's on our minds constantly. You think about it, I think about, the person next to you is thinking about it to some degree. People in every country on the face of the earth are thinking about this issue right now. What is it? Is it money, power, sex, happiness, wealth? No. It may include all of those things, but the single issue that we think about most is... freedom. I want to enjoy... what I want, when I want.

"Freedom. I want to enjoy what I want, when I want.

"Fortunately for us, freedom ties into true goodness, heaven, judgment, and being known by Jesus. There is a common thread that runs through all of them.

"Now, what do I mean?

"Well, let's look at freedom under two headings. First, are you free? And second, how do we get true freedom?

"First, are you free? Am I free?

"You may say, 'That's silly, of course I'm free.'

"We are living in a time in history that is unprecedented, when people virtually have unlimited freedom. Job choices, careers, entertainment, technology, computers, travel, hobbies, activities, purchasing power,...the choices are unlimited.

"And yet, when I talk to folks today, especially young people who are free to do anything they want..., watch movies, listen to music, play on computers, video games, texting, YouTube, social media, etc..., more often than not, they tell me they're bored. Can you believe that? Bored. With the zillion options available to people today. How is that possible? Do you ever get bored? Of course you do, we all do.

"So what's the cure for boredom?

"Some say, read a book, or watch a movie, or get a hobby. So then we watch the latest movie, and buy the newest gadget..., but sooner or later...we're bored again.

"Is there a cure for boredom?

"The answer is 'yes.' And here's what I tell people. I say, your problem is not a boredom issue, it's a freedom issue. They look at me and say, 'What?' That's right. It's a freedom issue. You're free to do everything, but you end up doing nothing. You have too many options, but you end up doing nothing.

"So what's the cure for boredom? The cure for boredom is...purpose. A person is bored, because they don't understand their purpose in life. If you understood your purpose in life, you would never be bored again. Think about it. What is your purpose in life?

"Now purpose is related to freedom, but that's another topic for another time. I just wanted us to start thinking about this notion of freedom.

"So let's get back to our original question, Are you free? Because this is really the heart of the matter.

"If I ask most people, 'Are you free?' They say, 'Of course I'm free.'

"And then I say, 'You may think you're free, but you're not free. In fact, you may be a slave, and you don't even know it.'

"And then I have a person's attention.

"You see, the problem for years was, that our grandparents and even religious people in general always emphasized, 'Be good. Be obedient. Do the right thing.' But the problem is, being good doesn't resonate with today's generation. If you talk to people today about goodness, they look at you and say, 'Who's to say what's good? What's good in one culture is different than what's good in another.' They basically say, 'Who cares?' But instead, their mindset is focused…, not on goodness, but on personal fun, and personal freedom.

"That's what we all care about…, personal freedom…, having a good time.

"So I tell a young person, you think you're free, but you're not free. And then they perk up and say, 'That's interesting.'

"In fact, not only are you a slave, but you're the worst kind of slave. You are a slave, and you don't even know it.

"Look around society, and you can see the things that people are addicted to, things they have to have, things they live for, things they work forty, fifty, sixty hours a week for. People are being dragged through life by a nose ring, by things they have to have. They have to have the perfect girlfriend or boyfriend, the cool clothes, or their own individual style, a great job, a great car, a great apartment, a big house, a house at the beach, money, sex, power, respect, my friend's approval, my parent's approval, cool friends, a prestigious job. Other folks are addicted to food, beauty, jewelry, shoes, physical appearance, social status, pornography, drugs, alcohol, partying, personal pleasures, fame, recognition, the latest gadgets in technology, big screen TVs, your own personal happiness, and the list goes on.

"You think you're free, but you're not free. Advertisers know you're not free, and they work very hard to press your buttons.

"So someone says, 'So what. What does freedom have to do with heaven? And the answer is everything.

"We are not free, because we are slaves. And our slavery is rooted in self-centeredness. I have to have these things. I live for these things. In the same way, people are rejected from heaven because of their self-centeredness. If heaven were filled with self-centered people, it wouldn't be heaven... it would be chaos, fighting and bloodshed, it would be hell.

"Are we self-centered people? Am I a self-centered person? Are you a self-centered person? The answer is, 'yes,' of course we are. If we say, "No," then we're in denial. All of us, deep down are self-centered people. We're just not willing to admit it. The Bible says that God opposes the arrogant and proud, but gives grace to the humble. God loves the poor in heart.

"So our first point is...Are we free? And the answer is 'No.' We may think we are, but we're not. We are being dragged through life by our self-centered desires.

"So what's the solution? What's the answer? That leads us to our second point, how do we get true freedom?

"There are two steps to true freedom, and fortunately, these same two steps give us true goodness, lead us to being known by Jesus, and usher us into heaven.

"What are the two steps to freedom? First, you need a wakeup call, and secondly, it is God alone who gives you freedom.

"What do we mean by a wakeup call? You and I need a spiritual wakeup call.

"What does that mean? Slavery comes in two main forms. Some people are slaves to things, possessions, items of wealth..., we talked about those things. But there is a second kind of slavery which is far more deceptive, far more slippery, and far more hidden...and ultimately..., it destroys you. It's called relational slavery, or relational self-centeredness. What is relational slavery? Relational slavery is when a person either feels superior to other people, they despise people, or they're caught up in their own personal happiness so much, that they ignore people. Let's talk for a moment about this hidden type of slavery, this relational self-centeredness.

"Someone says, 'relational slavery? I can already tell that's not me.'

"Well, let's see. Maybe this is your wakeup call. Let's put you to the test and find out.

"Think for a moment, of the worst person in the world. Now I'm not talking about tyrants in history, or mass murderers, I'm talking about people that you know personally, in your life right now. Is there a co-worker that you avoid, an annoying neighbor, a boyfriend or girlfriend who cheated on you, someone who lied to you or stole from you, someone you can't trust, or someone who let you down? Be honest with yourself. If you're honest, you know that we all have someone like that in our lives. Think about someone who has hurt you in the past, your worst enemy, someone you despise. Your wakeup call is this: When you think of that person, you must realize in your heart and mind… that you are no better than them. In fact, you are worse. Do you believe that? We live in a world where democrats despise republicans and vice versa. Ethnic groups don't care about other ethnic groups, instead they only care about their own people. Other religions look down on each other, rich people don't care about poor people, and poor people despise rich people. But when you look at people you despise, and say, "I am no better than that person," then you are on your way to your spiritual wakeup call. Or here's another example… , when someone cuts in front of you in line, do you call them a jerk? Do you? Do you think that in your mind? Now, they may be wrong for doing what they're doing, but you mustn't look down on them.

"Or answer these questions: Who has wronged you in the past? Who can you not forgive? Who lied to you? Abused you, stole from you, cheated on you, stepped on you to get ahead, took advantage of you? Is someone's name or face coming to mind? Of course it is. Is it true that they were wrong in how they treated you? Sure. But you must not look down on them, thinking you are better. If you can't forgive someone, no matter how vile and despicable they were... if you can't forgive them, it's because you think you're better than them.

"So the first step to freedom is to admit the problem of self-centeredness within you. When a person thinks that they are better than their worst enemy, then they are elevating themselves above them, and that sense of superiority stems from self-centeredness.

"Do we see the problem of self-centeredness in our own lives? If we say, no, then we are trapped in slavery. We are neither free, nor do we understand heaven.

"Let me give you an example, because the Bible is filled with examples of people who did not see their own self-centeredness.

"For example, what was Satan's problem? His problem was that he didn't see his problem. He wanted to be in charge. He looks down on everyone, even God. He wanted all the power. He was self-centered. He thought too highly of himself. Jesus said, "I saw Satan fall like lightening." When Satan tempted Jesus in the wilderness, he said to Jesus, "Bow before me, and I will give you all these things, riches, kingdoms, pleasures." Satan's problem is that he wanted to be the Most High.

"And what about us..., you and me? Are you the Most High in your own life, in charge of deciding what is good and bad, right and wrong for you, based on your own self-centeredness?

"Or have your eyes been opened...do you see your selfishness?

"If you see the problem, then what is the solution... how do we get Jesus to be present, as the Most High in our lives?

"And the answer is, we need to see His love at work, and understand how much He loves us.

"There are two steps to true freedom. The first is that we

are worse than we think we are, and secondly, that God's love is greater than we realize. We are worse than we think we are, and God's love is greater than we realize.

"Let's take a look at how great God's love truly is.

"In the book of Ephesians, God calls us His treasure, His inheritance. He says, that those who are united to Christ, are marked with God's seal of ownership, the promised Holy Spirit, who is a deposit guaranteeing our inheritance until the redemption of those who are God's possession. God actually calls us His treasure, His possession, His inheritance.

"What is an inheritance? An inheritance is the bulk of someone's wealth, their possessions... their valuables.

"Let me give you an example. Imagine a couple..., and they own one of the most valuable pieces of art in the world. And this art piece has an assessed value of over one hundred million dollars. Now, even though it is valued at over one hundred million dollars..., which is their complete net worth, the value is actually misleading, because the couple finds it to be priceless. They would not part with it for anything. Because when they look at it, sit before it, drink it in, and marvel at its beauty..., it envelops their emotions, stirs their passions, and delights their hearts. To them, it is priceless, and they wouldn't part with it for anything.

"Well, in the same way, that's how God looks at you. The Lord of the Universe, that owns all the galaxies, and all the stars, and all the wealth under all the planets in the universe, considers you, those who are in Christ...His treasure. When He looks at you, He feels rich.

"And if God loves you that much, if He treasures you that much..., that He was willing to die a horrific death on the cross in order to be with you..., what will His expression be like that first moment when we see Him face to face. We will be swept up in a hurricane of love. We will be swimming in His love...breathing it in, overwhelmed by indescribable joy.

"C.S. Lewis says, if we let Him, he can make the feeblest and filthiest of us into dazzling, radiant, immortal creatures, pulsating all through with such energy and joy and wisdom as we cannot now imagine. He will make us a bright stainless mirror which reflects back to God perfectly, though of course, on a smaller scale, His own boundless power and delight and goodness. This is what we are in for, nothing less.

"Everything you've ever wanted, everything you've ever longed for times a trillion, will be present in your heart, the first second of His embrace of you, when we see Him face to face.

"Has anyone here ever been in love? Have you? I mean, honest to goodness, one hundred percent, head over heels, you want to be with this person forever type of love? Well if you have, then you know that if you experience something wonderful in life...a great event, an unforgettable concert, a great movie, an extraordinary achievement..., that your happiness would not be true happiness... in the fullest sense..., unless your true love was there to share it with you. If you are truly in love, you want to share your greatest moments in life with that person.

"Jesus prays to the Father in the book of John, and He says, 'Father, I want those you have given me to be with me where I am.' In other words, He longs to have you with Him..., the passion of His heart is to have you with Him in heaven for all eternity.

"The Bible says that those who are united to Jesus will live forever.

"So how do you become united to Jesus... what is the process?

"The answer is, you need to see His love for you. The eyes of your heart have to find delight in His great love for you.

"So, let's take a look, and consider His love.

"How many of you have ever heard someone say, "I love you?" We all have. And it's wonderful. Words are important, especially words of love. But we also know that it's one thing for someone to tell you that they love you, and another thing for them to show it. Saying they love you is one thing, but isn't it true, that *actions* speak louder than words?

"Have you ever come across a person who was really in need? Maybe a homeless person, or a someone who was going through a hard time? We all have at some point, haven't we..., maybe not every day, but once in a while. And what are we willing to give them? Maybe a dollar here, or a dollar there... a few bucks, right? And that's a good thing. But isn't it true, that most of the time, our fists are so tight around our wallets that we don't like to part with our money for anything... unless it's to buy something for *ourselves*. Isn't that true? Of course it is. And we tell ourselves, 'Hey..., I'm just barely scraping by myself.'

"But what was Jesus willing to give up to be with you, to bring you to heaven, to spend eternity with you? The answer is..., He was willing to give up everything. He gave up riches, splendor, and glory beyond our wildest imaginations. He gave up His freedom, His power, the comforts of heaven, respect, honor, majesty, and even His own life...for you. The all-powerful Creator took on a frail human body and made himself vulnerable, susceptible, killable.

"Is there anyone here who was present at Jesus' crucifixion two thousand years ago? Of course not. But when we read about the historic event in God's Word, and we talk about it, and ask questions about it, and think about it, and talk to God about it, then His Holy Spirit works the significance of Jesus' death into our hearts.

"And why was His death so significant?

"The Bible says that Jesus' death saves not only you and me..., but all of creation... that the whole universe is being renewed from a single purification point in history. And that purification point is the life, death and resurrection of Jesus.

"And the Bible says that the magnitude of His death, the cosmic horror of His death, and the enormity of His suffering was far worse, and far more excruciating than our tiny minds can ever comprehend.

"What do we mean?

"Well, the Gospel of Mark says that when Jesus was

crucified, He wasn't holding it all together, on the contrary, he went out screaming! Mark 15:34 says, 'He cried out,' and verse 37 says, 'with a loud cry.' What was going on here? On the cross, Jesus was screaming out for reasons you and I will never fully understand. What do we mean?

"When Jesus, the God of the Universe, was crucified, He was screaming out, not because he had been tortured beyond belief, which he had... he was whipped over and over again with a whip that tore the flesh from his back. And he was screaming out not because they forced a crown of thorns into his scalp, piercing his skull...which they did. He was screaming out not because people were mocking him and spitting on him, laughing at him and cursing him...which they were—the military guards, thieves and even the religious leaders—the good people. He was screaming out not because his garments were stolen from him... which they were, he was completely naked, with no covering and no place to hide. He was screaming out not because his family and friends deserted him... which they did, he was denied and betrayed by those closest to him.

"He was screaming out not because he hung on the cross for hours, which he did, gasping for breath, with his rib cage jutting out, in excruciating pain. He was screaming out not because sharp nails were hammered into his hands—piercing his flesh, or because spikes were driven into his feet—slicing through muscles and tendons...which they were. When Jesus screamed out, he did not cry, 'My hands, my hands, my feet, my feet, my head my head...' but instead, Matthew 27:46 says, Jesus cried out in a loud voice, 'My God, my God..., why have you forsaken me?' The reason he was screaming out was because His own loving heavenly Father, who He had known from all eternity, turned his back on Him. God the Father abandoned Him.

"Psychologists will tell you that being rejected by someone can be a painful experience. And many of us know that feeling. But if an intimate friend or spouse rejects you, someone you are emotionally attached to at the heart, the pain is far deeper.

"God the Father turned away from the Son whom he loved from all eternity; and not only that, Jesus willingly gave up his life to be deserted and forgotten... Why?

"Jesus was abandoned, so that you and I would never be abandoned. He was rejected, so that you and I could be welcomed in. He was separated from His Father, so that you and I will never be separated from His love. We are His treasure, and He was willing to take hell for us, if it meant that we would be with Him forever.

"Does that move you at all?

"See him suffering for you, loving you... the treasure of His life, and that will melt your heart into selflessness. Think about it, talk about it, read about it, ask questions about it, talk to God about it, and let His Holy Spirit transform your heart.

"The good news is that not only did Jesus' death wipe away your self-centeredness, but God also covers you with all the righteous things that Jesus did in His life. Jesus lived a perfect life, and His record of perfect love is transferred to us.

"When Jesus came to earth, two thousand years ago..., from the moment He entered the womb, until the time He died on the cross when He was around thirty-three years old... His entire life was one of obedience and pure joy and unity with our Heavenly father. And his earthly life, the time that He lived here on earth... those thirty three plus years, is substituted for my self-centered life. It doesn't matter if you live to be one hundred and two years old, Jesus' life from the time He entered the womb, until His last breath on the cross is substituted for your entire life. And now, a perfect God can relate to us, because our lives are united to a perfect Jesus.

"And someday, when we stand before Jesus, He will see His perfect, spotless record of goodness in us, and He will say, 'Welcome, my child... welcome home.'

"Pray to Him, and first, admit that you are worse than you realize. Admit that your selfishness runs even deeper than you know. Admit that you need Him, and ask Him to be the Most High in your life, in charge of your life. Thank Him for taking away your self-centered heart. And thank Jesus for suffering and dying on your behalf and taking the separation and isolation that you deserved. And thank Him for giving you His perfect record of righteousness that unites us to God and Him. A spotless record of generosity, goodness, and obedience that you don't deserve.

"Romans 8:38 says, 'For I am convinced that neither death nor life, neither angels nor demons, neither the present nor the future, nor any powers, neither height nor depth, nor anything else in all creation, will be able to separate us from the love of God that is in Christ Jesus our Lord.'

"Do you want to go to heaven? Do you want real freedom? Do you want joy? Do you want to be swept up in this universal renewal? Do you want to be known by Jesus personally? The way to freedom is to submit. The way up is down. The way to find your life is to lose it. The way to power is to serve, and the way to the heavenly crown is by way of the cross. Go to Him, and say, 'Jesus, I need you. I need your substituting death on the cross. I need your life's perfect record. I need you to be the Most High in my life. 'Jesus, I need you.'"

Mitch's eyes were locked on the pastor, his body temperature rising—adrenaline pulsing through his veins. He was flabbergasted, hearing things he had never heard before. His ears were on fire, trying to make sense of a God who turned his back on his Son. He had never heard the account of Jesus' crucifixion presented that way, and it intrigued him. He always thought of God as an all loving Father, but for Him to abandon his dying Son, to reject Him… this gave Mitch reason to pause.

He closed his eyes, not sure what to think, inhaling a few deep breaths, then peering out the window.

A soloist onstage began to sing.

"There is a redeemer, Jesus God's own Son,
Precious Lamb of God, Messiah, O Holy One.
Jesus my redeemer, name above all names;
Precious Lamb of God, Messiah; O for sinners slain."

Mitch stared at the clouds, feeling self-conscious. What just happened here? His original intention was to simply sit in church for forty-five minutes, listen to a few songs, say a quick prayer, and then jet back home for lunch. This wasn't what he signed up for; he wasn't supposed to be reflecting on his life. Everything in his mind seemed hyperaware—the room, his thoughts, his past and future—everything felt surreal. As he looked out the window, he noticed off in the distance, a commercial airplane disappearing behind the clouds. He shuffled in his seat, feeling strangely unsettled; the pain medicine inside his body began to wane—his heart thumping against his rib cage.

'Tomorrow is guaranteed for no one,' the pastor's words resonated in his ears and in his heart.

"What happens the second you die?" the pastor asked.

"The very second you die... you will stand before a man with nail scars in his hands.

"The question you have to ask yourself is... 'Does Jesus know you?'"

Chapter 53

Mitch limped up the dark staircase, clenching his jaw to stave off the pain. The spasm shooting up his leg felt like a thousand needles piercing straight into the bone. He was desperate for a quick fix, even if it meant sucking down a whole bottle of pain pills.

He leaned heavily against the banister, hyperventilating to try and boost his energy. He regretted not listening to his wife, who insisted he move his belongings to the first floor.

He climbed halfway up, when his lungs suddenly seized up. His body shuddered with an internal earthquake, jolting him forward as if he had been punched in the stomach. He clutched his ribs, gasping for oxygen, and fighting to stay conscious. He was afraid he was going to fall, so he reached for the banister, flailing his arm and steadying himself for the moment. The light at the top of the stairs blurred into a floating chandelier. Was this the end?

His legs collapsed beneath him—his ribs slamming against the banister. Black spots clouded his vision, as he inhaled sharply, forcing his lungs to inflate.

The cast on his leg felt like a thousand pound anchor—dragging him like dead weight toward the bottom of the stairs. He massaged the area around his heart, trying to stimulate the blood flow—desperate to jumpstart whatever muscles were locking up inside. He hyperventilated until he sensed his lungs responding to his efforts.

The chandelier grew brighter with every extended breath. The pain shooting up his leg spurred him to keep fighting—clearing the cobwebs in his mind, and feeding his adrenaline. He clawed his way toward the top, pausing at every other step to allow his breathing to catch up.

When he reached the top, he leaned against the banister, exhaling a deep sigh of relief. He wiped the sweat from his brow, and waited for his lungs to return to a steady rhythm—he was just happy to be alive.

The chest pain slowly subsided, but his leg was still quivering from the spasm that was shooting up his leg. He let out a silent scream, clutching his thigh, and massaging the cramping muscle.

He set his sights on the bedroom door, trying to stay active, and keep his blood circulating. If only he could reach his pain medicine, then at least he would have a small semblance of relief. The stabbing pain intensified, driving him forward as he crawled through the darkened hallway.

Once inside the bedroom door, he collapsed from exhaustion. He clutched his ribs—worried that his lungs were going to seize up again.

Darkness clouded his vision, whipping his mind into a state of confusion. Where was his medicine? Did he leave it downstairs? The pain in his chest flared up—first in his torso, then his leg, and then it was burning all over. He rolled onto his back, staring bleary eyed at the ceiling—terrified to close his eyes lest he never wake up.

The air grew thin, closing in around him—he knew his brain wasn't getting the oxygen it needed.

The moonlight knifed through the curtains, casting a glaring spotlight onto his guilty conscience. His mind started playing tricks on him, conjuring up images that were stirring his memory. He envisioned his wife staring deep into his eyes, her face was marred by betrayal, and her eyes were filled with tears.

He reached out to comfort her, but she turned and fled. He tried to run after her, but his legs were sluggish, as if he was running through sand. He chased her through the haze, screaming her name and begging for forgiveness. The harder he pushed, the slower he ran. Finally, he lunged forward, stretching out his hand in desperation, falling to the ground.

He inhaled several deep breaths, shaking his head, and trying to clear the visions. His eyes lit up when he spotted his medication on the nightstand. His adrenaline kicked in, realizing that relief was in sight. He crawled along the bed, grimacing as he dragged his cast behind him.

When he reached the nightstand, he tipped the table over, knocking all the bottles onto the floor. He sorted through the capsules—popping off caps and tossing the empty bottles aside. He picked up the last remaining bottle, shook it, and heard something rattle inside. He unscrewed the cap, then let out a gasp. A single pill and a ball of cotton rolled into his palm—not even a quarter of his normal dosage.

He choked the pill down, gritting his teeth, and throwing the capsule across the room. He shook his head, cringing in disgust, when suddenly, he turned and noticed a bottle of vodka sitting on top of the dresser. His eyes widened as he focused on the bottle—there was no hesitation about what he was going to do. He knew the risk of mixing meds with alcohol, but at this point, did it really matter? He pulled himself onto the bed, then struggled to stand, balancing on one leg with a crutch under his arm.

He could already taste the vodka on his lips—the cool, crisp alcohol on his tongue, soothing away the pain.

He limped to the dresser, snatched up the liquor, and filled a small glass till it spilled over the rim. He chugged it without breathing, feeling the alcohol roll smoothly down his throat. The vodka stirred his senses, coating his tongue, and providing a moment of relief.

After gulping down a second glass, he stumbled toward the bed with bottle in hand, wincing from the pain that was burning in his chest and leg.

He collapsed onto the bed, groaning louder than before, trying to push the stabbing pain out of his mind.

"Ah!" he moaned.

The walls began to sway, the shadows creeping through the window. His heart beat faster, the blood rushing to his face. Would his heart even make it through another night?

He leaned against the headboard, desperate to find a comfortable position to alleviate the pain—even for a few seconds. He gnashed his teeth, rocking back and forth, then finally conceding—the bottle was his only relief. He stared vacantly at the floor, his heart thumping against his sore ribs, and his head feeling like it was about to explode.

He set his glass on the nightstand, when he noticed a picture of Rachel and the girls. He stared at it for a long moment, transfixed, as his daughter stared back at him—her warm eyes telling him that she was daddy's little girl. He chuckled to himself, hearing her high pitched laughter as she jumped between the waves. He missed his old life; their vacation seemed so long ago. The alcohol made him dizzy; he was tired of thinking of the past. His smile died away. Everything he knew was gone.

The specter of guilt gnawed at his conscience. No matter how hard he tried, he knew his family would never be the same. His wife would never forgive him, and his daughters would never trust him. His breathing labored once again, but this time it had nothing to do with his lungs. The pain he caused his family far outweighed any good he might bring in his few remaining days. His subconscious searched for any ray of light, but the longer he stared, the deeper he sank into darkness. With tears welling up in his eyes, he leaned over to the cabinet, and pulled open the bottom drawer. He dug beneath the pile of clothes, reaching toward the back, and pulling out the one thing that could put an end to his suffering.

The cold steel weighed heavy in his hand. He dropped the pistol onto the bed, then rubbed his temples, trying to suppress the throbbing pain. He stared at the gun, contemplating the unthinkable. His breathing grew heavy, his lungs laboring to inflate, the pounding in his chest made him more anxious by the second. He refused to live as a vegetable—being kept alive by a single plug was not an option. But what else was there to live for?

He clutched the gun in his hand, eyeballing the cartridge to confirm it was loaded, then pressed the metal barrel underneath his chin. He squeezed his eyes shut, tensing every muscle in his face—his hand shaking as he secured his finger on the trigger.

At that moment, he heard a faint knock on the door.

"Daddy?"

He gasped, but didn't answer.

He closed his eyes, cowering in the silence. Maybe she would go away.

"Daddy?"

He froze, holding his breath, and clenching his teeth to stave off the pain.

He heard the doorknob turning, so he snapped the gun underneath the pillow, and knocked the bottle of vodka off the other side of the bed.

"What is it, honey?" he said quickly.

Cindy poked her face inside the door. "Daddy, will you sing me a night night song?"

He squinted into the light that was peeking through the doorway.

"Can you ask Mommy, honey? Daddy's not feeling very well."

Cindy ran to the bed and crawled next to him.

"But I like when you do it, Daddy," she whispered.

His body shivered when she snuggled against him. A wave of compassion swept through his senses, like a cool breeze breathing life into his soul. His heartbeat slowed and his pain suddenly became bearable. He closed his eyes, trying to hide the anguish that was twisting inside.

"Are you okay, Daddy?" she wrapped her arms around his waist. The compassion in her eyes and her loving embrace began to melt his heart. For the first time in his life, he felt like a coward, like he was letting her down.

He kissed her on top of the head. "Go put on your PJ's, honey, and Daddy will be there in a minute," he whispered.

Cindy ran out leaving the door slightly open.

Sitting alone in the dark, a wave of guilt surged through his conscience. Remorse seized him so strongly that his hands began to shake. He reached for the pillow, hesitating, then flipping it over. He stared at the gun, realizing how close he came to never hearing his daughter's voice again. He bent down and picked up the bottle of vodka. It was empty, having spilled into a puddle beside the bed. He sighed, tipping it upside down, pouring the last few drops onto his tongue.

His pain turned to anguish, his body trembling at the thought of abandoning his daughter. He imagined her crying out in the dark, screaming for help, with no one to answer her. He cocked his arm back and whipped the bottle across the room, smashing it against the wall.

An eerie silence lingered in the air. He sat frozen, holding his rib cage, listening to his breathing going in and out.

At that moment, he heard music in the hallway coming from another room.

"There is a redeemer, Jesus God's own Son
Precious Lamb of God, Messiah, O Holy One.
Jesus my redeemer, name above all names,
Precious Lamb of God, Messiah, O for sinners slain."

He hung his head, realizing that he should be lying there, dead. And his daughter would have walked in and found his bloody body. His hands shook uncontrollably, as he stared at the gun. Overwhelmed by shame, he buried his face in his hands and wept bitterly.

He limped through the dark hallway toward Cindy's door, then cracked the door, and peeked in. He saw Cindy kneeling beside the bed, saying her prayers.

"... and please protect Piggly, Boo Boo, and Mr. Jammers. And Goldie, and Christy, and Mommy and Daddy. And Jesus, please give Daddy a new heart..."

A lump caught in his throat, as tears rolled down his cheeks. He quietly closed the door, and took a step back.

He squeezed his eyes shut, and whispered, "Forgive me, Jesus."

The music continued playing in the background, as he wiped his tears. He inhaled a deep breath, then reopened the door as Cindy was lining up her teddy bears, and climbing into bed.

"All right, does everyone have their PJ's on?"

"Uh-huh."

"Good." He pulled the covers up, tucking her in.

"Daddy, did you say your prayers?"

"I did, honey. Did you?"

She nodded. "And I asked Jesus to give you a new heart."

He kissed her on the cheek, and whispered, "He already has."

He sat beside her, brushing her bangs to the side.

"What are you going sing, Daddy?"

"What would you like to hear?"

She thought for a second. "Jesus, loves me."

He smiled. "Will you sing it with me?"

"Uh-huh."

Cindy started singing, and he joined in.

"Jesus loves me, this I know..."

Chapter 54

Rachel curled up on the sofa, then closed her eyes, pausing to enjoy the late night calm. The silence in the family room was a welcome respite after dodging the paparazzi all day. She was tired enough to sleep, but wrestled through her fatigue. She wasn't going to miss out on her quality alone time.

She picked up her book, anxious to escape into the world of her latest heroine. She flipped back a page to recall where she had left off, sipped her latté, then immersed herself in her story.

As midnight drifted into early morning, her eyelids grew heavy. She laid her head against the cushion, yawning occasionally, and balancing the book on her knee. She struggled to stay awake, hoping to finish one more chapter, before weariness claimed her for the night. The TV flickered softly in the background—the glow from the plasma screen casting a calm over her like a warm blanket.

As she wavered in and out of consciousness, a news bulletin flashed across the screen. The program switched abruptly to a live broadcast from a remote African region.

A reporter scrambled in front of the camera, his eyes wide with horror, peering anxiously over his shoulder. Black smoke billowed from an orphanage behind him; villagers scurrying back and forth, trying desperately to escape the flames. An elderly woman cried out, as she fled with a baby in each arm; she was choking from smoke inhalation, then collapsed in the middle of the street.

Gunfire erupted from the far side of the orphanage, sending the crowd into a chaotic stampede. The villagers screamed hysterically, pushing one another, and ducking behind cars and anything else they could hide behind.

The reporter flinched when he heard the crackling gunshots, his face turning ghost white when a spray of bullets ricocheted just above his head. He ducked behind a burned out truck along with his cameraman, cowering in the shadows—the sobs building inside his throat. He peered sheepishly into the camera, his eyes straining to mask his inner terror, struggling to find the words to file his report.

"Government militants continue to attack this border town, bombarding it with firebombs, and sniper fire. Hundreds of people have been murdered...the bloodshed..., the barbaric savagery at the hands of these extremists, is the worst I've ever seen," he turned away, coughing from the dust caught in his throat. "Sometimes, we think of ourselves as being so modern, so twenty-first century, and yet, nothing could prepare me for this."

As he continued gagging, the camera panned toward the orphanage, revealing the carnage unfolding along the roadway. Women wailed over bodies that were dragged from the burning huts. The corpses of children were scattered in the street—some unrecognizable, others covered with burlap tarps, as the unmistakable stench of death lingered heavy in the air.

The camera panned back to the reporter who had collapsed in the dirt. He stared bleary eyed at the chaos, paralyzed by a sense of helplessness. Fighting through the nausea, he forged ahead with his live report.

"The shock... the carnage, the murder..., it's like nothing I've ever seen. Whole villages have been wiped out. These people..., we are told, were targeted because of their religious faith, professing Christians..., whole families, children, and babies... all murdered, and their homes burned to the ground. The brutality is unimaginable."

The reporter shook his head, staring at the elderly woman lying face down in the dust. Her body lay motionless; the children beside her also appeared to be dead. He snapped a picture of the nameless victim; he had no idea who she was. To the government militants, she was a faceless nobody, a worthless old woman, discarded in the street like garbage.

Chapter 55

The elderly woman rubbed the anguish from her eyes; her withered hands scratching along her cheek. She was afraid to open her eyes—her mind was scarred by images she would rather forget.

She pressed her forehead to the ground, a position of oppression that she had known far too long. Her body shivered, curling into the fetal position. How much more would she have to endure?

Her threadbare clothes hung from her emaciated frame; her fatigued muscles were too weak to support her body. Her battered feet were bruised and bloody, bearing the marks of a calloused journey.

She listened intently for the sound of babies crying. She winced in the silence, conceding that there were probably no survivors.

Her lungs languished inside her rib cage, inflating just enough to keep her alive. She had all but given up hope, tired of being humiliated day after day, exhausted from a lifetime of brutality and hardship. Too weary to lift her head, she buried her face in the dust.

At that moment, she heard a compassionate voice calling out to her.

"Well done, my child."

She gasped in disbelief, startled by what her ears were telling her. What was happening? She mustered all the strength she could, lifting her chin to see where these words were coming from. Before she could focus her weary eyes, she heard the voice again.

"Come my love, I have prepared a place for you."

The old woman burst into tears. She collapsed face down, sobbing uncontrollably, releasing a lifetime of heartache. Jesus kneeled beside her and helped her to her feet. With his scarred hand he reached out, then gently wiped the tears from her cheeks. She gazed into His eyes as His strength became hers. He wrapped his arms around her, embracing her in His love.

A Post Note from Ernie Frederick

I write this note, as a Kingdom partner with my son, Eric, and together we pray that God will use this book as an avenue for those who are seeking to know God. As you read the book, were you aware of the costly extent in the suffering of God's love to open the gate to eternity? And did you know that Jesus, who in lifting our sins from us, and taking them on Himself in His sacrificial, sin removing death on the Cross, was separated from God, to pay the price for our forgiveness? We pray that the realization of the depth of God's love, and the sacrifice of Jesus, for us to be reconciled to God, and to experience the Holy Spirit's transforming Presence and working in us and for us, will motivate you to receive the peace, joy and hope that He offers.

Ernie Frederick

Acknowledgements

This book was written to bring glory to the covenant love of my life—the Father, Jesus and the Holy Spirit. Every breath, every heartbeat, every righteous thought that passes through my mind flows from your gracious love. I love you Jesus. It is your righteousness alone that sustains me and makes life worth living. Your love and beauty is a wellspring of living water that flows from within all of us who have been saved by your grace.

So much love and gratitude to my father, Ernie, for his loving support, endless prayers and countless sacrifices. Your spiritual fervor and love for Jesus is a constant reflection of our Heavenly Father's heart, and I thank you for the joy you have in Him. Thank you to Dr. Timothy Keller, pastor of Redeemer Presbyterian Church, who's teaching ministry has opened the Scriptures in a way that has set my heart ablaze with a passion to love and serve our Creator and Redeemer.

A special thanks to all my family members for their unconditional love through the good times and the difficult times. Thanks again to my father, Ernie, and his wife, Sue, for their faithful prayers and generosity. Thank you to my brother, Mark, his wife Julia, and their children, Phoebe, Brielle, Jenena, and Ethan. Thank you for your love for Jesus and your kindness and generosity. We don't see each other enough, but when we do, it's a family blessing and a gift from above. Thank you to my brother, Chris, and his wife, Sarah. I've been blessed to have an older brother who has always been generous and supportive of me. You are a gift of God in my life, and thank you for your love for Jesus. Thank you to my sister, Nena, and her husband, Curt, and their children, Artem and Lina. I see the selfless generosity of our mother in you, Ne, and having you as my sister has shaped my life in monumental ways. Thank you for your love for Jesus.

A special thank you to my Aunt Nena and Uncle Will for your loving support of our family over the years. Thank you to my cousins and their spouses and families, Luis and Wendy, Neil and Kim and their children, Christina and Max. Thank you to Steve and Leonora, and their children, Kirsten, Kelsey and Joel, and to Philip and Jaci, and their daughter, Allison. Thank you Steve and Leonora and family for opening up your home and hosting all of us for Thanksgiving celebrations. You have been a blessing to our family and I thank you for your love for Jesus.

Thank you to my cousins in the Philippines, the Abutons, Lucila, Gilda, Remedios, Ike, Gilbert, Estela, Dennis and his family and their parents, Guillermo and Demetria. Our Heavenly Father has made us a family, and we are part of an even greater family in Jesus.

A special thank you to Amy Hair who assisted me with the final editing. Your suggestions and encouragement were invaluable. May God pour out His blessings upon you. And finally, thank you to EMI CMG for permission to include song lyrics in the book, and the cover credit: Photographer: Peter Adams/photos.com.

"May His beauty rest upon me, as I seek the lost to win; And may they forget the channel, seeing only Him."

Comments and feedback are welcome. Please visit our **Facebook** page: Keyword: **Tomorrowcomestoday**

Made in the USA
Lexington, KY
21 January 2013